Resonance

Dianne J. Wilson

Resonance
COPYRIGHT 2018 by Dianne J. Wilson

Contact Information: titleadmin@pelicanbookgroup.com

All scripture quotations, unless otherwise indicated, are taken from the Holy Bible, New International Version(R) NIV(R) Copyright 1973, 1978, 1984, 2011 by Biblica, Inc.™ Used by permission of Zondervan. All rights reserved worldwide. www.zondervan.com

Cover Art by *Nicola Martinez*

Watershed Books, a division of Pelican Ventures, LLC
www.pelicanbookgroup.com PO Box 1738 *Aztec, NM * 87410

Watershed Books praise and splash logo is a trademark of Pelican Ventures, LLC

Publishing History
First Watershed Paperback Edition, 2019
Paperback Edition ISBN 978-1-5223-0026-7
Electronic Edition ISBN 978-1-5223-0024-3
Published in the United States of America

Dedication

To Mom, who taught me to see more than what is visible. I wish you could read this.

Spirit Walker Series

Affinity
Resonance
Cadence

1

"I want Bree to be alive as much as you. But even if she is, we can't get back." Kai sat on the windowsill of Torn's office, his feet drawn up underneath him. He avoided looking at Elden, who glowed enough to make Kai's eyes ache. Sunlight streamed through the windows, but it wasn't enough to warm the chill in Kai's bones.

Elden paced. "But Zee opened the doorway before. She can do it again. I don't see what the problem is."

"I can't believe I'm hearing this from you of all people." Kai's nostrils flared. "Zee hasn't moved from the bed since we put her there. She's so pale she's nearly blue. Have you seen her?"

Elden nodded, "I know but—"

"She's wiped out," Kai continued. "You have no idea how much that took out of her. She's resting now, but even when she recovers, we can't ask her to do it again. We have to find another way." Kai didn't say what he was really thinking—if she recovers.

"But you crossed over. You got yourself back to the spiritual realm. How did you do it? Maybe we can all do whatever you did!"

"I got hit by a bus, Elden. Are you suggesting we line ourselves up at the bus stop and take turns stepping out in front of them as they pull in to park?"

Elden ran fingers through his hair. "Well no, not

exactly." He paused for a moment, nose wrinkling, "Wait. Do you think that would work?"

"I'm not even going to answer that." Kai pushed himself off the windowsill, rubbing the back of his neck. A dull ache was building, creeping up his scalp. "We'll come up with something. I know we need to try and find Bree. I feel the urgency, too."

Elden's eyes narrowed. "Sure you do."

Kai let it slip. Being drawn into an emotional argument would be the last thing Bree needed. Mounted on the wall just behind Torn's desk, the automatic air freshener released a puff of lavender scent into the room. Strange. Kai wouldn't have thought of Torn as a lavender kind of guy. He sneezed as the fragrance curled up into his nostrils. "So we agree that it'll just be you and me going back, yes?"

"Agreed."

"It's been a long day. Give me until morning to come up with something. Try and rest."

"Sure. Rest." Elden prickled with impatience as he spun on his heel and left the room.

Kai rubbed his temples in a vain attempt at pushing away the pain that had his head in a death grip. He craved silence, time to think. So much had happened on the roof and the room below. He needed to process and figure it all out. He eyed the window. It wouldn't be too hard to climb through and down. Just maybe he could get away and…

A knock sounded on the door. Without waiting for an invitation, Runt poked her head in. "They want you downstairs." Humming a tune he didn't recognize, she skipped across the room, grabbed his hand, and twirled herself under his arm. Her brown hair was tied up into two shiny pigtails that bobbed as she moved.

"What do they want? And who are *they* anyway?"

His sourness appeared to bounce off without denting her happy mood. "The kids from the school, silly. They don't know what to do now. They're a bit lost. You need to tell them what to do." She stopped twirling and tugged on his hand until he nearly tripped over his own feet. ""Don't be grumpy. You're important now. Just as I told you, you would be." She gave his arm an extra hard tug.

"I dunno, Runt. I wouldn't call this place a school. You're being very generous." The OS: Open Sessions in the natural, Obsidian Square in the spiritual realm—a seedy nightclub to anyone passing on the street. Those recruited knew it as a cover for a dark Affinity training facility whose methods leaned toward more torture than training.

"Whoa, careful. You'll break my nose. I'm coming." Kai tripped on the mat and nearly face-planted.

Still holding Kai's hand in a death grip, Runt skipped out the room and hauled him down the passage toward the lift. She seemed to ignore his reluctance.

They took a lift one floor down and got out. He knew this floor well. Runt led him straight to the room where he'd first played guitar the night the real guitarist had gotten drunk and passed out. A low buzz of muted conversation filtered through the air, and it was hard to judge how many people waited for him.

Runt led him to the door, spun around, and blocked his way inside. "Wait! You need this." She reached into her pocket and pulled out a necklace. A pendant hung from the chain—a small glass bottle that appeared to be empty. Runt yanked on his T-shirt until his head was low enough for her to reach, slipped the necklace over his head, and patted his chest. He straightened up. Runt skipped into the room ahead of him, and he stepped away from the open door to tuck the necklace under his shirt so it couldn't be seen. He could only hope that she wouldn't be offended.

In a blink, Runt came back. She pulled him in line with the doorway, stood behind him, and shoved. Kai flew into the room with arms pin-wheeling. He only just managed to stay on his feet. Silence snuffed the conversation as all eyes focussed on him.

He walked to the stage feeling like a cancer cell making its debut under a microscope. Sunlight streamed in through the high windows, taking the menacing edge off the place, but highlighting how old and dirty it all was. Tables had been pushed to the back of the room and chairs had been brought forward—lined up in messy, semi-circle rows, which covered most of the floor space. As far as he could see, not a single chair remained open. There was no sign of Elden. He was probably back at Zee's bedside.

Zee's friends sat in the front row, arms tight across their chests. They'd all been through Affinity training with her, and Kai could only imagine that her absence would make them suspicious. They glared at him hard enough to drill holes through his chest. Kai resisted the urge to cross his arms in retaliation and avoided meeting their eyes. He took to the stage, palms itching for his guitar. What should he say to a room full of people who'd just been rescued from something they may not have wanted to be rescued from?

Kai scanned the crowd, trying to gauge the mood. Some of them eyed him with suspicion; others seemed happy but bewildered. Most of them just looked lost, staring up at him with their bright eyes as if seeing their savior. Nearly all of them glowed a faint green. Broken. It had always been this way for Kai. Glowing green was a clear sign that something—or someone—was messed up inside. His Affinity meant that he knew how to fix it. If only he had time, he could do something about the murky sea he faced. But for now, they wanted answers. Answers that he didn't even have questions for.

A girl with her hair scraped into a bun stood at the back and wiped her hands on an apron. There was something different in how she carried herself.

Kai waved her over. As she approached him, he read her name badge—kitchen staff. In a flash, he knew where to start. He pulled her close and whispered in her ear, "How fast could you feed these kids?"

She glanced across the room with her nose wrinkling in concentration. "We have tons of frozen meals ready for the trainers. I just have to warm them. I'd guess about twenty minutes."

"Great. Do it. Take some kids to help you."

The girl grinned and gathered a few younger ones to go with her as she left.

Kai held up both hands and waited for the room to quieten down. The green glow across them all made his stomach turn. "I know you have many questions. For now, I'm going to ask you to hold onto them and work with me. You've been in a training program to enhance your ability to see and operate in the spiritual realm. Some of you would know it as Affinity. Here's what you might not know: this school has been training you in what I think of as dark Affinity. Your experiences here have been carefully designed to taint what you see, hear, and feel. I want you to know there is another way. You'd gotten a taste of it when your greentube turned amber. Do any of you remember that?"

Across the room, kids leaned toward each other whispering, nodding. When they turned back to him, some of their faces had softened a degree. Kai took the moment and carried on. "It will take time to undo your training, and we're going to start in the most practical way I can think of. If you trust me, I want you to bring back the tables and set up chairs around them. In a few minutes, we're going to have lunch. This time, all of you get to eat the good food. Nobody goes hungry. As long as there is food in this building, you will all get to eat."

The crowd sat in silence. One girl jumped to her feet and cheered. She was so skinny her arms looked as if they might snap.

A tall boy with hollow cheeks and blonde hair that stuck out like an exploded feather duster stood to his feet, fists clenched. He snarled at Kai but addressed the crowd. "Are you all idiots? What makes you think we can trust him? Haven't we been told this before? This is another one of their tricks. Can't you see it? What is wrong with you all?" The cheering girl deflated and sank down into her seat with a fist half-raised, blinking in confusion.

Kai turned and forced patience into his tone. "And you are?"

"Ruaan. What's it to you?"

Runt scrambled up onto the stage and stood in front of Kai with her arms crossed, staring down Kai's challenger. Kai leaned down. "Go to the kitchen and tell them we need the food now," he whispered into her ear. "Don't you glare at me, too. Off you go. Run."

Runt stood, torn between protecting him and doing as he'd asked. With a stomp of her foot, she made her choice and jumped off the stage. By the time she'd worked her way through the crowd and out of the room, half of them were on their feet, twitchy and agitated. The rest stayed sitting.

It was only a matter of time before they started throwing chairs. The noise level climbed. There was no way they'd listen if he tried to speak. Every instinct told him to run, find somewhere to hide, go back home and leave this bunch to sort themselves out. But he didn't. He stood facing them, his face grim.

Ruaan picked up his chair. As he lifted it over his head, a metallic clatter rattled down the passage. The room hushed, and they all turned to see what monstrous nightmare would make such a noise. Kai sniffed the air...roast meat. Food was coming. "Quickly, get the tables set out!" He yelled, taking advantage of the moment of silence.

Zee's friends leapt to their feet, a tall blonde one leading. "Come on, everyone. Tables, now." The room full of kids who'd been a breath away from a full-on riot now scrambled to get ready for food. It took five minutes. Food trolleys rolled in and tin foil containers of steaming food were passed around the room until each one had roast beef and veggies sitting in front of them, a knife and a fork to eat it with, and a cup of clean water.

The girl from the kitchen came over, checking on all the trolleys as she passed. She slipped Kai a plate of his own with a shy smile.

"This is incredible. How did you organize this all so quickly?"

"The kitchen is kitted out to feed a small army. I can't tell you how good it feels to actually be able to serve proper food to everyone." She turned away from Kai, but he heard the emotion quivering in her voice. She was not a willing party to the OS training methods.

"Listen, that is all over now. Things are going to be different."

She smiled but her eyes remained sad. "That would be nice."

Kai stood. His heart swelled with emotions he didn't dare explore. *Tau, thank you for this food.*

~*~

Hours later, Kai pulled the office door shut behind him and sat on the couch, looping his arms around his knees. For some reason, he'd adopted Torn's office even though he didn't like the man at all. Maybe this was one way to make sure that Torn didn't try to sneak back in. He'd disappeared after the rooftop spectacle, but that was no guarantee he wouldn't try to come back and cause trouble.

Kai had wanted to check on Zee, but Elden had grown roots next to her bed. Kai backed off noiselessly rather than have to deal with all the man's angst. He had no desire to tangle with Bree's brother again. Elden had always struck him as cool and collected. But right now, he was so tightly wound, Kai feared he might snap. In this state, Kai wasn't in a hurry to go anywhere with him.

Kai stretched out and kicked the desk leg, finding satisfaction in the rhythm of his foot connecting wood. If he could figure out a way of getting back and looking for Bree by himself, he would. It had taken himself, Runt, Zee, and Elden to open a doorway and send all the darKounds back through to the other side. Nasty things, darKounds. Slick, blue-black dog-like creatures with acid-laced claws and a tendency to fill ones head with rotting thoughts. It was a sweet victory, but the story didn't end there. Now they sat with a building full of displaced kids who all needed to be reoriented to light Affinity and then sent home. As for those who couldn't go home...he didn't want to think about them.

His kicking nudged a desk draw open. Kai leaned over to shut it, but something caught his eye: a flat circular dome the size of his palm, with a separate inner and outer circle on the one side. It was stored in a harness of sorts, with a strap that looked long enough to go over one shoulder and tie around the waist.

Kai picked it up and turned it over in his hands. It didn't look particularly menacing. He pushed the inside button first. Nothing. He pushed the outside and nothing happened either. Maybe it needed batteries. He dumped it on the desk and flopped back onto the couch. It was a puzzle that intrigued him, but right now, his brain was mush.

Kai's eyelids grew heavy, and he eased himself over sideways, stretching out on the cushions. Today had been a victory, but it had cost them all. He fumbled for the threadbare throw over the backrest and pulled it over himself, tucking the edge right up under his chin.

A sharp knock at the door woke him out of sleep that had sneaked up on him. Sunlight streamed through the window, and he shielded his eyes. A full night's sleep on the couch had tied a knot in his neck and laced cottonwool through his brain. He swallowed against the dryness of his throat and coughed. With all the mush in his head, he couldn't figure out how to invite the knocker in, but he didn't have to. The handle swung downward without invitation.

"Kai, is that you?" Pete Zappiro, AKA Zap, poked his head nervously around the door. A wide smile cracked his face, and he bobbed into the room in his customary bouncy way.

Kai pushed himself upright, tossing the throw over the back of the couch. "Pete. Come on in. I thought I saw you on the roof. I've been dead worried about you." A skullcap of bright green lines criss-crossed Pete's skull. Affinity training had done some significant damage.

"You've got company, I see." Pete thumbed toward the end of the couch. Runt lay curled up at Kai's feet, her small body tucked into a ball.

Kai didn't remember her coming in. He took the blanket he'd discarded off the back of the couch and covered her, happy to see the contentment spread through her features and colour return to her pale cheeks. "I didn't think I'd see you again."

Pete shrugged. "Seeing you here is even more surprising."

"The day they took you from school, I should have come after you or something."

"Apparently, you did."

"No, I meant sooner. I should've gotten you out before they could mess with you." Kai searched his friend's face for any sign that he'd caused offense.

Pete dodged the unspoken questions in Kai's comment. "Speaking of messes, that's quite a mess you made downstairs."

Between his frown and his grin Kai couldn't tell if he was impressed or disgusted. Kai slapped the couch, "Honestly. If one more person says that was my fault, I'm going to lose it."

Pete waved a dismissive hand and dropped into an open chair. "No worries. What now?"

"And again, you're asking me. Why me?"

"Aren't you in charge of this lot?" Pete waved a hand up and around.

The weight of responsibility crashed down on Kai. Pete might as well be referring to the universe.

"There's talk amongst the rabble of you starting a school or something. Try and get our heads right and save our souls." His fingers drew invisible quotes in the air, sarcasm thinly veiled.

"Oh, please. For a moment I thought that might be a good idea. Replace the dark Affinity school with one that can show a better way. Sounds fantastic, don't you think?" Kai didn't look up to see if Pete was listening. "Now, I just want to go back and see if there is any chance my friend might still be alive."

"That's noble."

"Geez, why the sarcasm? What have they done to you? I don't remember you being like this."

"Ah, don't mind me. Let's just say that you were right. Coming here has been...hard." Pete sat forward in the chair and sniffed the air. "Can you smell that? Smoke. Something's burning."

"I don't think so. It isn't normal smoke. Smells more like a vaporised damp forest." He eased off the couch, careful not to disturb sleepy Runt. "There's something coming in under the door, look."

Tendrils of green vapour curled up from the floor. Wisps trailed down from the air vent on the wall near the ceiling and rapidly spread toward the passage outside the office.

Pete stood. "Man, I don't like this. I know this smell."

Kai was mesmerised by the curls of soft green drifting toward him. His brain slowed and thinking became difficult. Pete smacked him on the shoulder. Focussing on his face took effort.

"Kai, we've got to get out of here. I know what this is, and it's not good. Don't breathe it in. We have to go." He scanned the room. "The window!"

Thick billows of green covered the floor to knee height. Kai fought the fog enveloping his mind. "Won't work, too high. We'll have to use the passage." He felt his way across the room, using his fingers like a blind man. Halfway across the desk he picked up the harness with the contraption. He hung onto it and moved toward the couch, where Runt lay sleeping.

"Just don't breathe it in." Pete coughed and sneezed.

Kai strapped the harness around his body to free up his hands. It fit neatly under the necklace Runt had given him. He scooped up Runt off the bed and threw the blanket over her face to keep the fog away.

Pete tugged at the door handle. "It's locked from the outside!" The whites of his eyes were showing, tinged green by the rising vapour.

"Who would do this?" Kai choked. The green mist had risen to chest height. He could taste it in his mouth, "I don't feel right. What is this stuff?"

Pete stumbled across the room and worked on the window catch. "Affinity enhancer. An adapted version of what they've been injecting into us. I worked as a trainee in the lab and watched them develop it. Well, a version of it anyway. This, though, is slightly different." He ran a hand through the vapour, "I don't know what changes they've made."

"I don't plan on hanging around long enough to find out."

Pete smacked his fist into the window frame. "Window's jammed. We're trapped."

Kai's muscles strained under Runt's weight. "Throw something. Break it."

Pete shook his head. "They smash-proofed the windows long ago when drunk people started throwing things."

The vapour now filled the room, blocking morning light from the widow. It billowed thick enough that they couldn't see the floor. The floorboards under Kai's feet begin to slide, and the walls grew hazy. The circle of his vision tunnelled in closer, darkening around the edges. Runt was slipping. *Don't drop her.* He fell to his knees and eased her to the floor. His mind floated free from his leaden body. He keeled over sideways and felt the jolt through his shoulder as he landed.

I'm going to pass out. Any moment now.

Kai lay on his back watching the swirling emerald cloud pressing down on him. The ground shifted, rippled. His arms stretched out. He'd never been bucked off a floor before, but this might be the first time. The carpet beneath his fingers grew prickly, soft fibres morphing into sharp blades that bent at his touch. Grass.

A breeze picked up beneath his feet, billowing through the gas until the edges grew ragged, torn. Beyond the haze, there should have been walls, a ceiling, a window, a desk. Kai squinted through heavy eyelids, forcing them not to close. His eyeballs rolled back in his head. Do. Not. Give. In.

A small part of his brain was aware of Runt as she lay curled inside the arch of his outstretched arm. Where were the walls?

Wind blew harder, blowing over him and through him, clearing the fog in tattered strips. A midnight sky curved away above him.

2

Grass and sky.

Midnight.

He knew this place. Something in the fog had transported him to the spiritual. Almost like the recruiters' injections, yet the effect of those seemed like a cheap party trick in comparison to this.

This felt dark. Thick and heavy.

A scream ripped through the silence. Pete! Kai folded himself in half, forcing his heavy limbs to bend, and rolled onto all fours. Standing seemed impossible. He crawled in the direction of the sound, feeling his way forward with his hands. This was too weird. His hand came down on someone small, probably Runt.

Kai navigated around her, following the rough sound of Pete's bellowing. "Pete! Stop screaming like a girl, and tell me where you are."

Pete let out another terrified yell and bellowed words fast, making no sense.

"Stop yelling!" This wasn't working. Kai sat on his rear and tried to get his bearings. It would appear they'd arrived in the spiritual realm without needing a doorway, but Kai didn't recognize anything around him. He lifted a hand, waiting for LifeLight to flood through him and push back the darkness, but his skin remained opaque.

"Kai is that you? I'm in a hole. I can't get out. It's

too high. I can't see."

"I'm coming to find you. Just stay put."

"Oh sure. I'm not planning on moving from here. Just hanging around." Panic laced Pete's words.

Kai picked up speed, crawling blind, aiming at where he thought Pete's voice might be coming from. The ground in front of him shifted with a low groan, and he bit his fist to stop the squeak that bubbled up from his belly. He reached out, flinching. His fingers found soft, long hair. It felt like Zee's. She sat up as he touched her.

"Where are we?" It was Zee, dazed and sleepy. "Whoa! Who turned out the lights? Is this the testing lawn? No man, this is a bad joke." She flopped sideways, wriggling to get comfy on the prickly grass. "I'm going back to sleep."

Pete's voice came from the left. "Great, there are two of you. Can one of you come get me out of this hole?"

Kai stopped crawling. "OK, this is ridiculous. Who else is here? So far we have Pete, who is stuck in a hole, Zee, Runt and me, obviously. Zee, why are you whispering to yourself? Please don't tell me you've lost it."

Zee clicked her tongue in annoyance. "This is my dream, so you can't be rude to me. I'm talking to Peta. She's here, too."

A different voice spoke from the darkness on the other side of Pete's hole. "Um, I think I might be losing it? Where the flip are we? It's morning time. Who stole the sun?"

Kai tilted his head, someone familiar but he couldn't figure out who. "Who are you?"

"Who wants to know?"

Who could pack so much bad attitude into four words? Kai had had a run-in with that attitude not too long ago. Right before dinner in fact.

"Let me guess. Ruaan." What couldn't get worse, just had. "How did you get hauled into this?"

Pete snorted from below ground level. "How did any of us? Oh, and by the way? I'm still stuck in this hole."

"Sorry, Pete. Coming. Ruaan, help me get him out." Kai crawled along in the dark. Somewhere close by there was shuffling, and Kai hoped it was Ruaan moving in to help. By now some night vision should have kicked in, but it was still as dark as if his eyes had been plucked out.

He bumped into something warm and solid. Ruaan. They'd missed Pete's hole. "Pete, where are you?"

"Right here, man. This hole ain't budging."

Alongside Ruaan, Kai shuffled in the direction of Pete's voice. His deprived senses scrambled for anything real to latch onto. Even Ruaan's arm brushing his was welcome. Then Ruaan's arm smacked his chest. Kai let out a grunt and dropped. A loud crack rang out from below, followed by a hollow thud.

Pete roared wildly, "Are you trying to kill me? You nearly split my skull in two." He grunted and stamped his foot.

Ruaan groaned. His voice came from down below. "Your head is so hard you could tunnel your way through a mountain using nothing but your forehead."

"Excuse me? Your head is so hard they could use you to...to...knock down buildings. Or something."

"Ruaan? What now?" He couldn't see anything. Kai's belly knotted.

17

"I tripped and joined pit-boy here in his hole. At least he broke my fall."

"Yeah, and you broke my skull," Pete muttered.

"Apparently, neither of you is too hurt to whinge." Kai reached the edge and lay on his tummy, one arm trailing down into the pit. The hole seemed freshly dug, the soil still soft and crumbly. He stretched as far as the length of his arm would go, feeling for the bottom, nearly tipping himself in. Pete was in over his head. "Pete, give me your hand. Ruaan—push."

With Ruaan pushing from behind, Kai hauled Pete out of the trench. Together, they grabbed Ruaan's hands and pulled him out, too.

"Why is it so dark?" Zee asked. She seemed nothing like the Zee he'd known the last time he'd been stuck here. She sounded small and scared.

It rattled Kai's nerve to hear her sounding lost. "Can you light up, Zee?"

"I don't know. It used to just happen. Now, nothing."

"I'm not getting anything either. Runt?"

There was no answer. The girl could sleep through anything. A patch of warmth spread from the middle of Kai's chest, and he reached up to find the cause. He felt the device he'd taken from Torn's office. Snug in its harness, it was cool to the touch. Just next to it, his fingers closed on the bottle pendant Runt had given him, and he lifted it out. A small glimmer of blue appeared and seemed to float in mid-air. He unhooked the chain from his neck and held the necklace in his hand with the small glowing bottle hanging off it. It glowed brightly in the dark. The brightness built and grew until Kai could see Zee's face in the glow.

The pool of light coming from the pendant spread.

Pete stood shivering, covered in fine grey dust from the hole he'd fallen into. Kai brushed some off his hair and rubbed it between his fingers. Not soil or dust but ash.

"What is that?" Zee sat up, blinking in the light.

After the blind darkness, a small bottle of light was so beautiful, Kai nearly cried. "Something Runt gave me. I thought the bottle was empty but there must be something inside."

Zee blinked against the brightness. The intensity increased. "Water from the Healing Stream, maybe."

The group drew closer and huddled around the light as rescued hikers would around a fire. All but Ruaan. He hung back in Zee's shadow, covered in ash just like Pete.

Kai hunted around for Runt. "Runt, this is brilliant. Well done you." He shuffled over to the small lump he'd thought was Runt, but what should have been brown hair was silvery white. It was Zee's friend, Peta. Kai scanned the area for his small girl, but she was nowhere. Runt hadn't come back with them.

~*~

Zee hugged Peta to make sure she was OK with the strange shift. Peta stood like a statue, head turned away from the light. At least she wasn't freaking out. Zee turned her back to the others, scanning the area to figure out what and where this place was.

As far as she could see by bottle light, the ground stretched flat all around them. There were more holes, just like the one they'd rescued Pete from. Sharp rectangles dotted the ground randomly. No orderly rows, no pattern. She shuddered. The only thing they all had in common was a slab of rock at one end. Some were hemmed in by a tall metal fence that ran along the edges, just a step away from each side of the pit. There was no doubt in Zee's mind. They were in a graveyard.

Zee shuddered. "Kai, bring the light over here. I want to check something."

Kai shuffled closer and held it out. Zee tried to take it, but he gripped tighter.

"What's your problem? Give it here."

"What do you want to see? I'll hold it for you."

"Really? Don't you trust me?" Zee didn't wait for an answer but yanked him by the arm to the stone closest to them, the one right next to the hole they'd rescued Pete from. It was a tombstone, engraving clearly visible: Pete Zappiro. "Pete, what's your surname?"

Roused from her zombie-like state, silvery-blonde Peta answered instead. "Delmara. Oh, you were asking him."

"You were talking to me?" Pete thumbed his chest.

Kai put a hand on his friend's arm. "Pete, from now on we're calling you Zap. Pete and Peta are too similar. I hope that's not a problem for you."

Zee snorted, "And you don't think Zap and Zee are too close? You could actually call me *Evazee* you know. It is, after all, my name."

"Are you serious? Evazee is such a mouthful."

"For real. From now on Evazee."

Pete AKA Zap shrugged, unfussed. He leaned closer to where Evazee shone the light on the tombstone and swore. "What kind of sick joke is this? That's my name. And my birth date."

"It doesn't mean anything. Look, it doesn't even have a date of death, so it's fine." Evazee forced herself to sound cheerful. "It's nothing. Don't worry about it." She grabbed his arm and tried to pull him away, but he yanked out of her grip and pointed. Right next to the word *DIED,* engraving of a date began to appear. Kai stepped in. "She's right, it means nothing. Let's get out of here, I don't like this place."

Zap stood transfixed, watching the growing line. It moved so slowly, one's eyes could be playing tricks, but there was no doubt it was moving. "That's it. I'm dying."

Evazee smacked his arm, "Stop it. Just because we're in a graveyard and there's a grave with your name on it—"

"We're in a graveyard. At my graveside. This is not good. Not good at all." Zap began pacing in circles, his hands waving wildly as if he were chasing a swarm of bees.

Ruaan grabbed him by the back of his neck and lifted him a few millimetres off the ground. Zap's arms still swatted wildly, but at least he wasn't in danger of falling back into his own grave and killing himself by accident.

Kai had moved on to another grave, one with a metal railing all around, "I wonder what the metal railings mean? The hole is empty, just like all the rest. This one says *James Kirkwood.* Ring a bell for any of you?"

Ruaan dropped Zap, who fell to his knees and collapsed forward with his forehead in the dirt. Ruaan rubbed his hands on his pants, trying to get rid of the grave dust. "That's Elden and Bree's father. He was taken by darKounds. Does it have a—"

Kai squinted and turned his head sideways, "This makes no sense. There is a date deceased, but it's in three months' time. According to this, he isn't dead yet."

"Kai, you need to see this. It's Bree's grave, but there's something weird going on." Evazee blinked to focus.

Kai brought the light with him. They checked the tombstone. There was nothing written under deceased, but when he shone it into Bree's grave, Evazee's suspicions were confirmed. The level of dirt was slowly rising.

3

Kai had fully expected to find a grave dug for each of them, but they checked the stones closest to them and only found three: Elden's missing father, Zap, and Bree. The pull was strong to keep looking until he'd made sure there wasn't one with his name on it, but a deep unease in Kai's gut warned against venturing further into the graveyard. Searching the entire cemetery could have taken hours or days, as it was impossible to judge how far it stretched. Besides, Zap's date of death was slowly being carved, and Bree's grave was filling right before their eyes. They had no time to waste.

Kai thought he might throw up, as if he'd eaten hope and despair for breakfast and they were fighting in his belly.

Evazee pulled him to one side, just out of earshot of the others. "We need to pray. Seriously."

"Pray? How would that help?"

"Jesus will know what to do. We just need to ask. He'll show us. C'mon Kai, you know how this all works now."

"Last time you went on and on about me finding Tau. Strangely, that turned out to be good advice. Shouldn't we track Him down instead?"

Evazee shrugged. "Tau…Jesus…different names,

same person."

"But—"

Zap cleared his throat, "Are you two done? This place is creepy."

Kai frowned at Evazee, struggling to reconcile the cardboard Jesus he'd heard of in school with the enigmatic, unpredictable Tau he'd met. "He's right. Let's get out of here. Ruaan, take the rear."

Ruaan, who'd become strangely amicable compared to their pre-dinner showdown, stamped his foot and a cloud of ashen dust billowed from his shoes, curled up, and settled on his pants. "I can't get this stuff off. It just comes straight back."

Zap patted Ruaan's back, brushing the ash dust off. Just as with the shoes, the dust circled straight up onto his sweatshirt. "It's not coming off."

Ruaan pulled away as though Zap had fleas or a deadly contagious disease. "That's what I said, genius. Go pat yourself. You're also covered. This mess is your fault."

Kai clucked his tongue. "We'll find the river. It'll come off in the water." Kai frowned. Ruaan was still touchy, but far more co-operative than he'd been the day before. Almost helpful. What had changed? Being in a dark graveyard was enough to make him value his companions.

Kai chuckled, shook his head and began walking, carrying their only source of light. Which way should he go when he didn't have a clue? He just wanted to get out of this graveyard and then figure out what to do.

It was meant to be just him and Elden that came back to look for Bree. Now, because of some freak accident, he was stuck here with an odd collection of misfits that would take a lot of energy to look after. He wasn't great at keeping other people safe, which was why they were here in the first place. He clucked his tongue and kept walking.

Evazee followed with Peta behind him. Zap skittered from the back of the small group right up next to Kai, chewing on his nails and fretting. "I've figured something out. You know why this place is so creepy? Hmmm?"

"Um, Pete? Open graves, self-engraving tombstones, ash instead of soil. I mean seriously, take your pick."

Zap waved a dismissive hand, the whites showing all around his eyes. "It's Zap, not Pete and *psh*, obviously. But apart from that…" He rubbed his hands. "No noise. Have you noticed?" He wriggled his fingers over his ears.

"You've got a point." Silence, back home, was seldom truly silent. Crickets or wind or something was always blowing or buzzing.

"Listen. There's no wind, no crickets. It's like a vacuum, but so loud it hurts my ears."

"I was just thinking that. Those exact two things." Kai frowned at his friend. "You're right, though. Being in space would be noisier." More than the silence bothered him. He took the bottle light and checked the gravestone. "We're walking in circles. Look."

Ruaan pushed past Zee, took the light from Kai, and leaned in close. It was Zap's grave. "What? That's not possible. We've been going in a straight line."

Peta stared ahead, eyes unseeing. "We will never get out of here."

She spoke in a detached and hopeless tone. It was the first thing she'd said since they'd gotten here, and it sounded wrong coming from one so small. So cold, devoid of all emotion, it sent a shiver down Kai's spine that ended in his stomach as the urge to hurl. "Not if I can help it." He scrambled up onto the headstone, wobbling as he secured his feet beneath him and turned a slow 360 degrees. "There is something out that way, but I'm not tall enough to make out what it is."

~*~

Evazee had fallen silent. Her attempts at drawing out Peta had failed until this moment, and now she wished she'd left the girl alone in her silence.

"Evazee come get on my shoulders. You've got good eyes. I think heading that way might break us free from walking in eternal circles."

Evazee blinked at Kai, not sure she'd heard right. "You are insane. I'd prefer not to fall to my death in Zap's grave, if that's OK with you."

Zap nodded, rubbing his chin sagely. "She's got a point."

Ruaan punched the top of his arm. "C'mon, we'll hold her up. The sooner we get out of here, the better."

Zap nodded again. "He's got a point, too."

Ruaan swatted the back of his head. "You're wasting time."

"Stop hitting me!"

Together they lifted Evazee, who was too shocked to protest. Zap, however, mumbled under his breath— snippets of words, *punch bag, bully*... Then Evazee was in Kai's space, balancing on the stone, and all Zap's mumblings faded into insignificance.

Her heart pounded loud in her ears and Ruaan's clipped instructions blurred to a dull buzz of shoving hands and shaking muscles.

Kai crouched down, and she climbed on his shoulders. He lifted himself to a stand, supported on either side by the others, and then she was up.

Ruaan tucked the light bottle under Kai's shirt. Darkness rushed at them and pressed close.

Evazee squinted. "There are definitely lights out that way. Too far to see what or who, but anything with light has to be better than this." She slipped off Kai's shoulders, and they helped her to stand on her own legs with muscles that quivered. She faced the right direction. It would be too easy to get mixed up.

Kai took the bottle out from under his shirt. "So we agree. We follow the light?"

Zap bounced on his toes. "Let's do it, man. I want to get out of here." A bead of sweat rolled down his temple. It slid down his face and dripped off the edge of his jawbone. As it hit the ash below their feet, a muted rustling broke the silence. It started as a faint whisper from behind, as if the air had grown skin and bones of metal. Something was coming. Zap's wide eyes narrowed to slits, and he walked sideways, gesturing behind them with his thumb. "I don't think that's a good sign."

~*~

"We should probably leave. Maybe even run. Now!" Kai took off, leading them, torn between keeping the bottle light out and attracting attention or hiding it and stumbling in the dark. The first open grave across their path persuaded him to keep the light out, regardless of the danger.

Swishing metal sounded closer now. Whatever roamed this place had the advantage of familiarity. "Stay close. Don't get left behind." Kai glanced back and wished he hadn't. They didn't have just one follower. He could see movement between all the graves behind them. There were many lumbering, shadowed lumps. He resisted the urge to count.

The creatures following them were getting closer. The shortest one was twice as tall as Ruaan even doubled over, running in a loping stride that ate the distance. Vaguely human in shape, they wore tattered rags that flew behind them and exposed hands like metal branches, long stick fingers reaching toward the group as they ran. Grave Keepers.

Anything their steel fingers touched turned to ash and crumbled. The ash was sucked into the vortex of wind created by the creatures' movement and added to the swirling windstorm that was already building.

"Kai! Come on!" Ruaan grabbed and shook him from his daze.

Evazee held Peta's hand in a death-grip, hauling her along and ignoring the girl's reluctance. "Look! The boundary fence! There's an opening. We're nearly out!" Beyond the rusted metal of the fence stood a forest of tall, straight trees. If they could reach the trees...

They got to within ten paces from the gap. With a screaming rush of wind, the creatures swirled past them around the outside of the group and blocked the way out.

"You may not leave." The tall one stretched to his full height, towering above them. His voice rolled over them, the hiss of water on hot coals. His eyes gleamed as pits of nothingness, twin black holes that could suck you in. His mouth, nothing more than a gaping hole spewing out words that rasped through the air like vaporous acid.

Zap squeaked in fright and hid behind Kai. Evazee dropped to her knees next to Peta, who stared ahead as if already dead.

Kai swallowed hard, hoping his voice wouldn't abandon him. "It's not our time. Let us pass." The words burned fiercely in his chest, but they came out of his mouth as a whisper. He coughed and tried again. "It's not our time! Let us go!"

A swishing hiss rustled through the ranks of ragged keepers. Kai could almost swear they were laughing at him. "Foolisssh, foooolish. You're marked. You're ours. You can never leave."

Ruaan edged forward until he was next to Kai. He whispered, so quiet Kai strained to hear. "Use the light!"

Kai glanced sideways, wondering what level of idiot this kid was. He shut his eyes anyway and held up the tiny bottle, feeling like a fool. Then he thought of Tau and the fierce love in His eyes. He pictured Tau in front of him now, standing between them and what they faced—a strong wall of unyielding resistance. Waves of liquid courage rolled through him, and he swayed on his feet, thrusting the light even higher. Dare he look? He felt the light as heat down his arm, over his skin.

He braved a glance through squinted lids. The Grave Keepers cringed away from the light, which seemed to shine straight through them, reversing their solidity so that they appeared as negative images, not real creatures that could turn someone to ash at a touch.

Holding the light high, he inched forward one slow step. They shrank back. Another step, a little bolder this time. They shrieked louder but backed away. Kai kept walking, thrusting the light out in front of him like a sword.

Eight steps later, he stood between two solid walls of screeching creatures. They hissed and frothed but didn't dare come any closer. The way out stood open. "Guys, get out. Go!"

They squeezed past him and stayed as far as possible from the thrashing claws on either side. Ruaan was the last to get through the gap. Kai's head ached from the high-pitched noise. He swung around, holding the light high and backing toward the gap, resisting the urge to run.

Kai cleared the fence, turned, and ran to catch up to the others. All along he'd assumed that the Grave Keepers wouldn't be able to follow them out of the graveyard. Running with his back to them now, he furiously hoped his assumption was right. Judging by the dip in the volume of their noise, he'd been right. He reached a fork in the road. A tall tree stood between the two paths, dry and long dead. He hesitated for a moment. Which way would they have gone?

A ball of blue flame whizzed past his head, singeing his hair. It landed at the base of the dead tree, which erupted in a spectacular fountain of ash and blue flame. The dead wood yielded quickly to the fire, crackling and snapping in glowing surrender. Heat unlike anything Kai had ever felt washed over him from head to foot.

The second fireball popped with an ear-splitting

whoosh before it flew past him and landed in a shower of sparks amongst the undergrowth. Powdery ash filled the air like dust. His throat burned from breathing it in.

There was no time to waste. He held his breath and veered right, instinctively following the path that led in the direction of the light he'd seen from the top of the gravestone. Ash and sparks landed on his skin, but he ignored the burns and kept running. The light bobbed and danced, dangling off the chain around his neck. He let it bounce and kept on. Another ash bomb landed somewhere behind. He glanced back and saw the forest path blazing, cutting him off from the fork. If the others hadn't taken this path, he was on his own. There was no going back now.

Kai turned away from the burning chaos and ran. The explosions had messed with his vision. A vivid technicolour replay blazed across the inside of his eyelids when he blinked. He ran, rubbing his eyes and collided with someone. They stumbled together and grabbed arms to stop themselves from falling. Ruaan. He'd caught up to the others. Relief washed over Kai.

Ruaan let go of his arm. "You made it. For a moment, I thought you'd gone up in flames."

"That was the tree, not me. Is everyone here?"

"We lost Evazee and Peta. I don't know how—" Ruaan broke off in a coughing fit.

Zap patted him on the back and picked up Ruaan's story. "Evazee and Peta went left. I didn't even realize it until a moment ago. They must have taken the other fork. We can go back—"

"The forest is burning right across the path. There is no going back." Kai swallowed bile at the back of his throat. *Not again. Please, Tau.* "The best we can do is keep going until we come out the other side and head left to find where the other path comes out the woods."

Zap sniffed the air close to Kai's head. "You smell like a barbeque. What happened?"

"I don't know. The Grave Keepers went nuts. They started throwing blue ash fireballs at me. I dodged, but the first one was so close." He motioned to them. "C'mon. We have to get to the girls."

4

Evazee was wheezing from the run. The air felt thin here, as if they were high in the mountains. She doubled over to catch her breath and felt Peta do the same next to her. Without Kai's light, the dark was deep and solid. Evazee reached out to Peta, and the girl didn't pull away as she had been doing.

"That was too close. How is everybody?" Evazee's words bounced off the trees and fell to the leaves at her feet. "Hello? Kai. Ruaan! Zap?" She stepped closer to Peta, slipped an arm around the girl's bony shoulders, and waited for one of the others to respond. She checked the ground with her feet, but it didn't seem as though anyone was there either.

"I think we went the wrong way. We're going to have to go back." Running from the graveyard had happened so fast, yet Evazee had a vague memory of the road branching off in two directions. They'd been the first ones out, and she'd stuck to the left without thinking. Now it seemed that all the others had probably travelled to the right. They simply had to retrace their steps, and they'd find them.

Evazee dreaded facing the Grave Keepers, but maybe if they crept quietly, they could move past undetected. After all, it was only the two of them, and they were both small and light on their feet. Peta said nothing but followed her without resistance.

They retraced their steps and soon saw flickers of blue flashing through the gaps in the trees.

"That doesn't look right." A few steps closer showed the forest blazing in blue fire. White ash filled the air and burned their throats and noses. A burning tree had fallen across the path, blocking the way. They wouldn't be getting back to the others this way. Peta took in the flames with no comment. Another tree went up in flames, sending sparks flying in a shower of blue and white.

"Let's get out of here. We'll have to use a different path to find the others." Peta stood rooted, her eyes on the fire. She still said nothing. Surely, she understood what this meant? A wave of homesickness washed over Evazee, but she tucked it away and turned back toward the dark path. She dragged Peta with her as though the girl had grown roots, mesmerized by the flames. Only once they were out of sight did she turn and follow.

They walked in silence, testing the perimeters of the path as they went. They could cut across the forest and keep walking until they found the other path, but Evazee broke out in a cold sweat at the thought of it. Straight lines had become circles back in the graveyard, and there was no way of predicting where they'd end up if they left the path. If they just kept on until they cleared the trees, they'd find the others waiting for them. Surely.

As they left the crackling fire behind, silence fell as deep and complete as the dark, until all that filled Evazee's ears was the sound of her own breathing.

Her brain ran wild. The last time she'd stood in this place, she'd been full of light and could do all sorts of things. Now things were different, but what had changed? The possibility that she'd burnt out her gifting while opening the gate on the rooftop was becoming more real than the ground beneath her feet. It might come back to her with rest—

Wait.

What was that noise?

She kept walking as if she'd heard nothing, but she slowed her pace. There it was again—rustling in the trees just next to them. It could be the others coming to find them, or it could be something looking for a snack. Evazee had no intention of being eaten just yet.

Leaning down, she whispered in Peta's ear. "Can you run?"

Peta did not respond.

Evazee tightened her grip and broke into a run with her arms stretched out in front of her as her only guide.

~*~

Kai couldn't think straight. As they walked, thoughts buzzed inside his head like LightSuckers trapped in a bottle. If he were a superhero, his superpower would be losing things. Correction, people. He lost more people on any one day than others lost in a lifetime.

The three of them walked in a row, the path too narrow for any other formation. Ruaan trailed at the back, humming a tune that Kai strongly suspected he might recognize if it had been anybody else humming it. Kai didn't know what to make of this tall boy who had been ready to rip his head off back at the OS, but since then had been nothing but friendly and helpful.

The fierce confrontation was still too fresh in his mind.

Something growled in the gloom behind Kai. He stopped walking to listen.

Zap inched closer. "Did you guys hear that?"

Kai shoved a finger to his lips, "Shhh!"

Ruaan coughed, "Sorry, guys. It's just my stomach. We left before I could have breakfast."

"Wow. Is that even normal?" Zap's question was innocent enough, but it came out with as much force as if Ruaan had sprouted an extra ear on his head.

"What are you saying? Don't you ever get hungry?" Ruaan's voice dropped in pitch. He puffed out his chest and sounded more and more like the boy who'd solved things with his fists.

Kai had no desire to play referee for a daft argument. Diversion might work. "I'm wondering if we should cut straight through this forest to the other path. I'm not happy leaving the girls alone with no light."

Zap shrugged. "It can't be too far."

Ruaan was already shaking his head as he eyed the tall trees. Deep shadows hung thick between the trunks, resistant to Kai's bottle light. "Are you both nuts? We don't know what's in there."

"Let's rescue the girls. We'll be like heroes." Zap's chin tilted up, and he stared off into the distance. "We need a theme song."

Kai held the bottle up towards the trees. "We don't know what waits at the end of this path either. We could be walking straight into a trap." Kai shrugged. "Besides, it's two to one. Sorry, Ruaan. You're outvoted. Look, I'll even carve a mark in this tree to make you feel better." With that done, he aimed himself between the trunks and plunged into the thick.

Zap followed him without question.

"Wait! We didn't even vote! That's not right. Come back here." The thought of being left behind must have gotten the better of Ruaan. He followed them, muttering under his breath.

~*~

Evazee lost track of how long they'd been jogging. In a moment, the darkness around them felt different, and she knew they'd cleared the forest. They stopped to catch their breaths and figure out what to do now. As far as she could tell, whatever had been rustling in the trees had stayed put and decided not to follow them.

A low rumble passed underneath their feet and the rock began to glow in gentle, broken light. Evazee knelt down for a closer look.

They stood on a flat stone surface, pock-marked and rough, shot through with random sparkling patterns that glowed and pulsed. Raised bumps the size of bowling balls dotted the ground at regular intervals like miniature volcanos, complete with a hole at the centre. The light given off by the rock barely reached their knees, but after being sightless for so long, Evazee drank in the sight gratefully. Peta stared off into the distance. She may as well have been blind. Evazee was losing the girl.

"Come on. Let's see if we can find the boys." Evazee aimed right and followed the line of the trees.

If the boys kept walking along the right fork of the path, they would soon be out of the forest as well. Unlike the silence of the graveyard, this place hummed in a way that was almost musical. Evazee kept her eyes on the ground as she walked, fascinated by the tiny sparkles in the rock. Must be minerals, though not any she'd learnt about in school. Whatever they were, they made her heart happy...and that was more than she could say for anything else they'd come across in this grim place.

"So, Peta, I was just thinking that we don't know much each other. How about we pick out some things to chat about?" Evazee didn't wait for the girl to respond. "What about happiest memories?"

Peta trudged along next to her and didn't answer.

"I'll go first. I was home sick from school one day, and my mom had to work, so she brought my gran over to keep an eye on me. Gran moved all the lounge couches and made the lounge into an aeroplane. She pretended to be the air hostess and brought me snacks and let me choose the in-flight movie. She nearly set the carpet alight with the tiny candles she used to mark the runway. We had to put it all back before Mom came home, but Gran giggled and told me that it would be our little secret. I'm sure Mom knew what we'd got up to, but she didn't mind and never let on." The memory warmed Evazee. "How about you?"

Peta continued her walk in silence. Evazee's usual response would be to fill the awkward dead air with a stream of chatter, but she bit her tongue and waited. Suddenly, with no warning, Peta began wringing her hands, her face crunched up, and she shut her eyes. "I don't remember good. The sun has gone down in my brain. There is only night and memories of darKounds, LightSuckers, and the man who fixed my ankle." A sigh shuddered through her, and her face went slack as she turned away from Evazee.

Evazee watched helplessly as the window of opportunity slammed shut in her face. Her hand on Peta's back seemed like cold comfort. She'd seen Shasta bring a dead LightSucker back to life, only to watch it die a few minutes later. Shasta led the OS training school and even though Evazee hadn't had much to do with him, she'd seen enough to know that his miracles were a sham that came at a high price. With the grim reality of Shasta's failed LightSucker healing fresh in her brain, she'd watched him go to work on Peta's broken ankle. Her bones may have knit back together, but something else had been let loose in her body that made Evazee's skin crawl.

There was nothing else to do but find the boys, and maybe together, they could find the Healing Stream.

~*~

"You know, maybe this wasn't our best idea. We've been walking this forest forever. We're not getting through." Zap cleared his throat. There was a quiver to his voice that Kai knew well. He was terrified. "Maybe we should just go back."

Ruaan patted his growling stomach wistfully. "Can I just remind you both that I was against all this in the first place? Maybe next time you should consider listening to me."

"Look! There's the path." Kai couldn't stop a tinge of I-told-you-so coloring his voice. They stepped clear of the trees, and Kai clicked his neck left and right, stretching his arms overhead to ease out the muscles of his back.

"Well done, genius. We're back where we started." Ruaan pointed to a mark they'd carved into the bark of a tree.

Kai rubbed his eyes and held the light bottle up close, "What? That's not even possible! We should be able to cut straight across. We walked straight, didn't we?"

Zap had his hands on his hips and a philosophical slant to his eyebrows. "Makes sense, really. Think of the graveyard. There is nothing natural about this place. Back home, you could assume walking in a straight line would get you where you wanted to go. Here? Not so much."

Kai frowned. "That makes sense. When did you get so smart?" He slapped Zap on the back, "So what now, smartypants? We have to get to the girls."

Zap crossed his arms. There was just a hint of swagger in the lift of his chin. "Well, if you must ask me..." Moments in the spotlight were not to be taken lightly.

Ruaan slapped him on the belly with the back of his hand. "There's a path. We follow it. It's not that hard. They'll probably be waiting for us when we get through." With that, he turned and headed into the darkness, leaving the other two gaping in the pool of bottle light.

~*~

A low rumble groaned through the rock beneath their feet, building to a shudder that made Peta stumble. Evazee reached out to steady her, but Peta pulled away as if Evazee's skin scorched her. The shaking settled, and one line of glowing pattern brightened. It started at their feet and sparked a bright path away from the trees, cutting across the vast expanse of rock. The intensity of the glow was so bright that it lifted the reach of the brightness from their knees, to hips, up past their shoulders.

Evazee felt the light dance on her skin, tingling and sparking, a Jacuzzi of radiance. It washed over Peta, and the muscles in her face visibly relaxed.

"Should we follow it?" Evazee asked.

Peta met her eyes and nodded.

Evazee grinned. It was a hint of the old Peta. This had to be right.

Starting slow, they followed the glowing line as it weaved around the mini volcanoes. Each step they took echoed through the rock. Laughter bubbled up inside Evazee, and she grabbed Peta's hand as they started to walk faster. Wherever this led was going to be glorious. Maybe it would even take away the gloom that had settled into the girl's soul.

It began as a slight tremble. A shudder beneath their feet. Evazee looked ahead and saw one of the mini volcanoes in their way. The glowing line they were following went straight across and carried on to the other side. Evazee hesitated. Another tremble shuddered through the rock, this one nearly shaking them off their feet.

"Get off! Get off! It's going to blow!" Footfall slapped the ground behind them like gunshots.

Dazed and blinded, Evazee squinted. Who was it? In a moment, a tall figure burst through the brightness and threw an arm around each of them, shoving them to the side. They landed hard.

The bubbles left her skin, and she felt cold and

empty. "What are you doing? Who do you think you are?"

It was Elden. He was an Affinity trainer, and one that she may or may not be able to trust, but that didn't stop her heart from double-thumping.

"We've got to get off this rock. Haven't you felt the tremors?" Elden helped them both to their feet. With a hand on each of their backs, he pushed them along.

Evazee let herself be shoved along, still stunned at his sudden appearance, "When did you get here? Were you in the graveyard? Why didn't we see you? Why didn't you say anything?"

"Good grief, girl! All these *whys*. Can we get to safety first, please?"

Evazee pulled away from his hand and folded her arms across her chest. "How do I even know I can trust you?"

"Look at it this way. If you are torched by one of these jets, you'll never know, now will you?" A faint whoosh sounded behind them. Elden spun and peered through the gloom. "It's started. Run, run now!"

Evazee glanced past Elden. What had him spooked? One of the mini volcanoes shot out a steaming stream of sparks and fire taller than both Elden and Kai balanced on top of each other. As she watched, it spread to the next one and the next, as if it were fed by some underground stream of flame inching relentlessly towards them.

"Running is good. Let's do that." Tearing her eyes away from the jets closing in, she grabbed Peta's hand, but the girl stood rooted, sparks and flames reflecting in her unblinking eyes.

"Elden, help!"

Elden scooped Peta up in his arms, just as the jet at

her feet blew. He turned away and hunched over her, using his body as a shield against the rain of liquid flame.

5

Elden wouldn't let them stop until there was dirt, not rock, beneath their feet. He eased Peta out of his arms, and she sank down, almost hugging her legs but stopping short of touching. Her breathing was too fast.

The jets burned all across the rocky surface behind them, casting an eerie glow where they huddled. Evazee knelt next to Peta. "Are you hurt? Or just shaken up?" Evazee moved in close and lifted Peta's hands away. All down the front of her legs, from the knees down, were raised blisters, the skin an angry red. Elden had shielded her body with his, but he hadn't managed to protect all of her.

He sat next to Peta, his arms resting on his knees, head down.

"Elden are you hurt?"

"A bit. My back. I'll be fine." He spoke through gritted teeth.

"Let me see." Evazee hobbled closer. The eruption had burnt holes in his T-shirt, and each fabric hole surrounded a blister. "I don't know what to do. We need the Healing Stream." Evazee thought back to when Kai's LightSucker bites had been healed just by her touch. He'd been so insistent that it was the LifeLight inside that carried healing power, and he'd been right, even though she'd thought him crazy at the time. But now? Everything was different. There was no evidence that she was filled with LifeLight—no means of staying safe in the messed-up place. Maybe she was burnt out beyond recovery.

Peta cried softly. Tremors wracked her body in response to the pain.

Jesus, I don't know what to do. I don't even know what to ask You. I can't help these people. I need you.

Elden gently eased his arms under Peta and lifted her. She folded herself into his neck and hung on. "I think we should get away from this place."

Evazee rubbed the back of her neck as they walked away from the burning rock. She wished her sense of direction were better. "We split up from the others. I don't know how we're ever going to find them. Do you know your way around this place?"

"Not this section. Things work differently here. You can't expect things to be predictable or logical. Where were you aiming to go before you split up?"

"From the graveyard, we could see lights in the distance. We aimed ourselves at those, and we would have been fine if the Grave Keepers hadn't shown up."

"How do you know that would have been safe?"

Evazee shrugged. "Can one ever be sure?" Her feet *schlurped* with each step she took. The ground was becoming soggy, making walking hard. "How do we know any of this is safe? None of it is. Even the beautiful things are apparently lethal." She waved her hand behind her and toward the fiery field. "We're here to find Bree, and that's about all I know. We have to start somewhere. What about you? Where do you think we should start looking? Maybe the fact that I've just asked you four questions in a row is a fat clue to how freaked out I'm feeling. None of this feels safe.

Your question is stupid."

Elden shook his head. This semi-gloom seemed to weigh him down even more than the girl he carried. "I guess so. Let's keep going until we find someone."

Evazee shook her head as they walked, turning over the same question lurking in the back of her mind since she'd woken up here. "What I'd really like to know is how we got back here. Last time, Kai was unconscious, and he was stuck here sort of permanently."

"Yeah, I know. Hit by a bus. So he kept telling me."

She ignored his comment. "As for me, I kept fading in and out. It seemed like every time I prayed, I found myself here. But in between, I went back to normal life. It doesn't make sense. What could have happened to get a bunch of us here—stuck like Kai—but all at the same time?"

Elden didn't say a word. He grunted under Peta's weight and the pain of his blistered back.

"And then there's you. When did you say you came across?"

"I didn't." His breathing came in short gasps, and his footsteps slowed in the sticky mud that seemed to be getting deeper. It was over their feet now, with a layer of liquid sludge lapping their ankles. They were back in deep shadow, far enough away from the burning field that it was merely a glow on the horizon.

"But we were all together in the graveyard. If you came back with us, why weren't you there? Or were you, but you didn't say anything?"

Elden stood still, the sudden stop in movement causing a mini-wave that sloshed up Evazee's legs. "Is it just me, or is this watery stuff getting deeper?"

Evazee clicked her tongue. "Are you avoiding my questions?"

"You ask so many, if they were bullets, I'd be bleeding. Can we not do this now, please? Also, we're up to our knees, and it is getting deeper."

"You know something. But you're not telling me." Evazee slopped closer, wishing she could look him in the eye.

"I'm in pain. This girl needs help. Stop it."

"Fine. But we will pick this up when you're better." A wave of hot shame flushed through Evazee. She'd been so caught up in *how* and *why* that she'd forgotten that she was the only one not injured. "I'm sorr—"

"*Shh!*"

"Don't *shh* me. I'm not—"

"Keep quiet woman. Can you hear that?"

From far off to the right came a steady sloshing noise, rhythmical and unhurried. Slosh, pause, slosh, pause. It continued, getting louder each time. Whatever was making the noise seemed to be coming directly towards them. Evazee shuffled closer to Elden. A tremor ran through her body, not entirely caused by standing in the cold mud. Soon, a light appeared, floating above the water, weaving and bobbing with each subsequent swoosh. It was a longboat. The oarsman sat up front, paddling left then right.

"Should we run?" Evazee stood close enough to Elden that his body heat warmed her. She wished she could tuck her hands under his arms to thaw out her fingers.

Elden shook his head. Sweat beaded on his forehead.

They waited while the boat drew steadily closer,

almost hypnotised by the beat of the strokes of the paddles through the water. As far as Evazee could make out, there were two people onboard.

A man's voice drifted across the surface of the marshland towards them, low and gravelly. "Can you see them yet?"

"*Yebo*." The second seemed a man of few words.

"Uh, Shrimp...I need more info than just a yes. What are we dealing with?"

The one called Shrimp sat closest to the front of the boat. He paused rowing to squint through the gloom, "From here it looks like two Unlit's and a Cover-up."

"Safe or risky?"

"I dunno, Beaver. Injured, I think."

Beaver took up a spare pair of oars and settled down toward the back of the boat. "All right. Let's bring them in. Paddle hard left, and we'll coast in sideways to load them up."

"Yebo."

"And stop with that foreign lingo. Have you been hanging around the Zulu again?"

"Ye—"

"No! Don't say it!" Beaver aimed the back of the paddle at Shrimp's back and gasped with fright when cold liquid ran down the paddle and down his arm, soaking his pants. He was still spluttering and shaking his legs in turn when the boat pulled to an expert stop a hair's breadth from bumping into Elden and Evazee.

"You folks in need of some help, perhaps? The name's Beaver, and this here is Shrimp." He didn't wait for them to respond but stood to take Peta from Elden.

The boat rocked alarmingly, but the two onboard stayed steady. Elden hesitated for a fraction of a second before handing the small girl over. For Elden to accept help from strangers meant he was close to being done. Right now, this seemed to be their best option.

Elden boosted Evazee from behind, steadying the boat with his other hand. Evazee almost tipped in head first. Her water-logged feet were cold and stiff from being submerged for too long. Elden climbed in after and lifted Peta onto his lap. The boat was small and the three of them huddled in the middle section, all knees and elbows.

Elden drew Evazee closer to himself with an arm around her shoulder, "It's a bit squishy in here."

Heat crept into her cheeks, and she let him tuck her closer, only because it meant he couldn't see her blushing face. "Where are you taking us? If you don't mind me asking." She threw the question out, not sure which one of the men was in charge.

"Not at all," Shrimp answered from the front, paddling as he spoke. "You're coming to our home so we can do something about those burns before infection sets in."

"How far is your home? Where do you live?"

Shrimp paused rowing. "Not too far now." He waved his hand over the rippling water. "In fact, you could call this our backyard."

"You all had a run in with the rock lava, I see?" Beaver spoke up from behind them.

Evazee pointed. "These two did. It missed me somehow."

At her comment, Shrimp swung around and winked at Beaver. "Cover-up. Told you."

Beaver threw up a hand, his flat palm aimed straight at Shrimp. "Honestly. Did I even argue with you? No, I didn't. So can you just shut it?" For all their arguing, the vibe between the two men was good-humoured.

Evazee pressed closer to Elden. Angling her head towards his ear. "Do you think those are their real names? Beaver and Shrimp?"

Shrimp chuckled, and Evazee wished she'd swallowed her curiosity.

"Of course not. Real names are powerful. Those with wisdom keep 'em secret amongst strangers." He kept his eyes focussed ahead, peering through the murky gloom, lit only by the half-hearted lamp light.

Evazee stared out over the water and pretended she hadn't asked the question or heard Shrimp's answer. Nope. Not her.

"We're close now," Beaver spoke up from behind. "Pay attention, kids. You don't want to miss this."

Peta roused from Elden's lap. For a moment, they paddled in gloomy silence. Suddenly, sparkles of colour like a thousand tiny stars dotted the air in front of them. Were her eyes playing up? Each spot of light glowed, grew, and started spinning as one until the edges blurred and the sparkles merged, transforming the sky above them to an iridescent dome of shifting colour that dissolved the gloom.

Evazee drank in the light as it washed over her in waves, stripping off oppression that she hadn't realized was pressing down on her. The water they floated on stretched as far as she could see in all directions, reflecting the rainbow colours of the sky in a rippling dance that made her heart miss a beat. She sat forward, twisting all around to absorb the beauty. "Beaver, where do you live? I don't see anything." Evazee glanced back, caught sight of Beaver's face, and froze.

When they'd first climbed into the boat, Beaver had looked craggy and old, somewhat weather-beaten and neglected. Seeing him in this light transformed him. He probably wasn't much older than her or Elden.

Beaver caught her eye and grinned. He pointed up ahead. "Welcome to our home."

Evazee turned and gasped. Instead of empty water, an enormous dome-like structure floated on the water in front of them. The mirrored surface reflected the sky, but with a wave of Shrimp's hand, it cleared to transparent, revealing the insides.

A multi-story home, complete with furniture, bookshelves, a kitchen, plants, carpeted floors…everything that made a place a home. The base of the structure was built from a dull grey material that appeared to be buoyant enough to keep the whole thing floating. As they drew closer, a section of the base split apart and the top drew back to reveal three steps leading to the front door.

Shrimp steered the boat and stopped alongside the stairs. Connectors appeared from below the base with a mechanical whine, securing the boat to the dome.

Beaver stepped off first, pressing his palm to a rectangular, marked section on the dome. With a hiss, the door popped out and slid sideways. "Come on in. We've been expecting you."

~*~

Zap leaned in close, whispering so furiously that Kai feared spit would fly and his ear would catch the worst of it.

"I'm telling you now, if we don't find food for him, he's going to get worse. Look at him. He's stalking around like a demented bear with an infected bladder."

"Bladder? Why bladder?"

Zap's face crinkled. "I dunno. It sounded impressive at the time. And it's really sore. You ever had a bladder infection?"

"If I did, I wouldn't be telling you. That's for sure." Kai shook his head and went back to squinting in the direction they were heading, hoping for some clue that they were travelling in the right direction.

Ruaan stomped along behind them, muttering under his breath and kicking anything in his path.

"There has to be food here somewhere." Zap dashed ahead of Kai, peering through the gloom at the bushes that dotted alongside the path they walked on.

"I don't get it, Zap. Last time I was here, I didn't need to eat. It wasn't even an issue. I never got hungry, never saw food, and never ate. I don't think one has to eat here."

Zap's face skewed in the way it always did when he was trying not to hurt feelings. "From what you've been saying, this time has been nothing like last time. So I'm not sure why you keep using that as some sort of guide for what is happening now."

Kai sighed. "I guess you're right. Are you also hungry?"

"A bit." A loud growl echoed through the air. "OK, maybe a lot." He rolled his eyes like he did when he was five years old. Now as an eighteen-year-old, it just made him look daft. Ruaan ambled behind them and spewed a stream of unhappiness, none of it loud enough to make any sense.

Kai shrugged. He didn't know where to start looking for food in this place.

Zap grabbed his arm and pointed. "Maybe we don't have to know where to look for food. Let's ask them."

"Did you just overhear my thoughts again?"

"No. I don't think so. Don't be weird, Kai."

Huddled together and moving quickly, a group of people came over the rise and saved Kai from having to respond. They came to a sudden stop, silently staring toward Kai and his friends.

"Get down!" Kai dropped to the ground, hiding the light underneath him.

Zap knelt slowly. "But—"

"Shh! We don't know who they are. I don't want them to know we are here." Kai squinted. He couldn't see through the gloom.

Ruaan shuffled closer on his knees. "Those are kids from the OS. That's Morgan in the front."

"How can you tell?" Kai's spoke louder than he'd meant to. He clapped his hand over his mouth but removed it again to whisper. "Can you see?"

His eyes glowed faintly, a luminous grey, just visible.

Ruaan shrugged. "I can see everything. It's all greyed out, but it's clear. Can't you?"

Zap grabbed Kai's arm and hung on as if a whirlwind was about to hit. "Dude, that's creepy."

Ruaan turned toward Zap. "What's creepy?"

"Your eyes. What is going on with your eyes?" Zap's fingers slipped off Kai's arm as he backed away.

Ruaan's belly rumbled, and he patted it. "Just so you know, Morgan and her bunch are all looking toward us. If you were aiming to hide, you failed. They're listening to every word we say, trying to decide if we're safe. So go right ahead, keep yakking."

"And you're sure that's Morgan?" Kai asked.

Ruaan rolled his eyes.

Kai frowned, "I saw that."

"You were meant to." Ruaan put a hand to his mouth and yelled, "Morgan! Come on over."

Kai's head hung. He pushed back onto his knees and light bloomed from the bottle around his neck. "Seriously? Did you have to?" The situation was getting worse. It was only meant to be him and Elden who came back to find Bree. Now it seemed that more of the kids had been brought back. With no Affinity, no Tau, and Evazee missing, the last thing he needed were more people trapped here. Whether it was his job to look after them or not.

"Ruaan? Is that you?" Morgan and her companions inched closer, hunched over, wide-eyed and wary. Her face relaxed and she straightened up. "It is you. What are we doing here? I thought all the training was supposed to be over." She took in the other two with a brief nod. The rest of her group huddled behind her. Her gaze flew back to Kai and her eyes narrowed. "You. This is your fault. You're a liar! What did you do to us?"

Kai's head tilted, and his eyebrow rose. "Excuse me? I could ask you the same thing. Why are you here? It's not safe. You should be taking care of this bunch back at the OS. What were you thinking?" He regretted his outburst the moment the last word left his lips. He opened his mouth to apologize, but before he could say a word, a deep drumbeat shuddered through the ground, vibrating up his legs. It pounded into him through the air and shook the ground beneath his feet.

Morgan and her friends turned away from Kai. Another deep boom rocked the ground. Kai, Ruaan, and Zap staggered to keep their footing, but Morgan and her friends stood rock steady, staring into the distance like a regiment of soldiers carved from stone. The drum beats picked up a rhythm, coming faster and stronger. The sound rippled through him.

Morgan's group started walking, each step in time with the drumbeat.

Kai reached for Morgan. "Don't listen!"

Her eyes glazed over, and she pulled from his grasp with shocking strength.

Kai swung around to check on Ruaan and Zap. "Are you guys falling for this?"

Zap's mouth hung open, and he crouched low with his legs spread and arms wide as if he were trying to surf on solid ground. He wobbled as each drumbeat hit. He blinked at Kai, eyelids flapping, "I'm trying not to fall!"

Ruaan stood with his arms tightly folded, sneering at the group as they marched off. "I bet you they'll get food."

Kai looked from one to the other. Then he shook his head and walked. "Enough. Let's keep moving." As the deafening drumbeat hit, the ground rocked beneath him, but other than steadying himself, he ignored the noise and drama and aimed himself in the direction of the light. He just had to get there, and everything else would sort itself.

6

Evazee curled up on a beanbag and fought the heaviness of her eyelids. The oblivion of sleep seemed so tempting.

The lounge of the dome house was on the same level as the boat bobbing outside the front door. The only seats were randomly dotted beanbags in shades of sea-blue and green. The glass panes of the dome were clear, and from her vantage point on the bean bag, she could see out over the river, which stretched lazily away into the distance. The dome spread light that pushed back darkness in a wide circle. The dome itself was a strange contradiction, seeming at once fragile and indestructible. She felt safe. But could she trust her feelings? She'd been wrong before.

She wriggled upright and placed both feet on the floor. Her head lolled back.

Shrimp brought in a tray and propped a glass on the short, mushroom-shaped table next to her. The liquid glowed, five different coloured layers in all. "Drink up. It will help you relax." Shrimp's sandy-blond hair stood out in all directions as if it objected to being rooted to his scalp. His skin was golden with a dusting of freckles across his nose.

Evazee eyed the drink, not convinced something that cheerful could be safe to drink. "Where are my friends?"

"Do you want to see them?" If Shrimp was offended at her suspicion, he didn't show it. He smiled. There was kindness in his eyes. "Come."

He held out a hand, but she ignored it, preferring instead to awkwardly push herself to a stand.

A winding staircase ran through the centre of the dome, leading to the upper floor and disappearing into the base of the structure below. Evazee eyed it with suspicion. The steps were see-through, connected to each other by metal rods that zig-zagged beneath each step. Shrimp followed the staircase down, two steps at a time. Evazee hung back. They seemed too fragile to hold her weight, but Shrimp was heavier, and they'd held him without breaking.

Evazee took a deep breath and followed, walking on her toes to make herself as light as possible. Only as she stepped off the last step did she look around.

"Oh my word. Are we underwater?" The entire lower level was fashioned from glass. Her feet tingled as she walked on the cold surface. Tiny fish darted beneath her. It was like being in a reverse fish tank, only she was in the glass bowl for everyone to gawk at.

A small, cold hand slipped into hers. It was Peta, pale and shivering. Evazee squeezed and wrapped the girl's hand in both of hers, sharing warmth.

The water all around shifted and bubbled, and rays of light broke the surface, slicing through emerald with dazzling slashes of turquoise. The sound of water bubbling seemed louder inside than what it should. Shrimp waited for her off to one side, a strange smile on his face.

"Your boyfriend is here." He moved to the side and waved her over. Behind him were two glass pods suspended from the ceiling and half-filled with bubbling water. Elden floated in one, the other one behind it stood empty.

Elden's face was radiant. He opened his eyes as she came close and grinned at her. The pain must have lifted, as his features were relaxed and calm. He was dressed in a baggy blue jumpsuit. It flapped around him, loose enough for the water to get to his skin but covering enough to be modest.

"What are these?" Evazee stepped closer, but Peta hung back, still holding onto her arm like a lifeline.

Shrimp looked smug. "The water is from the Healing Stream. Another couple of minutes and his back should be all better."

"Would it work for Peta's legs?"

Shrimp nodded. "If it were up to me, she'd be in already. But she was a bit reluctant."

Peta had tucked herself in behind Evazee. Another tremor ran through her from top to bottom and her nails dug into the palms of Evazee's hand.

"And what if I go in with her? Will that work?" Evazee twisted to look into Peta's eyes. *Should we do this?* Peta blinked rapidly, and her nostrils flared. She was breathing too fast. Evazee sunk to her knees and wrapped her arms around the girl. She pushed away to study Peta's legs. The wounds were angry, red, and seeping.

"We've never tried that before." Shrimp's head tilted sideways as he frowned at them both. "You're both quite small. You'd fit. Still, I don't know if it's a good idea."

"I've been in the Healing Stream. I know the water. Please." The thought of Peta in pain was too much for her. The risk of infection was high. Maybe if she had her first aid kit she could prevent it, but she hadn't been given the luxury of packing for this little adventure.

"I'm going to ask Beaver. I'll be back."

He made it halfway up the stairs and turned back, rubbing his chin. "Once I seal you in, it takes ten minutes to pressurize. I can't open for you until those ten minutes are up. Think about that before you decide." He ran up the stairs two at a time.

Evazee thought back to the first time she'd taken Runt into the water. She'd not only been healed, but she'd been changed from the inside out. Maybe this was Peta's hope of getting rid of whatever had been transferred into her when Shasta fixed her ankle.

"Peta, do you trust me?" She twisted herself around in the little girl's arms and crouched to eye level.

Peta glanced from Evazee to the pod and back again. She didn't shake her head or nod, but her eyebrows dropped low into a fierce frown.

"Here, look at Elden. Look at his face. He's happy in there. His pain is gone."

The girl breathed deep and took a small step forward. Easing in front of Evazee, she walked alongside the pod. Evazee kept an arm around her shoulders, willing courage into the girl. Elden floated with his eyes closed, thousands of tiny bubbles collected on his skin. As they burst, more bubbled up from below to replace them. Peta's muscles relaxed beneath Evazee's fingertips. Peta's frown lifted, and she reached out to touch the pod.

"Don't touch the p—" Evazee spoke too late.

As Peta's fingers met the glass, a jolt of heat shot through Evazee. Her eyes burned, and she pinched them shut. Images flashed in her head: a sticky black spider web, melting, flowing along the ground and seeping up into her feet, slipping into her veins; black goo pumping through her cells, her lungs, to her heart, flowing through her system, tainting cells and turning healthy flesh grey. It threaded all around her spine, up through her neck, branching out over her scalp, a skullcap of hemlock.

A curtain was drawn over her mind. She gagged and fell back and the vision cut off. The room had turned a sickly green. Peta clung to the pod as if all the strength had gone out of her legs. Elden thrashed inside, hands pressing the glass. The water had turned a dirty, murky brown.

"Peta! Get back!" Evazee pushed off the floor and staggered across to Peta, pulling the girl off.

Shrimp and Beaver ran down the stairs. Shrimp flew to a lever on the side of the pod. "One more minute."

Elden was on his knees, back pressed against the lid of the pod. He stared at Evazee with wild eyes. A trail of blood trickled from his nose.

Shrimp hovered over the timer as if he could speed it up through the sheer force of his will. A single, clear beep rang out and Shrimp leaned on the lever, all his muscles straining. It shifted with a metallic screech and the lid flew back with a hiss.

Beaver tried to help Elden, but he shot up out of the water and clambered over the side. His foot hooked and he came down head first, breaking his fall with his left arm. Elden lay there, moisture from his jumpsuit spreading into a puddle on the floor. The moment he left the pod, the water changed back to the sparkling emerald that it had been.

Peta had curled up in a ball on the floor with both hands covering her ears, her eyes squeezed shut. Evazee crawled over and stretched out a hand to stroke her back but stopped just short of touching her, remembering the awful vision. Her little friend needed the comfort, but the memory was still too raw.

Shrimp ran a hand through his hair, shaking his head with a low whistle. "Beaver, take the girls upstairs. I'll check on the boy."

Beaver reached down and helped Peta to her feet. She flinched at his touch but didn't fight him. Evazee followed him, looking over her shoulder at Elden, searching for some sign that he was going to be all right.

~*~

"We've been walking forever. I tell you now, we are not getting any closer. How do we even know for sure that we're going the right direction?" Ruaan had seemingly unlimited stamina for complaining. He never missed a beat and constantly found new ways to whine about their current dilemma. "I can't see lights. I'm beginning to think that it was some weird trick or illusion. Like an oasis but no water, just light. We don't need a desert to end up as carcasses."

Kai halted so fast that Zap bumped into him.

"Hey! Why'd you stop?"

"Mostly to glare at the one sprouting rubbish here behind us. What do you suggest, hey, Ruaan?"

"That's not a fair question."

"But filling our ears with your moaning is?"

"Oh please. I don't moan that much. Anyway, you

asked for my suggestion. I say we ask him." He pointed up ahead to a tree.

"A tree. Seriously?" Unlike the purple trees of Kai's first visit, the bark of this one was quite ordinary, all in regular shades of brown. At least it looked ordinary until a whole section of the tree moved and spoke.

"Greetings, travellers." The man's clothes rippled and shifted from tree bark to worn, soft leather that carried the dust of travel in its creases. The man wore his long hair scraped back and caught up with a leather strip at the nape of his neck. His face was a lined roadmap of the years he carried in the curve of his spine and the strength of his hands. He held a black metal knife, which he slipped into a pouch on his belt as he waved them over. "Anyone hungry?"

Kai frowned, trying to see if the man had any other weapons. "We can't stop. But thanks for offering."

Ruaan shuffled close to Kai and tapped him on the shoulder. He blinked fast against the moisture gathering on his lashes.

"What? Are you crying?"

Zap cleared his throat and pointed at Ruaan's belly. Ruaan's shoulders hung forward, and he cradled his stomach with the tenderness most people save for newborns. Zap snorted a laugh. "You forget that thing has been talking to us for hours now. We should stop and feed it, Kai."

The man leaning on the tree threw aside a cloth to reveal a spread of food unlike anything Kai had ever seen before. "It won't take long. Lunch is ready. There's too much here for me to eat. Come on. Have a seat."

Zap and Ruaan didn't need a second invitation. They each picked a different side of the square table cloth and sat staring at the food as if they'd been eating gruel since birth.

Kai took his place opposite the man and tucked his legs underneath himself, shying away from touching the cloth spread beneath the food. The food itself looked more like a deconstructed bridal bouquet than something that would put some meat on their bones or fill their bellies.

"Trust me. It's more filing than most of the stuff you're so fond of on the other side." A faint trace of amusement coloured the man's speech.

"How do you know what we're fond of? Who are you anyway?" Kai kept his hands tucked firmly in his armpits, though his eyes roamed from item to item on the blanket.

"All in good time, friend. I've been sent to help you."

Zap had torn his eyes away from the food to stare at the man. "You're a Seeker! I've heard of you. They warned us about your lot back at the OS. You're like bloodhounds but for people. Whoa." He frowned at the man, glanced at the food, and shrugged.

The man smiled, and it transformed his face. He almost looked kind. "Some call us that. You may call me Gallagher. "Please eat. I brought it all for you."

Zap checked his hands and tried to brush the dust off. Ruaan tucked his behind his back.

"Would you like to wash your hands before eating?" Gallagher's eyes flicked over the dust that stubbornly clung to them. He brought out a pitcher of water and a bowl, and tipped it over their outstretched hands. The grey dust was no match for liquid. Zap laughed in delight, rubbing his clean hands together.

Gallagher waved towards the food. "Help yourselves."

Ruaan reached for a perfectly round, lime green blob, with dimpled skin much like a strawberry. He sniffed it and bit into the soft flesh. Purple juice dribbled down his chin and his eyes rolled. "Oh my! You guys have to try this one."

Zap waved a royal-blue stick under Kai's nose. It vaguely resembled celery but gave off a sweet and salty scent. Zap nibbled one end with long teeth. He sighed and a goofy smile crept over his face. "Now this is what I call the food of the gods. Here, try it."

Kai sneezed, and Zap snapped his hand back. Zap studied it to make sure he couldn't see any moisture all down the length of it. Then he bit into it, chewed, and swallowed.

Kai stared from one to the other and back again. His shoulders itched, and he glanced up to find Gallagher staring.

"You're not hungry. You weren't hungry the last time you were here either." Gallagher's eyebrow lifted and changed his statement to a question.

Kai shook his head. It bothered him that Gallagher had picked up on the same thing that was puzzling him. Worse than that, Gallagher probably knew why, but Kai couldn't bring himself to ask. Pride or caution? Either way, he kept his mouth shut tight.

A strangely satisfied smile pulled at Gallagher's lips, and he nodded slowly. "Good."

"You said you were sent to help us. Who sent you and why?"

"I'm glad to see that you are cautious, Kai. Let me ask you one question, though. What does your heart say about me?"

"I don't trust my heart."

"Fair enough."

"Who sent you?"

"I can show you the way to the one whom you seek."

Kai leaned back, unfolding his long legs to ward off a cramp threatening to knot up his left foot. He wiggled his toes inside the canvas of his sneakers. At least this time he wasn't barefoot. So, Gallagher thought he knew who they were here to find. Kai bit back a dry laugh. Bree was meant to be the whole point of this trip until they'd lost the girls and seemingly Tau himself. "That, right there, is the problem. I don't think you know as much as you think you do."

Gallagher shrugged. "If you're worried about your two female companions, they're safe for the moment. You need to get to your friend."

Kai shot up. "How did you know—"

"I know what I need to. However, as slow as you're moving, you aren't going to get to her in time. She's inside Stone City. You're heading in the right direction, but the way is treacherous and long."

Zap swallowed his mouthful of food and his jaw dropped. "Whoa!"

"You speak as if she's alive." Kai narrowed his eyes. "So what can we do?"

"There's another way." Gallagher held up a hand in caution. "Or I should say, there used to be another way, but it's broken beyond repair."

"Broken? Like a holey bridge that we'd fall off?"

"It's not a path like that. Think of it this way. In space you get wormholes. Pinches in the galaxy that bring point A and B closer together and let you cut out years of travel. Are you familiar with the concept?"

Kai nodded. Zap and Ruaan were arguing over the last crispy flat cake. Hunched over, each of them had one end of the cake in hand as they glared at each other over the top of it. Neither seemed to have been tracking the conversation.

Zap pulled the cake a few millimetres closer. "We know about wormholes. Can we find a wormhole home?"

Gallagher shrugged. "I don't know about that. Brio Talee, spirit cuttings. They are quick paths through the spiritual world. But if you were listening properly, you'd know that you can't use them anyway. So the point is moot." He slipped the knife from his belt, hoisted it overhead and slashed the flat cake in half. The boys landed on their backsides, still hanging onto their half of the cake.

"Whoa! That thing is dangerous, man!" Blood drained from Zap's face. "I heard you. But the thing is, Kai fixes broken things."

"What are you talking about?" Kai asked.

"Oh, come on. We lived in the same dormitory for how long? You were always fixing broken things."

"But I was careful. I made sure nobody saw."

Zap bit into his section of flat cake, waving his hand in a circle while he chewed and swallowed. "I guess that means I'm nobody." He grinned. "You told Phil how to fix the microwave. That was cool. And there was that time Matty was in the sick bay. You sneaked out in the middle of the night. I didn't dare follow you, but it was pretty obvious. He'd been gone for a week. The next day he was back. Coincidence? I think not. It's all you."

"But you never said anything."

"So you admit it?"

"Come on, Zap. Why didn't you say anything?"

"I was waiting for you to tell me yourself. After that? I never found the right moment. Why do you think I wanted Affinity so bad? All I wanted was to be able to do what you do."

Gallagher leaned forward, rubbing his chin. "Are you telling me that you're a Restorer?"

Kai peered at him out the corner of an eye. "Maybe? I don't know."

"All the signs are there. Living things, inanimate objects—you've fixed both?"

"I can see what's broken, and I know what to do about it. That's all. If this shortcut wasn't broken, could we use it to get to Bree?"

"In theory, yes."

"How is it broken?"

"Broken is the wrong word. More like infected. Tainted is even more accurate."

Kai shut his eyes and pinched his forehead. A headache crept across his skull from the base of his neck. "It seems that point is moot, too. My Affinity isn't working this time." He held up Runt's glowing light bottle. "I need this to make light. Can't even do that anymore, let alone fix invisible pathways."

Gallagher leaned back, resting on the tree. "How did you get back this time? The first time was a run in with a bus, if I'm not mistaken."

Ruaan had stretched out on his back with his hands on his belly. He snored softly, his chest rising and falling like a metronome. Zap leaned on his elbow and sucked the last traces of food off his fingers. He stuck his hand in the air the way they used to at St Greg's when they wanted the teacher's attention. He shook it around as if to say, "Me! Me! Pick me!"

Kai rolled his eyes and put on his best teacher voice. "You there, boy. The one on the floor. What?"

"We were sent back with the help of a serious dose of dark Affinity enhancer." He sat up, stretched, and looped his arms around his knees. "Whoever did it pumped enough of the stuff into the building to bring five of us back."

Kai pinched the skin above his nose. "More than just us. Morgan and her friends, too, remember? We don't know how many were brought back this time."

Zap nodded. "You're right. It's worse than we thought. Normally, it should have worn off by now. I don't know why it hasn't. Apparently, it's having a bad effect on our boy here, who is some sort of Affinity superhero. He keeps going on about all the things he could do before that he can't do now. Cleansing a tainted bridge may be a little beyond him right now. No offence, Kai."

Kai waved off the insult. He clicked his fingers and sat up straight. "It's that air freshener thing. That's what's causing all the trouble. Why didn't I think of it before?"

"Excuse me?" Zap's forehead crinkled. "What are you talking about?"

"You know the section of the OS where we were sitting when the green vapour got us? It has those air freshener things mounted on the walls that are supposed to send out puffs of freshener at regular intervals. If someone loaded Affinity enhancer into those..."

"It would just keep pumping into the rooms until the canisters emptied."

"Exactly. That could take months. All my light

Affinity is powerless under the influence of that chemical cocktail."

Gallagher picked up the corners of the cloth and folded it over the empty containers. The cloth flattened out the way it would if there were nothing inside. He took the next set of corners, folded them in and kept going until he had a tiny square of fabric, which he pocketed.

He stood up, brushed himself off, and held a hand out to Kai. He pulled him to his feet and leaned in close. "You are not as powerless as you think. Use what you have. Stop being a victim."

Before Kai could respond, Gallagher turned to the tree, placed both hands on the bark and muttered under his breath. A shudder ran through the tree from roots to leaves, and the tree shook, filling the air with rustling. It began as a creaking whisper and built to a groan of ancient wood.

Ruaan woke mid-snore, shrieked, and rolled onto his feet. He backed away too fast and tripped, landing on his rear. The tree was moving.

Kai blocked his ears and resisted the urge to run. Zap sat with his face blank, head tilted to one side, pinching the skin on the back of his hand.

Gallagher moved aside with a wide sweep of an arm, "Gentlemen, I give you the entrance to Brio Talee, the spirit cuttings.

7

Evazee sat on the floor next to Peta's beanbag in the blue-green lounge, careful not to touch the girl. Peta lay curled up, her eyes shut tight. She'd stopped crying and withdrawn inside herself. More than anything, Peta needed the Healing Stream but after seeing what had happened to Elden in the water, Evazee couldn't imagine her agreeing to go in. Maybe if they could find the real thing, it would be different. But where would she even start looking?

Evazee studied her surroundings. It was easier than deciding what to do. The mat on the glass floor seemed to be woven of sea-grass. It was see-through, green, and soft to the touch. Apart from the beanbags, the only other decoration in the room was a life-size statue of a black man crouching in the corner. His carved ebony skin shone as if polished, his body lean but muscular. A scar ran down one side of face, slashing through his right eyebrow and down his temple and cheek, missing his eye by millimeters. He had the look of a warrior, fierce and merciless. Evazee dropped her gaze. Looking at the statue made her uncomfortable.

"You're worried about your friend," the statue said.

Evazee shot upright, adrenalin pumping through

her system. "You scared me. I didn't think you were...er, never mind."

The man unfolded himself from his crouching position and crossed the room with the grace of a panther. He towered over Peta and then knelt down next to her, the frown on his face deepening. Evazee could pick up Peta and run, but trying to outrun this guy didn't seem like a bright idea.

He reached toward Peta's forehead. His hand was big enough to cover her whole face, but his fingers were gentle.

"Don't touch her!" Evazee shook at the memory of the vision, at what had happened to Elden.

He stopped and his eyes flashed. "I'm not going to harm her."

"Oh no, I didn't mean it like that. I just meant it's not safe for you. We had some trouble downstairs." The thought of explaining was too much. "Never mind. I'm sorry. I'm Evazee. You are?"

A broad smile slashed across his face. In a moment, he shifted from fierce warrior to kind stranger. "They call me The Zulu. I know what happened."

Evazee blinked, "What do you mean?"

He pointed toward the stairway, his finger circling in a downward spiral.

"You mean downstairs? I was there, and I don't know what happened. It was awful." *Painful, confusing, frightening.* She could go on and on.

"The water, it changed. Yes?"

"I don't know if I should be talking about this."

"Did it turn black, green, or brown?"

"Brown. What difference does it make?"

"The colour speaks. Brown means..." He rubbed

his fingers by his lips as if to tease the right word off the tip of his tongue.

"Zulu! Downstairs quick!" Beaver's head poked up through the hole in the floor.

Zulu shot to his feet, whispering as he rushed past. "We'll talk."

"Is he going to be all right?" Evazee's words bounced through the room and returned to her unanswered. Beaver and Zulu were gone. She sank to her knees on the seagrass mat, leaning on Peta's beanbag, careful not to touch the girl. Evazee's body felt heavy and her heart was sore. The vision had left a residue of dread in her that she was too scared to examine. It simmered just below the surface of her consciousness. Peta was not right, and Evazee had no idea how to fix her.

Jesus, I don't even know if You can hear me. At home I can talk to You at any time, about anything. I know what it feels like to be near You. Here, I feel nothing. Well, nothing good anyway. I can't feel You or see Your miracles. I don't know what to do. I don't know how to help Elden or Peta. If I close my eyes, all I see is the spider web. I can feel it oozing through my veins. I'm scared.

She buried her face in her arms and cried. All the emotions of the last few hours washed over her in thick waves, and she drifted on the edges of tattered consciousness, slipping in and out of sleep. She was so far gone that a warm hand on her back seemed to be more dream than reality.

"Evazee, wake up."

She knew that voice. It took her straight back to stolen fruit and the testing grass. "Elden?" His hand spread warmth across the small of her back and made her shiver. Evazee eased herself upright, stretching out the kinks in her spine and neck.

He sat cross-legged next to her on the sea-grass mat. He had dark patches under his eyes. He'd changed out of the blue jumpsuit into his own clothes, even down to the holey T-shirt.

"Oh my gosh. It is you. How are you?" His face was paler than she'd ever seen, almost chalk-white. Evazee checked the room to make sure they were alone. "Where are they?"

"Researching. They're trying to figure out what went wrong. They told me to find you, that we should make ourselves comfortable until they can help us. I doubt they'll return for a while yet."

"What happened? What did they do to you?"

Elden shrugged. "I don't remember much."

"Turn around. I want to see your back." She wiggled her fingers in his face, waving tiny circles in the air.

He enfolded her small hands in his, gently, as if catching butterflies. "Can we get out of here? I don't want to be here."

The sadness in his eyes tugged at Evazee. "I think we can trust these people. They seem good to me."

He looked away, his eyes roaming over the room with all its soft curves and gentle colours. "I know. I just want to go." His cheeks were hollow and raw emotion cracked his voice. She'd never seen him like this before.

"Show me your back."

Elden sucked in a deep breath and held her gaze as he let it out. His eyes seemed to search for something in hers. He turned his back to her, lifting his holey shirt.

Evazee bit her cheek. His back was a mess of

raised scars. She fought off the stars that twinkled on the edges of her vision. The burns had healed but the scars remained.

"You're not burnt anymore. That's something."

Elden turned back with a wry smile. "The pain is much less. So that's good. Right?"

"I would have thought the Healing Stream would have finished the work. It's weird."

He shrugged. "I wasn't in there for the full time. They said about half an hour should do. It was cut short."

Evazee cleared her throat. "Was it Peta?"

"Peta? How would she affect the process?"

How could she transform her vague suspicions into words? She checked to make sure the girl was sleeping. "Peta touched your pod. That's when everything went wrong. I think there's still some residue of what was released in her when Shasta healed her leg. I think it affected you. I'm so sorry."

"How could it have?"

She shut her eyes to avoid his, but residual images of liquid spider webs sliding through her veins flooded in. It could have come from Peta alone, but what if it came from both of them? Was the vision a warning? If so, it was up to her to figure it out.

Peta whimpered in her sleep. Her face crinkled, and she clung to her belly. A single tear slid down her cheek, but through it all, she didn't wake up. Evazee reached for her forehead and stopped short before touching. Peta's skin blazed beneath her fingertips, hot enough to be felt across the gap between fingers and skin.

"She's burning up. I don't know how much time we've got. She won't go in a pod after tonight. I don't think I'd let her either. Her only hope is the Healing Stream." Evazee turned straight into Elden who'd moved closer without her noticing, "Can you take us there?"

"This is a different section—"

"To where you were before. I know. Can you find the stream?"

He reached up and gently separated a lock of her hair from the rest. He curled it around his finger and let it unwind as it slid off. "I can try."

"Let's do it. She doesn't have time for all their research."

"We steal their boat?"

"Not steal, borrow."

"That works, too."

"What else do we need? Do you think we could borrow a lamp as well?" A small smile tugged at the corners of Evazee's mouth, and Elden grinned back with a faint sparkle in his eye. For a moment, she saw beyond the gaunt pull of his cheeks, and her heartbeat doubled.

"I was about to suggest that." He held up a hand for a high-five, and she hit his hand, feeling excitement bubble in her belly.

"There's no time to waste. They could be out any minute."

Evazee nodded and eased herself off the floor, working life back into her ankles. Her only regret at leaving was that she wouldn't get to finish her conversation with Zulu. He would have told her the meaning of the colour of the water. But in the big picture, what difference would that knowing make? Probably not much.

She picked up a lamp off the table. It was shaped

like an hourglass that fit in her hand and the light reached as far as she could see into the rest of the home. It glowed with its own light and didn't need to be plugged in.

Elden scooped Peta up in his arms, grunting under the weight of the girl who slept so deeply that she hung in his arms like soggy seaweed. "Let's go."

~*~

Kai peered into the dark hole at their feet. A silvery staircase led down into the blackness. It was impossible to see what they would be walking into. "Guys, you know that we could die in these cuttings, right?"

Ruaan leaned forward, tilting his head at an angle, "That doesn't sound like something I want to do. I like living. I really do."

"You don't have to come. You can wait right here or go back to the graveyard. All I know is I can't leave Bree. If there's a chance I can get to her, even a slim one, I'm going to take it. Same for you Zap. You don't have to."

Zap pursed his lips, "Let me think this through. My choices are, go back and die at the hands of the Grave Keepers, or follow you into who-knows-what and potentially die. I think I'm going to go with potentially. It's a bit of a no-brainer really." He shrugged, "Besides, it's quite exciting, don't you think? I want to know what's down there."

Ruaan glared at him. "You truly are insane, aren't you? Here's the thing. There was no food where we came from. Nothing. However, there might be food where we're going. So I'll take my chances." He slipped his hands into his pockets. "Besides, Kai is the only one with light. I'm not going to hang around in the dark."

Kai sighed. "You're both nuts." He twisted his torso, clicking his back. Then he laced his fingers and pushed his palms forward as if he were warming up for a marathon. "Let's just do it." *Don't overthink, just walk. One step at a time.* He took a deep breath and stepped down. As his foot touched the first step, a dark flash rippled through the structure of the bridge from beneath his feet, swelling outward and then snapping back with force. The stinging rebound shuddered through his legs hard enough to make him stumble.

Kai caught himself on the rail, but the metal seemed acidic and seared his fingertips. He pulled away so fast he lost his footing and slid down the stairs to land at the bottom in an ungainly heap of arms and legs.

"Kai! You dead?" Zap sounded shaken.

Kai gingerly eased onto his back, checking for broken bones. "Not yet. I fell. That's all." He closed his eyes for moment and wished to have his Affinity back. "Get down here. I want to get through fast. Just don't touch the rail." It had always been so simple: know the problem and fix it. It didn't take Affinity to know that this place was broken, but there was nothing he could do. He hoisted the bottle light toward the stairs. The steps themselves were rusted, corroded, eaten right through in places. "Walk carefully. There are holes."

Ruaan pushed Zap out of the way. He made his way down, feeling his way with his feet before stepping. He moved efficiently, avoiding the holes without much fuss. Only when Ruaan reached to the bottom closer to the bottle light could Kai see his jaw clench and the white in his cheeks.

Zap stood alone at the top. He leaned in, but his feet stayed rooted. "The darkness looks hungry. I don't think I can…"

"Get down here. Now."

"But—"

"I'm not listening. Get moving." Kai shoved his hands over his ears, feeling like a three-year-old.

"But…"

"No! We can't wait. Go back or come. Choose." *Stop being such ninny.*

"I am not a ninny. What a fine friend you are, wanting me to die." Zap stepped down, his foot narrowly missing a rusted hole. "So much for an adventure. This is more like the dentist and the principal's office all rolled into one."

Kai leaned over to Ruaan. "Did I say ninny?"

"I didn't hear you say ninny. Did you want to say ninny?"

"He is being a ninny. I might have thought it."

"This isn't the first time he seems to have heard your thoughts, is it?" A tremor snaked through the structure, cutting off their conversation. Ruaan shuffled closer to Kai. "Do you think this thing can carry our combined weight? It seems too weak."

"It will hold." Kai avoided Ruaan's eyes. He focused on Zap, who gingerly picked his way down the damaged stairs, blinked hard, and chewed his lips as if trying not to cry. "Two more steps, Zap. Keep coming."

8

The door to the dome house was unlocked. At Evazee's touch, it slid back. The boat bobbed at the foot of the stairs just where they'd left it a lifetime ago. The catches that held it shifted back automatically as their feet touched the first stair. Evazee hung the stolen lamp on the hook mounted at the front of the boat. It swung with the movement of the boat, casting strange shadows that seemed to have a life of their own.

Elden motioned Evazee in to sit in the middle. He straddled the gap with one foot in the boat and the other on the landing and leaned over Evazee to deposit Peta into her lap. Evazee shrunk back, still scared of touching the girl, but Elden gave her no choice and even less time to object. Peta curled herself up against Eva's chest. She breathed in deeply and settled down with a slight smile tugging at the corners of her mouth.

"You got her?" Elden settled in behind Evazee with his feet prodding her in the back. Somehow today, it didn't matter. Evazee fought the urge to pat his feet. He unhooked the oars and used one to push away from the dome house. The front door slid shut as the gap between them and the floating house widened in time with each dip of the oar.

"How are you going to find the Healing Stream?"

"Don't ask." Elden grunted with the effort of

rowing.

"Why not?"

"Because I don't know."

Evazee shivered at the tingling across her skin. The light from behind them dimmed. She looked back to find the dome house was gone, cloaked once more behind an invisible shield. The light it cast had been cut off too, leaving them in the same deep gloom they'd been stumbling through when Beaver and Shrimp had found them. But for the light hanging at the front of the boat, they'd be in complete darkness.

Time lost meaning as they sliced through the water. Oars dipping and dripping, as steady as a metronome, the rhythm of it filled Eva's head. At first, she found herself tensing at each pull of the oars, waiting for a crunch of collision. There seemed to be nothing around them but water, and soon, she grew more relaxed and her thoughts drifted.

Their progress through the water slowed. Elden was having difficulty breathing. Evazee imagined his back, the cross-cross roadmap of pain, and she shuddered, "You must rest if you need to."

He said nothing but picked up the pace.

Peta still slept, her eyelashes casting dark shadows on her cheeks. Her arm underneath Peta had gone numb.

"So is Bree your only sister?"

"Correct."

"And where are your mom and dad?"

"Why are we talking about this?" Elden grunted with each swing of the paddles.

"Just interested, that's all." Silences were always uncomfortable for Evazee. Her natural response was to fill the void with words. Questions. The void left by the absence of noise sucked them right out of her. "Were you happy growing up?"

"Seriously?"

"I'm sorry. I'll stop." The marshlands around them gave off the smell of sulphur. It hung at the base of Evazee's throat, and she fought the urge to throw up. To take her mind off her queasiness, she peered ahead. The river forked in three directions. *Now what?* Elden swore under his breath, and she knew he'd seen it too.

"So Evazee, which one do we take?"

"I was about to ask you."

"Yeah, but I beat you to it, so you have to choose."

"That's a bad, bad idea."

"OK fine. We'll rock, paper, scissors. Loser chooses."

"That is completely flawed logic. You're letting the loser choose."

Elden rested the oars across the boat in front of him, stretching sideways. "Fine. Winner picks. I don't care."

"But you can't make that decision if you don't care. It doesn't work like that."

Elden hid his right hand behind his back, his eyebrow demanding that she do the same. Evazee shut her mouth. No point talking if he wasn't even going to listen.

"My hands are stuck." She pointed at Peta with her chin.

"Rubbish. Balance her on your knee and you can slip that one out."

Evazee sighed and did as he said, sliding her hand out and hiding it behind her back.

"Rock, pap—" The boat spun suddenly, nearly tipping Elden out. The oars slid off and fell into the water with a splash that wet all three of them. Elden gripped the sides with both hands. "Whirlpool. Hold on! It's getting worse!"

Evazee folded herself forward over Peta as the boat jerked hard, changing direction. It picked up speed, hurtling along out of control. It spun round and round, tilting them precariously before it dropped back level, pitching Evazee and Peta forward. Before Evazee could recover, it dipped again and spun. The nose of the boat hooked on a submerged rock and the timber shattered, breaking the boat into hundreds of tiny pieces and dumping the passengers into the icy water.

Cold slammed through Evazee, and she lost her grip on Peta. Her thoughts froze, drifting through her mind like snowflakes, none of them making sense. As heavy as stone, her body started sinking. Darkness blurred the edge of her vision, spinning to a closed tunnel.

~*~

Kai held up the tiny bottle of glowing water so that he could see what they were getting themselves into. The silence sliced through his head, no insect noise, no birds, not even the sound of wind blowing. "As far as I can see, we have to follow this bridge to that central landing. From there we have to figure out how to navigate through." His voice echoed.

"You've left out the part where we die." Ruaan hunched over and leaned in close to Kai. "You might recall that I'm not so keen on that."

"You make it sound like there's no other option." Zap stepped forward and tried to make himself taller than Ruaan. It failed and left him looking like nothing more than a cheeky younger brother.

"Cut it out, you two. Come on." Kai walked without waiting. Each step sent another ripple through the bridge beneath his feet. He ignored it and kept walking anyway.

The bridge curved up and over and Kai stuck to the very centre so as not to have to look over the edge. Behind him followed Ruaan, who walked with ease. Zap brought up the rear in odd bursts of tiny running steps, and then he froze. After a patch of silence that seemed too long, Kai looked around. Zap wasn't moving at all.

"Come on. We don't have time for this. What's that smell?" Kai squeezed his nostrils shut and gagged. "Did one of you let off? Must have been that weird food you ate."

Ruaan shook his head, and Zap's mouth worked but no sound came out. His lower lip shook, and he pointed at his feet. Kai moved closer and bent down so that the bottle light could reach. Zap's feet were buried in black goo up to his ankles. A faint shimmer threaded away from the puddle he was trapped in. Kai ran the light up, following a web-like trail of black goo that stretched off the edges of the bridge into the shadows beyond where Kai's light reached.

"It's a web." As Kai brought the light back down, the goo at Zap's feet crept higher up his leg. "And it's growing." A bubble formed in the puddle and popped, the first sound they'd heard in the cuttings other than their voices and the sound of their own breathing.

The pop broke the spell and Kai grabbed Zap's arm. "Ruaan, help me. We've got to get him out of here now. This stuff is spreading."

Ruaan grabbed Zap's other hand, and together they pulled. Zap yelled, a guttural bellow that started in his belly and echoed through the open space around them, bouncing and rebounding back to them, filling the emptiness with bellowing on an audible loop.

The goo clung tightly, stretching as Kai and Ruaan sweated to pull Zap out. Just when Kai thought they'd have to hack off Zap's feet or leave him behind, the web snapped back nearly throwing them off their feet. The web oozed toward them with a metallic hiss.

Kai ran for the platform, picking his way around the holes. "Follow my steps. Run!" The closer they got to the central platform, the worse the holes became, until at last the platform was within reach. The bridge broke through completely, leaving a broad gap.

The ooze made up Kai's mind before he could even consider any other option. He took a deep breath and ran, launching himself off the broken edge of the bridge. He landed on the other side, tripped and rolled. He lay on his back watching the stars dance. The fall had knocked his wind out.

Something landed next to him, a thud of a body...one of them had taken the chance. A loud "oof" and a scream. Ruaan hung in by his fingertips.

"Kai, help." Zap's voice was low, strained. He crouched near the edge, holding on to Ruaan's wrist.

Kai rolled to his side, onto his hands and knees, and crawled. *Don't pass out.* He grabbed Ruaan's other arm and together they pulled. As Ruaan shot over the edge, his shoe hooked and slipped off. The three of them watched it disappear into the shadows below.

The oozing web reached the crack in the bridge. Each string slid along the edge like tentacles, feeling for a way to get across. The boys stood mesmerised, breathing hard.

"It's stuck on the other side. Haha! Take that stupid webby slime!" Zap fist-pumped and started happy dancing with arms and legs swinging wildly. As he spun, his arm thwacked across Ruaan's chest.

Ruaan caught it, putting an end to his jig. "I wouldn't be celebrating just yet. It's starting to cross the gap."

Kai watched the threads melt together, slowly reinforcing, building, growing. It would only be a matter of time until it was across to their side. "Come on. We're nearly at the platform."

Kai stepped off the bridge onto the round island; a circular ball suspended on nothing, covered in intricate patterns carved into the ebony surface. Kai leaned down and traced the patterns with his fingertips. There was nothing gentle in the carving. Harsh lines and jagged edges protruded from the surface. If torture could be captured in a surface, this was it.

Many bridges led off the ball at all angles, poking out like short spikes and ending at a door. Some were elaborate, carved and exquisitely detailed. Others were plain and undecorated. Kai guessed there were at least fifty. How was he going to pick just one?

"This is weird. How do we get to the other side without falling off?" Zap stood like a surfer, legs spread and bent, waiting for the next ripple under his feet.

Ruaan appeared behind them. "Try walking."

"What? Are you completely insane?" Zap tapped his temples.

"Apparently not. I just walked right around the whole thing. Gravity sucks. Literally."

Kai frowned. "Are you sure?"

"I'm not going to answer that. Try it."

Kai started walking, his eyebrows huddling together in the middle of his forehead. His tummy flipped as he got close to the edge of being upright but he took another step. Then another and another. It took one hundred steps to get back to where he started, and he managed without falling off.

"That's all very well, but it still doesn't show us which bridge to take." He glanced toward the spreading black goo and urgency clenched his gut even as the hiss grew louder. The black tendrils were nearly across the gap. The bottle in his hand glowed through his fingers and a plan hatched in his head. Maybe there was a way to fix this. Risky, but it might work.

He uncorked the bottle of light, whispered a quick prayer to Tau, and allowed a single drop of the light to fall from the bottle before corking it again. The light droplet hung suspended for a moment and then slowly slipped down until it landed with a quiet *plop*. Another shudder rippled through the ground beneath their feet. This time it flashed silver and left a gleam of residue in the metal below their feet.

Ruaan slapped his forehead. "What are you thinking? You can't waste that stuff! What are we going to do when it's all gone?"

"I know. I hoped it would show us the right door." He scuffed the ground beneath his feet. "It was a gamble that didn't pay off." He cast a glance towards the web. It was more than halfway across the gap and closing fast.

Zap stepped back, pointing at Kai's feet with his eyes wide, "What the heck? What's up with that…"

The ground where Kai had let the drop of water fall was shifting before their eyes. Ebony gave way to white-silver, the jutting angles smoothed out to soft curves. The patch of transformation was growing. It spread beneath their feet and Zap's eyes looked ready to pop out.

Loud sizzling hissed behind them. The web had bridged the gap and was spidering towards them.

"I might sound crazy, but that web seems to be able to think. That's not possible, right?" Ruaan sounded calm, but by the glow coming from below them, Kai could see just how pale he was.

"There's no telling what's possible and what isn't down here. We have to go." Kai spun around, trying to decide which way was right.

The web reached the edge of the glowing patch and recoiled. A single sliver of brightness branched off from the patch, trailing a direct path toward one of the bridges.

"I think we should trust it." Kai didn't wait for the others to agree but took off following the light. The faster he moved, the faster the path ran ahead, leaving the platform to curve along one of the bridges. There was no argument from Ruaan or Zap. They ran right on Kai's heels.

The black web snaked alongside the light-path, flanking it and travelling faster. Kai threw himself off the bridge at the foot of a door that seemed carved of ancient stone. There was no handle or any other visible way to open it. He banged on it until his palms stung. "Help me push."

The three lined up, put their hands on the door, and heaved. It swung back easily, and they fell through, rolling in the dirt on the other side. The silvery pathway stopped at the doorway's edge, but the web crept out. There was light on this side of the door.

"Shut it!" Kai scrambled to his feet and eased himself behind the now impossibly heavy doo.

Zap stood rooted, eyes fixed on the web that seemed to be growing straight toward him. Ruaan ran to help Kai, and together they heaved the door closed, snapping two sections off the web. The bits left on their side of the door writhed and squirmed, turning Kai's stomach.

"Stand back!" An approaching man put a spear through the closest bit, bellowing out a war cry. Loud hissing filled the air, and the severed bit of web shrivelled to a floating wisp. The man reached into a pouch he carried on his hip and sprinkled some dust over the blackened air. He turned his attention to the other bit of web, yelled again, stabbed, and dusted that bit into oblivion, too.

The man stood a head taller than Kai, dressed in baggy maroon pants with the crotch that hung to just above his knees, barefoot running shoes, and a leather breastplate. His head was shaven all down both sides, leaving a central strip in a plait from forehead to halfway down his back. His jaw jutted out at an angle that was sharper than his sword. His spear got a liberal sprinkling of dust before he strapped it onto his belt. Everything about the man screamed soldier, despite his pants that made Kai bite back a chuckle.

Kai stepped forward and held out a hand to thank him, but the man looped a rope around Kai's wrists. In a blink, he had the other two hooked in as well. He tied the loose end of the rope to his belt. Then he stepped back and formality slid like steel down his spine.

"I am under oath to the powers that be to detain any strangers found around Stone City. The fact that you came via the Door That Should Never Be Used counts against you. The fact that you did not use the correct words of greeting counts against you."

"Is this a joke? We just need help finding a friend. You can't be serious." Kai looked around for a hidden audience.

"Speaking without being consulted counts against you. Your strange attire counts against you. Approaching an officer of Stone City without invitation counts against you. Withholding your business in our land counts against you."

"But you haven't even asked our business. Besides, he said it. We're looking for a friend." Zap's lip pulled upwards along with his eyebrow.

"Interrupting an officer of Stone City during a formal decree coun—"

"Let me guess!" Zap stuck up his hand. "Counts against us. Right?" He grinned.

Ruaan slapped his belly with his bound hands. "You're making it worse. Shut it."

"You actually think this guy is serious. That's priceless."

The officer glared at them in turn before removing a small object from his belt. The handle fit in his palm and the top was split into two narrow sections just wider than Kai's turning fork for his guitar. The soldier held it up and pressed a button. Blue sparks shot between the two narrow sections.

Fury flooded red into Ruaan's cheeks. Kai caught his eye and shook his head quickly. It seemed to get through to Ruaan, as he stayed on the spot, fingers working into fists.

"I hereby declare you lawful prisoners of Stone City until such time as your innocence can be proven beyond a shadow of doubt. You are to accompany me in silence. Failure to comply will be counted against you." The soldier turned and began walking, leading them behind him as he would a pack of tame dogs. The confidence he had in his authority was absolute.

Kai rolled his eyes but nodded at the others to go along peacefully. This could be the one time that something seemed bad but turned out for good.

9

Evazee came around, choking on the water in her lungs. Someone rolled her onto her side and rubbed her back. With each drop that left her body, Evazee breathed a bit easier. When the coughing stopped, she fell back and wiped her eyes.

Zulu's ebony face hovered over hers, tight lips and the deep scar making him seem fierce in the gloom.

"Peta. Elden. Are they—" Awareness crept back in slivers.

"Resting." A smile creased his cheeks and relief calmed Eva.

She pushed herself up, but her head swam and she lay back down. Elden lay sprawled on his back with Peta curled up at his side close enough that she'd touch him if she moved her leg. The lamp they'd hung on the boat sat midway between them all, still shining. Eva's damp clothes clung to her, and she shivered. Her hair hung in a soggy mass of knotted wetness. She squeezed it out and water dripped onto the grass. "What are you doing here?"

Zulu squatted easy on his haunches, back propped up against a tree. "Helping."

"You followed us when we left the dome?"

"I did." His face was an expressionless chiselled mask.

"Were you going to take us back?"

"You weren't prisoners."

"But we stole their boat. Well, we didn't steal, just borrowed." Her gaze slipped to the riverbank and the bits of boat bobbing along the edges. "That didn't work out too well."

"It's just wood. You are worth more than wood."

"Zulu, I wanted to ask you." She pushed herself up gingerly and pain flowered through her ribs. She bit back a grunt. "The water in the pod. It turned brown. What does that mean?"

"Brown?"

As brown as your skin. "Yes, brown. Do you know?"

"Brown is guilt. He is hiding something."

"Elden? He couldn't if he tried."

"I read it in his eyes." There was no judgment in his statement. He was simply stating the facts.

She glanced across to Elden, sleeping at her feet. He was relaxed and at peace. Her heart skipped, and she looked away quickly but not before catching Zulu grinning at her.

He shrugged. "This guilt, it doesn't make him a bad person."

Evazee angled her shoulders away from Zulu a fraction. She couldn't get side-tracked now with petty arguments. Peta needed her. "Do you know where we can find the Healing Stream?"

"I do not know of this Healing Stream you speak of. Is it for the small one?"

"But didn't the water in the pods come from the Healing Stream?"

"It did."

"But surely you'd know where the water came from? How they got it there?"

Zulu's head tipped to the side. "No."

Three different responses formed in Eva's mind. All of them included the words *frustrating, irritating,* or *stupid.* She shut her mouth deliberately and rolled herself upright. Cold and wobbly on her feet, she hobbled over to Elden. She bent down next to him and shook his arm. "Elden, wake up."

Her gentle voice did nothing but illicit a snore. She leaned in a bit closer to his ear. "Elden! We have to go."

His only response was a vague grunt. Evazee patted his cheek. His arm snaked up and drew her down towards his chest.

"Elden! No. Wake up."

Pressed up against his chest, his arms—two bands of heat—locked around her while she balanced precariously on her knees. His chest rose and fell in easy breaths, and he smiled in his sleep. This would not do.

Her toe cramped, and she toppled, head-butting his chin.

Elden sat up straight and yelled, "No! You can't make me. I didn't do it!"

He shoved Evazee and she rolled, bumping into the lamp from the boat, landing with an "oof."

"Oh no, Evazee! I'm so sorry. What happened?" He scrambled to his feet and rolled himself upright while rubbing his eyes.

"Is he always like this?" Zulu pointed sideways, his nose wrinkled up to meet his frown.

Evazee shrugged, brushing dirt off her pants as she stood up. "I guess so. Though I've never heard him shout so much." She stepped close to Elden and pulled down an eyelid to check his pupil response. "Any headache? Dizziness?" Her palm slipped to his forehead as she felt his temperature. Heat crept into his skin below her fingertips.

"Breathing is hard."

"Probably from inhaling water. I felt the same. It will settle."

A strange grin tugged at his mouth. "Oh, of course. You must be right." He reached up to remove her hand from his forehead. "Who is he?"

"He is Zulu from the dome house. He works for Beaver and Shrimp."

"The same Beaver and Shrimp whose boat we just trashed?"

"I don't work for them. I help. And yes, the same ones. It's like I told the girl, a boat can be rebuilt. Lives, not so much."

Evazee locked onto Elden's gaze. He mouthed something she didn't catch. Rather than risk getting it wrong, she changed the subject. "I'm worried about Peta."

"I'm worried about Bree."

"We need to find the Healing Stream. Zulu hasn't heard of it before. Isn't that strange?"

"What is he doing here anyway?" He turned his back to her as he spoke. "Is he going to take us back?"

Zulu had his back to them, holding Peta's frail arm in his enormous hands. Her pale skin looked translucent against his dark skin.

He turned to them and smiled. "There is not much time. Come. Let us fix your worries. Both of you."

~*~

The rope around Kai's wrist was rubbing away

layers of skin. This whole situation was beginning to annoy him. They'd been walking in silence behind the baggy pants soldier with the dagger-sharp chin for a while now, and Kai was about ready to ask where they were going. The only thing that held him back was the deep desire not to hear the words "counted against you" one more time.

Ruaan had long since given up complaining about his missing shoe, probably for the same reason. He limped along in silence now.

They cleared a rise and found another soldier sitting on a rock with his back straight, hands on his knees, eyes closed, and face lifted as a sunflower would bask in the sun. His entire head was shaved and he was dressed in the same baggy pants as their captor. He must have heard them coming. He shot up and stood to attention. As they got closer, his gaze ran over them and stopped at their bound wrists.

He pulled the soldier aside and hissed at him through clenched teeth, "What are you doing? These people are our guests, not our prisoners! Do I need to send you back to training?" His hand hovered in the air as if he were about to swat the one that had tied them up.

"But they came through the door and two of them are covered in dirt. You know what that means."

Kai felt Zap staring at him and looked over at him. Zap wiggled his eyebrows toward the thick bank of vegetation that ran along next to them.

"I'm keen to ditch these two and their ugly pants," Zap said.

Kai wasn't so sure. He glanced across to Ruaan and grimaced when he saw the look in his face. Ruaan's hands crept up toward his belly. He must be getting hungry. Off to one side, the two soldiers still whispered furiously.

Kai shook his head at Zap and leaned forward to whisper in his ear, "We should stick with these guys. I don't know why, but I have a feeling. It's weird because I don't trust them, but my gut says we're heading the right way. Gallagher said so too. Do you trust me?" He held out his open palm in a gesture they hadn't used since the first time they'd crept out of detention together at the age of ten.

Zap groaned and slapped his hand into Kai's. "Sneaking out of detention was a disaster. We got kitchen duty for a month, but fine. Whatever you want, hotshot."

"How do you keep doing that? Get out of my head."

Before Zap could answer, the two soldiers finished arguing. Their captor bowed his head, but not before Kai saw the flash of defiance in his eyes. The new soldier ran to them and pulled a knife out of his pocket. It was as long as Kai's forearm and sliced through their bonds with a single swipe.

"There. That is better." He faced them all and bowed deeply. "Welcome, honoured guests. Please accept my apology for my fellow soldier here. He is new and has been known to take his job a little too seriously. Please, will you do us the honour of accompanying us?"

Kai rubbed life back into his wrists. "Maybe you can help us. We are looking for a friend. She was last seen in the desert outside the Darklands. She's most likely injured." Hearing himself say it out loud made Kai realize how ludicrous their quest was. Short of a miracle, they were never going to find Bree. Kai cleared his throat and pressed on. "We don't know where to start looking."

"Also, I've lost my shoe." Ruaan cleared his throat before shuffling in behind Kai.

Deep lines creased the soldier's face, grave concern expressed by each one of them. There was something about this man that made Kai's hackles rise, even though he was the one showing them kindness. *Stop being paranoid.*

"That is a dangerous place. I fear your friend may be more than injured." He blinked rapidly, eyelids flapping like moth wings. ""However, our people routinely patrol that area, and they have rescued people from darKounds before. They bring all the survivors to our city for healing. If your friend is still alive, this is where she'll be. Come with me. Maybe Stone City holds the miracle you seek. We've got some ground to cover. Follow me."

Kai studied their surroundings as they walked, searching for anything that seemed familiar. It was a relief to be out of the thick darkness that they'd come from. This couldn't compare to the sun back home, but there was a glow from something in the distance that meant they could walk easy without fear of tripping. The terrain shifted from wild to tame in gentle degrees that almost went unnoticed. In a blink, long, wild grass and tattered hedges became trimmed lawn and clipped hedges. Order had been brought to bear on every blade of grass, every leaf. Trees grew in straight lines that shifted in diagonal chevrons as one walked past.

The two soldiers had split up to flank them. Sharp Jaw marched up front, while the bald one brought up the rear. They marched along, all pulled up and smart, dedication to the cause of looking soldier-ish oozing out of every pore. They carried themselves as if all the higher powers in the universe were watching to award promotion.

Zap dropped back and fell into step next to Kai. "I might have been wrong. This might work out."

Kai glanced at his friend to see if he were being sarcastic, but there wasn't a trace of it in his face. "I'm not so sure. Have you noticed?" His arm swung over all the straight lines, "What is up with all this? It can't be natural, can it?"

"What do you mean?"

Kai waved a hand that covered it all, down to a last point at their guards. "All the straight lines, all the smartness. Isn't it a bit weird?"

"I like it. It's neat." Zap bobbed his head up and down as if his neck were a spring.

Kai scrunched up his nose and peered around, "I guess so."

Ruaan walked ahead of them all slumped over as if his spine had resigned and left. Regular growls came from his mid-section, and he looked sadder with each noise that escaped.

"He's going to need food."

"Let's just hope they have food wherever it is they're taking us."

The light grew brighter as they walked, and soon the air around them took on a yellow tinge and seemed to grow thicker. Soon they faced a wall of swirling mist that stretched up high into the sky. The glow that lit it came from the other side of the mist bank, though the mist made it look sickly. The bald soldier up front stopped them all and motioned the guy at the back to meet him off to the side. They spoke in low undertones, and a few minutes passed before they turned back to the three of them.

Before they could say anything, a single drop of mist landed on Kai's bare arm. The droplet felt cool at first, but as it ran down his arm, it burnt his skin.

"Ow! What is this stuff?"

Both soldiers reached into their pouches for the dust that had dispersed the dark cloud left by the web when they'd escaped from the cuttings. The bald one sprinkled a fine layer over Ruaan, who sneezed, and then he moved on to Zap, who kept dodging.

Kai faced the soldier with the jaw and the plait. "What is that for?"

"The mist is toxic. This powder is a temporary antidote. If you tried to cross the mist without it, let's just say that the pain would drive you insane. But suit yourself." He moved to pour the dust in his hands back into the pouch.

"I'll have the dust." Kai rubbed at the raw patch left by a single mist drop and shuddered at the thought of his whole body being drenched. "I was just curious, I meant no disrespect. Zap, have the dust, man. Trust me."

Zap frowned but stood still and allowed the bald one to dust him. "Why aren't you guys getting dusted?"

"There are other ways of getting immunity." Baldy took the coil of rope off his belt. "Listen closely, you lot. I'm tying you up again, but it's not because you're our prisoners. If we get split up in there, we'll never find you. Also, if you hear things, just don't listen. All right?"

"Wait! What kind of things?" Ruaan's face went pale, and there were dark, sunken rings beneath his eyes.

Baldy and the jaw exchanged a look halfway between amusement and genuine fear. Kai couldn't read their expressions, and with his Affinity not operating, he had no means of telling if the mist was tainted, broken, or just plain evil.

10

Evazee slipped her hand over Peta's forehead. "She's burning up. I don't think we have much time."

Elden carried her in his arms, careful not to touch the sores all down the front of her legs. Sweat ran down his temples. "You're telling the wrong person." He grunted and flashed a look to where Zulu stood a few steps away with his eyes shut, hands raised and mouth moving silently. "It seems our guide is consulting his inner-GPS and the connection is dodgy."

"If I didn't know better, I'd say he's arguing with himself."

"Schizophrenia. Not uncommon. I wish he would hurry up and agree with himself so we can move on."

Evazee whacked his arm. "Don't be mean." Zulu had been nothing but kind toward them. Even so, she still felt weird around him. Interrupting him was the last thing Evazee wanted to do, but Peta couldn't wait. She strode across to him and poked him on the shoulder. His muscles were solid knots coiled beneath his ebony skin.

"Hold on." Zulu's eyes stayed shut and one of his hands came down on her shoulder, clamping her where she stood next to him. Suddenly his eyes shot open, whites showing all around his dark irises.

"I'm sorry to rush you. We need to get Peta to the Healing Stream. I don't think she has much time."

Zulu pulled himself up tall, his ebony skin gleaming in the lamplight. The light caught his cheekbones, casting a sharp shadow that emphasized the strength in his jawline. Evazee stepped back. Her pulse raced. Taller than her by two heads, he looked every inch a warrior king. Terrifying.

Yet he reached for her cheek but stopped just short of touching. His voice was gentle, "I'm afraid we cannot get to this stream you speak of. Not from here."

Desperation slammed through Evazee like a tidal wave. "How do you know? You can't just give up like that. No! I won't let you!"

"Calmness, friend Evazee. There is another hope for her." Zulu dropped his gaze, and Evazee heard him swallow.

"Well what is it? This other plan of yours."

"Follow me." Without any warning, he darted off into the trees like a spooked gazelle.

Evazee and Elden pushed through the trees, trying to keep up with the furtive shadow that was Zulu. He was completely at home in the forest, dodging roots and hanging branches, flicking off leaves that stuck to his chest without breaking his stride.

A deep boom rang out from up ahead. It shook the trees and made the ground quiver below their feet. "What was that?" Evazee grabbed hold of Zulu's arm to stop herself from falling. Elden tripped and stumbled, throwing himself backwards to provide a softer landing for Peta. Her head rolled back and bounced as they landed. She seemed to be nothing more than a ragdoll.

"Zulu, what's going on? What are we supposed to do?"

His eyes stayed fixed on the horizon where

nothing moved.

"You are freaking me out. Please don't go crazy. We need you."

He ignored her comment, still staring into the distance. "That was a boundary warning. We are close now." He turned to them. "These people have what the small one needs, but coming here is very dangerous." Zulu waved to where Elden sat with Peta tucked on his lap. They were close enough to the base of a tree to use it as a back rest. "Sit here with small one. We bring medicine."

"No. I should go with you. You need all the muscles we have. Evazee can stay with the girl. The forest's been quiet."

Zulu scratched his chin as if he were considering options. "No. This doesn't need muscles. Protecting the girl does. Do you think I cannot see she's marked? That you all are?" Zulu's gaze slid sideways. "This is not a village to be entered into lightly."

Evazee pulled herself up to her tallest, barely reaching Zulu's shoulder. "So I don't get a say in this. You just make all the decisions."

Zulu nodded once, meeting her eyes coolly and not rising to meet her bubbling anger. "*Yebo.*"

If he'd shouted at her, got angry in the slightest, she could have really let her hot-head fly. But he spoke with such calm, such authority, Evazee felt like a silly child for disagreeing. "Fine. Only for Peta's sake. Let's go." She marched off, determined to have some say.

It was Elden who called after her. "Er, Evazee? You're going the wrong way."

She spun back, feeling her cheeks flame, taking them both in with a sweeping gaze that dared them to comment. Zulu turned his back on her and shrugged, leading off in the other direction. Evazee wanted to talk to Elden before going with Zulu. She didn't feel right about splitting up. *Brown means he's hiding something.* It didn't feel right leaving Peta behind either. But the grin on Elden's face stopped her, and she straightened up and followed Zulu without another word.

~*~

Mist swirled thick around them as they walked. Kai shivered and rubbed his arms. The mist clung to his skin and soaked his hair until it dripped down his spine. Thoughts of what he'd be feeling if he hadn't been dusted kept popping into his head. The mist felt wrong, and it frustrated him that he didn't know why. They walked in single file, nearly toe to heel. They'd been walking blind like this for many steps. Without means to tell time or even the sun to hint at the time of day, Kai started counting steps. He'd tripped on a rock at around three-hundred-and-something, and in the mental scramble to work out how to count the shuffling mini-steps, he'd lost the actual number and gave up altogether.

Zap spoke out of the fog to his right. "Three-hundred-and-twenty-two before you tripped."

"I didn't ask you that. I didn't even say it out loud, did I?"

"Hey man, don't yell at me. I'm just helping a brother out."

"No, for real. Was I talking to myself?"

"You lost count. I didn't. It's not a big deal."

Kai shut his mouth. One more weird thing to deal

with. Apparently, his friend had become a mind-reader.

"It's not really like that, you know. It's not mind-reading. It feels more like absorbing thoughts. Kinda like osmosis or whatever it's called."

"Well can you stop? It's pretty rude."

"I don't know about that. What do you think Ruaan? Oh wait, give me a mo', and I'll tell you."

"Get out of my head, creepy boy." Ruaan was at the growling stage of hunger.

"Zap, stop it. I'm serious. Wait, can you?"

"Honestly? It fades in and out. I don't really have much control."

"Just don't do it. It's not cool."

"Fine. I'll think about sheep."

"Why sheep?" He shook his head and held up his hand. "You know what, I don't even want to know."

They trudged on blindly. Kai's feet cramped, yet they still marched on, the mist deadening all noise but Zap's deep sighs. Kai's thoughts drifted like bubbles. Some popped easily, like those involving pizza. Others kept bouncing on the edges of his consciousness.

Bree was one thought. Evazee and Peta, too. Gallagher had said they were fine, but Kai's stomach churned at the thought of the two of them standing against some of the things the boys had faced.

He sent out a test thought toward Zap. *Your breath smells worse than the ancient bulldog that lived at the St Greg's hostel.* No response. Maybe he'd figured out how to control it after all.

Runt. Runt filled a bubble that stayed front and centre. She even spoke to him, though he could just see her mouth moving. She really did ramble on, that one. It was fitting that he'd remember her chattering away.

Maybe if he focussed on her lips, he could remember her voice. He should, after all the hours he'd listened to her yakking. Kai chuckled to himself. He was going to tease her when they all got back.

Kai concentrated on her bubble, allowing the others to drift to the background. Runt's lips were moving slow and deliberately as if communicating with a deaf person. A fierce frown buckled her eyebrows. The memory must have been a deep one because for a moment he swore he heard her voice.

"Your cats have fleas. They are scratching themselves to pieces. What must I do?" She harrumphed with an exaggerated eye-roll. "Are you deaf or stupid? Or am I going nuts here all by myself?"

Kai slowed down. He had never discussed fleas with Runt. Maybe this was a sleepwalking daydream—it sure wasn't a memory. Then Runt held up his kitten. Her neck was a raw mess of scratches and the little thing looked twitchy and tormented.

"Runt? Are you there?"

Something hit him on the head. Zap's voice sounded hollow in the mist. "They said we'd hear things. You can't talk to her, you nit. Focus or you'll trip and send us all crashing." He felt a tug on the rope looped around his waist as a reminder.

Kai rubbed the smacked spot and did what Zap said. He focussed on the Runt bubble. She had a pasted-on smile, the kind that kids wear when their mom makes them say cheese for the camera and they'd really rather not.

Kai sent a tentative thought out into the bubble. *Can you hear me?*

"About time. Of course, I can hear you. How do I kill fleas?"

Kai's heart pounded, he formed another thought and imagined sending it into the bubble. *What's happening there?* He kept it short, not knowing how much would get through. Runt held up his cat with a look on her face that implied he had no brain at all. *I mean apart from fleas. What is happening?*

Runt sighed and pushed the cat off her lap, brushing at her skirt. She was dressed in a purple dress covered in enormous flowers. Kai could have sworn her lower lip quivered the tiniest bit.

"Everybody is out. They're all just lying around. On the floor, on tables. You're at least on a couch. The air is full of the green stuff they used to inject into me before you fetched me." Her features danced through a full range of expressions as she spoke. Then her face grew deadened. "This is boring. When are you coming back?"

Runt, listen to me. This is important. You need to find where they're pumping the green stuff out of, and stop it somehow. We're trapped here, and our imprints are useless. Can you do that?

Tears pooled along her lower lashes. "I want you to come back and help your kittens."

I'm trying, but I need your help. I think they might be using the air freshener machines like in Torn's office.

Baldy's voice boomed from up ahead and popped his bubble, taking his connection to Runt along with it. "We're nearly through, brace yourselves."

11

Kai stepped out of the mist into brightness that seared his eyeballs. It was clear that the mist was not natural. There was no gentle dissipation, just a solid cloud that *was* and then *wasn't*. From this side, it was a dirty brown wall that reached up higher than they could see. A fresh breeze blew over him, turning his skin to gooseflesh as the wind hit the droplets from the mist. A high melody floated on the breeze, dipping and swaying with each change in the air. It both pulled at his heart and sliced straight through his eardrums.

Baldy untied them and handed the rope back to Jaw with the same wariness as if it were a loaded weapon. "Use this appropriately."

Kai could hear the unspoken *or else* and coughed to cover the laugh that sneaked out. *Yeah, Jaw, it seems that arresting us for no reason counted against you. Ha!*

Zap yanked at his arm, pointing. "I swear that's the city we saw in the distance. Look at how much light it gives off! I haven't seen anything that bright since the Grave Keepers nearly burnt us to a shrivel." His whisper was the equivalent of a normal person's across-a-crowded-room volume.

Baldy spun around, his eyeballs appearing to pop out of his head. "You've been with the Grave Keepers." It was a statement, not a question and he seemed to take in the dust on their clothes.

Jaw smirked, self-righteous justification oozing from every pore. "I told you they're bad news. Did you notice that they are marked, too? Hmm?"

Baldy hissed. "They are still our guests. They just need to be decontaminated first. Come, you three. There's not a moment to lose." Out of the baggy folds of his pants, he produced a pair of folded objects for each of them, including himself. With the deft movements of many years of practice he unfolded his pair of what looked like sandals on stilts. "We made it through the mist, but now there is the small matter of crossing the field of glass grass." He stood tall and waved a hand across where they were heading.

The vast expanse shimmered in the light from the city, twinkling as if a million stars had fallen and had come to rest on earth. Each blade of glass grass was tinged green, shaped like normal grass, but much fatter and completely see-through.

The music came from the glass grass as it swayed in the breeze and sang with each movement. The song was haunting and reminded Kai of the siren songs that supposedly lured unwary sailors into the water and drowned them.

Baldy strapped the strange shoes to his feet and stood up. Balanced on such high stilts, he towered over the rest of them. He motioned for them to do the same. "Do you know about glass grass?" He glanced at them and must have seen enough blankness in their faces to persuade him that they didn't. "First, it's deadly. It may look pretty, but if you tried to walk through this field barefoot, you'd have bled out before you could reach the other side."

Zap's nose scrunched up the way it did when he

hit a hard problem in a math test. "So it's sharp?"

"Sharp is an understatement. Deadly is more accurate. And if you stumble? Not even the shoes can help you then."

"Perfect. My kind of backyard." Zap glanced back as if weighing up his odds against the mist, spirit cuttings and Grave Keepers.

Ruaan's stomach growled.

Zap jumped in fright and turned on him, arms waving like a pinwheel. "Dude! That's not even funny! What were you thinking?"

Kai swatted Zap on the back of his head. "Leave him alone, and get your shoes on." Kai towered over Zap whose head only made it to mid-chest height.

Ruaan had taken off his one shoe and strapped the stilts onto his bare feet. He was struggling to get up. Baldy and Jaw reached down and grabbed each of his hands to plant him on his feet. He wobbled a bit and grabbed Kai, bumping him off balance. They crashed down onto Zap who was still trying to figure out how the straps worked across his feet.

The soldiers watched them, their legs wide and their hands crossed behind their backs. As they disentangled themselves from each other, Jaw muttered under his breath and glared at them. Baldy shook his head and shut his eyes as if watching were painful.

It took some doing to get the three of them to their feet. By the time they were ready, Kai was sweating as though he'd run a marathon. He squared his shoulders and rubbed his palms together. "Right. Let's do this."

Jaw looked him up and down with a buckled eyebrow. He turned to Baldy. "I'm not taking rear. I don't want to watch these fools bleed."

Baldy shut his eyes, and his lips moved. Judging by the movement of his fingers, he seemed to be counting to ten. "Fine. Lead on. Try not to get lost."

Jaw turned and stomped into the field of sparkling grass. Each time his foot came down, glass blades shattered. The song on the wind twisted, becoming an eardrum wrecking cacophony of shrill glass-agony. Kai wanted to shove his fingers in his ears to block the sound, but he was too scared of falling over if he lifted his arms. *The sooner we're through this, the better.*

~*~

Evazee blinked and crept along blindly behind Zulu. They had left the lamp with the others, but Evazee's night vision hadn't kicked in yet, and she followed more by listening than anything else. Zulu's dark skin blended into the deep shadow they moved through. Evazee breathed deep to calm the panic that bubbled in her belly.

"Zulu, what is this place we're going to? Why is it dangerous?" Evazee whispered as loud as she dared.

"No talking. Not safe."

"I know. But I need to know what to expect. Are we talking quicksand or cannibals?"

"Probably both."

"What?"

"Follow me. Don't do anything I say you shouldn't, and hopefully, we can get what the small one needs. Now shush."

They walked on in silence. Evazee's ears grew sensitive to the sound of their feet on dry dirt, the rustling of leaves and grass. At least, it sounded like leaves and grass. She shut her eyes and flung her hands out in front of her like a sleepwalker. She daren't think of spiders, or anything else with more legs than her, that might be waiting up ahead. To keep her mind busy, she began reciting Bible memory verses that she'd learnt at Sunday school many years ago. She'd gone all the way through five of them when she noticed that the ground beneath their feet had turned soggy. Soon they were up to their ankles in chilly water. It all felt very familiar.

"Zulu, are we going back to Shrimp and Beaver's place?"

"Nope."

"But..."

Zulu spun around and clamped a hand over her mouth, pulling her into the undergrowth with him. Indignation shot through Evazee like a fiery dart, but before she could squirm out of his grasp, a group of people came walking through the trees to their left. They marched in single file, loops of rope strung between them. The guy who led the group carried a tiny flaming torch that flickered green. The pool of light it cast was just big enough for them to see where to put the next footstep.

Evazee's eyes drank in the sight of the light. She followed it as it weaved and bobbed through the blackness until it made her feel dizzy. The leader's skin looked as dark as Zulu's. She studied his face, smooth skin marred by pockmarks. The light threw strange shadows that highlighted a deep scar that ran across the length of his face. The more she looked at him, the more he reminded her of someone else. It dawned on her as his face creased into a smile.

Zulu.

The man looked just like Zulu.

~*~

Crossing the sea of glass grass left Kai with a splitting headache. Apart from a few stumbles, they'd all managed to stay mostly upright and made it to the other side without any shedding of blood. They stood outside a white wire-mesh fence that stretched up as tall as a three-story house, running off to the left and right as far as the eye could see. It was sealed with a gate wide enough for two trucks to drive in side-by-side.

Baldy was quick to collect the shoes they'd used to cross the glass grass field. He folded them up and packed them away in the hidden pockets of his baggy trousers before Kai could even think of hanging onto a pair. Kai glanced back over the sparkling expanse they'd just crossed and felt a wave of nausea. They were now completely cut off from the girls. They should have ditched these two and their ugly pants ages ago. The way back was now completely impossible.

Baldy took one pair of tall shoes in his hand and waved them at Jaw. "Why did you take these off?"

Jaw stood up from adjusting the strap on his barefoot shoes. "I'm taking these three to Decontamination."

"I'll do it. You should get back to perimeter patrol." He held out the shoes.

"I think it is your turn."

Baldy coughed and turned his back toward Kai and his friends. "I outrank you. Take the shoes." The power struggle turned into a full-on staring battle with each man drawing himself up taller as they locked eyes. Even their chests puffed out.

Zap chuckled, and Kai elbowed him. Ruaan stood cradling his belly, scowling at the two soldiers.

Jaw snatched the shoes without breaking eye contact. His eyes narrowed, the only indication of his rebellious submission. "Yes, sir."

Zap shook his head with a snort. "So much drama."

Kai smacked his belly and whispered. "Shut it."

Baldy didn't wait for the Jaw to get back into his shoes before turning to Kai and his friends. "I'm sorry you had to witness that. Please forgive my colleague for his lack of decorum." He adjusted his breast plate and waved them toward the gate. "Follow me, honoured guests." He pressed his hand to a rectangular palm reader mounted on the gate post. The gate drew back and slid sideways with a hiss of hydraulics.

Zap looked down his nose at Kai as he sauntered past. "He called me an honoured guest." Smugness oozed out of every pore.

Ruaan pushed him out the way and stomped through first. "He called us all that, you half-wit." He shook his head as he followed Baldy through the gate.

Zap smirked and wiggled his jaw sideways as a kid would do behind a bully's back. He seemed to have just enough wisdom not to push the issue with any further comment. Kai sighed and followed them in, cringing as the gate shut behind his back.

What had they gotten themselves into this time?

12

Evazee waited until the group of people had moved out of earshot before tackling Zulu. "Who are these people? You know them, don't you?"

Zulu's mouth remained a tight line.

"Talk to me. They could be your family. That guy, he could be your brother. What's going on?"

"Family is not always good. No more talk. We need medicine."

From the ground below came a scuffling sound and then a solid *thunk*. A purple glow rose up from a broken mushroom at the base of the tree. Zulu kicked at another mushroom. As it broke, the insides lit up in the same shade of purple as the other. A few more kicks and Zee could see the tall, graceful trunks of the trees that surrounded them. She leaned down to pick up some mushroom bits to take the light with them.

"Don't touch." Zulu's arm shot out in front of her so fast that she bumped into it. "Deadly poisonous."

Zulu ran his hands along the trunk of a nearby tree. The surface of the wood was smooth. Zulu patted it and bent down to look amongst the long grass at his feet. Avoiding the mushrooms, he turned in circles as he felt around, and straightened up with a piece of bark in his hands as high as his shoulder and wide enough for him to hide behind.

"Um, what is that for?"

"No talk. I'll show. You need one also. Hold this."

Evazee frowned but balanced the piece of bark. Zulu found a smaller one and held it up against her. "This should do." He took the larger one back from her and tucked both under his arm, forcing Evazee to walk inconveniently far behind him to avoid bumping into the wood.

Zulu rinsed the glowing mushroom light off his shoes in a puddle and waved for Evazee to follow him. They left the mushroom light behind, and the muddy sogginess beneath their feet grew gradually deeper until they were soaked up to their knees. Evazee waded with her hands waving out in front of her like a bad zombie impression. At least no one could see her right now. Her hands kept getting swatted by tall thin plants that bobbed and swayed out of reach.

The water was deep enough to lap at her thighs, and the ground beneath their feet sucked hard, threatening to remove her shoes. Zulu stopped and put the two pieces of bark down to float on the surface. They touched down with the slightest splash. Nothing else moved or made a sound. He held her bark steady and whispered, "Climb on. Boost yourself on my leg."

Evazee waded closer, grabbed his hand, planted her foot on his thigh and aimed her rear at the bark. It was surprisingly buoyant, and she floated, feeling safer than she thought she would.

"What do I paddle with?"

"No paddling. I show you." Zulu hoisted himself up onto his bark and grabbed onto a nearby reed. As he pulled it toward himself, the makeshift raft glided through the water without a sound. He waited for her to try and grabbed her raft as soon as she was within reach. He pulled her close and whispered, "Don't pull yourself same-same. They will know we're coming. Have to keep random. Yes?"

"You mean I must pull myself along, avoiding a regular rhythm?"

"That is the thing I said, yes."

"Who will know we're coming?"

"Not who. What. Come. It's nearly time. We must be there before they start."

Evazee opened her mouth to ask another question, but Zulu turned his back on her and pulled himself along. If she didn't follow, she'd be left behind. That was not going to happen. Not if she could help it.

There was a knack to driving the bark boat that Evazee just didn't have yet. She sat cross-legged in the middle, stretched forward and grabbed whichever reed she could lay her hands on. As she pulled back, most of them twisted the boat sideways. Let go too soon and the bark hardly moved; let go too late and she risked getting tipped into the cold water.

A purple glow lit the horizon—the same shade given off by the broken mushrooms—and Zulu aimed his bark towards it. If that purple was from the mushrooms and as poisonous as he'd said, Evazee couldn't imagine why he'd want to get closer. Asking him, though, was impossible. It took all her energy and focus to stay on the bark and keep up with him. By the light of the glow, she could see that Zulu's reed-pulling technique was much better than hers. He sat with his legs out in front of him and reached to the sides at the same time. His arms were long enough to catch reeds and pull forward evenly. Evazee copied his movements and stayed aiming forward.

The challenge now was to keep her movements

irregular so as not to wake whatever was sleeping deep beneath. An ugly tingle ran through her legs at the thought. Something potentially dangerous lurked below with just a thin strip of bark between her and the unknown nasty.

She trained her eyes on Zulu's back, refusing to pay any attention to whatever was underneath. Huts appeared in front of them, painted in glowing purple and floating metres above the water. Evazee squinted and tilted her head. They were all mounted on stilts. As for the colour, it was as if they'd crushed the poisonous mushrooms and used them to paint the walls. Some huts were completely covered, while others had the glow around doors and windows only. Of those she could see, one had been decorated with swirls and circles. Looking at it made her head spin.

Nothing moved in the hut village. The place looked deserted. She leaned forward and risked a whisper. "Where are the people?"

Zulu halted his bark raft. Turning it sideways, he somehow managed to shift her so that they ended up side to side. "Nobody can be out during the sacred ceremony. Only the priests. To be out of home is to risk death."

"Oh great. So we could die."

"Yebo."

His honesty threw her. "I don't see how that would be helpful. Are you sure what Peta needs is here?"

"Yebo."

"In that case, lead on."

~*~

The boys stood on a broad, stone road edged by a knee-high wall. The road ran alongside a wide expanse of water, a moat. On the far side of the water rose a towering city of stone that glowed, giving off light to all the surroundings. Bridges connected the road to the city at regular intervals. Elaborate stone arches marked the entrance to each bridge marked by strange symbols that glowed in white. Some of the arches they passed stood open, while others were blocked off by closed gates. Without exception, all of the arches were flanked by soldiers dressed the same as Baldy and Jaw.

The road was crowded with people all wearing soft cotton tunics that hung shapeless off their shoulders to just above the knee. The men's were cut in a V-neck opening, while the ladies wore their necklines in a high circle that covered their collar bones. As far as Kai could see, they were all identical but for the slightest variation in colour.

A young man clothed in a shade of eggshell blue, tipped his head in greeting as he passed them. Kai responded by tipping his head back in the same manner. Zap waved cheerfully, and Ruaan scowled at the stranger.

Baldy clicked his tongue, exasperated. "Come on. Let's get you where you won't cause more embarrassment. Please follow me." He continued left along the broad road and walked purposefully, avoiding all the other cotton-clad people.

Zap shrugged at Kai and mouthed, "What did you do?"

Kai frowned at him, poking his chest. *Not me, you.*

As they walked, Kai drank in the sight of Stone City. It was built of stone that glowed softly, setting alight the shimmery surface so that it sparkled. Kai wondered what kind of stone one would use to create this luminous effect.

They passed five different arches until at last they came to the one that Baldy was seeking. The gate to this bridge stood closed and locked.

"Wait here. I'm going to clear your passage with the Gate Guard." Baldy disappeared into the tiny room that served as a guardhouse.

Zap leaned close to Kai. "I really like his shoes. Do you think they'll give us some? I was thinking we should make a run for it while we can. But if we hang around we might get some shoes."

"Shoes? You are obsessing over barefoot running shoes?"

Zap waved a hand, swatting his bad idea away as if it were a fly. "You're right. Maybe we should just take off. Forget about the shoes."

"You want to make a run for it. And go where? Are you going to cross the glass grass with bare feet? And that whole mist thing. I think the dust has worn off by now. You seem to forget what it took to get here."

"Well then, the shoes make sense. Stick around for shoes and then run."

Ruaan's face was expressionless. "We won't mention that the guy in barefoot shoes needed the same platform boot-things we needed to cross. We won't say a thing about that." He peered through the gate, squinting to see what was happening on the other side. "Maybe they have food for us."

"And maybe they're going to drug that food before they give it to us. Have you ever thought about that?" Zap scowled.

"You're just sour about the shoes. I need them more than you. Anyway, right now, I don't care. They could probably feed me boiled water, and I'd be just fine."

"I can save us all some time and just shove you in the moat. How's that?"

"Hush, you two. Ruaan, hang in there. I'm sure they'll feed us on the inside. Do yourselves a favour and pay attention. Remember we're here to look for Bree."

~*~

Evazee hardly dared to breathe as they slid silently through the water toward the stilt village. Before she could ask, Zulu aimed his raft between the stilts of a hut on the outskirts of the village. They drifted in beneath the hut together and stopped. Muted conversation filtered down to them through the wooden floor above their heads. The whites of Zulu's eyes glowed in the light, and Evazee realized that the mushroom paint had a tinge of UV to it.

Zulu shut his eyes and grew silent. Tension knotted all down Evazee's spine and shoulders, causing her ears to buzz louder than a hive of bees. She was so highly-strung, her insides so jittery, that she feared she would do something daft to break the awful tension. She was a breath away from snapping. She pictured herself leaping to her feet and belting out a song. The only thing stopping her was that the roof over her head might be too low, and she could well knock herself out.

Zulu moved again. The reeds stopped growing on

the outskirts of the village, almost as if they'd made an agreement with the village people. Either that or any reeds that had tried to grow inside the enclosure had died from exposure to purple mushrooms.

She followed his lead, using the bracing on the hut stilts to move through the water. Together they moved from hut to hut until she lost count of how many they'd passed.

The light ahead shifted from pure purple to a mixture of purple and blue. The two colours wouldn't blend, but remained distinctly separate from each other. Zulu's breathing sped up and a tremor ran through his hand.

Her raft slid in next to his, and she knew instantly why he was so wound up. They'd reached the centre of the village, the place where the sacred ceremony was happening. Instead of a wooden structure on stilts, what they faced now was an enormous floating platform. Two clear glass tubes stood next to each other in the centre of the platform, completely out of place in the rustic, neglected setting. One was filled with glowing purple liquid, the other pure blue. It could only be from the Healing Stream. Evazee gasped at the beauty of the blue. Virtue rolled off it in waves.

Three men with shaved heads paced around the two tubes an equal distance from one another. They swapped positions as they walked, their low voices mingling in a hypnotic dirge. Each wore ragged pants, torn off around the knees, worn through and holey. They could only be the priests that Zulu had spoken of. As they walked around the tubes on the platform, they cringed whenever they came near the blue, just as she cringed looking at the purple. Sitting directly between the two tubes was a boy whose bones poked through his fragile skin.

A hollow drumbeat boomed through the village and, as one, the priests halted. Another drumbeat ripped through the water and made the timber stilts quiver. The shortest priest pulled on long leather gloves that came all the way up to his elbows. He picked up a glass jar and waddled toward the tubes. He placed it onto a spinning turntable between the two tubes, right above the small boy's head and connected a thin pipe from each of the tubes to the jar. The two different colour liquids flowed down the pipes and into the top of the jar. Purple and blue jostled inside the glass. As the jar reached full, the pipes dropped off and the turntable began to spin. It sped up until the edges of the bottle blurred. Under the force of the spinning power, the two colours met with a hiss and reluctantly blended.

The two colours glowed violently in a reaction that Evazee would have described as an all-out battle. Beneath the turntable, the little boy huddled with his head between his knees, quivering. A pure white flash shot from the jar, so intense that it was blinding. Evazee blinked back the stars that lit the inside of her eyelids. The chanting had built to a pitch that rattled her eardrums.

Zulu quivered next to her. His fingers were pale from gripping the strut. She put her hand on his shoulder, and he jerked as if her touch had burned through his skin.

"What are they doing?" Evazee whispered, hoping the chanting would be noisy enough to cover their conversation.

Zulu passed a shaking hand over his face. "The blue fights the poison in the purple so it's safe to use on the homes." He shifted onto his knees, causing the bark raft to rock. "We need the blue, but alone, it too, is toxic."

"How do we get past them?" She waved towards the priests.

"Patience."

"You are kidding, right?"

Zulu put a dark finger across his lips. "Shh!"

Evazee clucked her tongue and tried to settle down for a long wait. Knowing that Peta was in pain made her impatient. Whatever Zulu was waiting for needed to happen, and it needed to happen now.

The priests unhooked the first bottle of glowing purple. Two of them held the little boy steady, and the third tipped the bottle until some of the contents ran down his throat. The boy swallowed, and within seconds began shaking violently. He fell to the ground, twisting and writhing in pain. A high scream tore from him, and Evazee nearly passed out.

"Stop them. You have to stop them."

"The boy won't let me. He wants to be there. He wants to be priest."

The boy passed out, and the short priest lifted a lid to check his eyes. He mumbled something to the others, and they nodded and smiled. Passing the bottle around, they each drank long and hard.

Zulu's eyes narrowed. "Watch."

The first priest that drank the purple water keeled over sideways, landing with a dull thud. The second two followed at the same time, falling half on top of each other.

"Oh my word. It killed them." Evazee was horrified.

"Not dead. Part of testing. Come. Now's our

chance." Zulu pulled his bark from under the shack and steered toward the central landing where the action had all happened.

13

Zulu hauled himself onto the platform and gave Evazee a hand up. "They could wake up any second. Take a bottle and put it on the middle, just like they did."

"That's not right. We just need blue." Evazee wasn't sure she'd heard him right.

"No time for argue. Blue is too potent. You need the mixture. Small one needs the mixture." It must have been the look on her face that made up his mind. He pushed her out the way and took a bottle himself. He placed it on the centre section which began spinning as the glass touched it.

One of the priests twitched and moaned. They were waking up. Evazee ran to the pile of bottles, uncorked one, and knocked off Zulu's half-full mixture. It hit the ground and shattered. Evazee ignored the mess and placed her bottle under the stream of pure blue.

Zulu's nostril's flared. He was angry, and Evazee's heart pinched. Peta was her friend, and there was no way any of the purple was going anywhere near her. Evazee's bottle was full. She slipped it out from under the trickle of blue and corked it. All three downed priests stirred. A pile of leather harnesses hung from hooks along the wall. Evazee grabbed one and slung it across her body. She slipped the bottle into the harness and pulled it tight.

"Let's go." Evazee jumped off the platform onto the bark. She landed too hard and nearly tipped off the edge. Zulu was close behind her. One of the priests sat up rubbing his eyes, and Evazee's heart pounded in her chest. She steered her bark boat beneath the closest hut, pulling herself in far enough that no part of her or her boat could be seen by the priests.

Zulu had one leg off the platform, foot stretching towards his bark.

Their eyes locked, and Evazee saw raw fear. Zulu's toes hooked the wood and it slid closer. The priest behind Zulu sat lost in a stupor, his eyes glowing a deep purple where there should have been white. He blinked and shook his head, rubbing his hand over his face.

Zulu fell onto his bark raft and pushed off the platform with all his might. It was a good push. The bark slipped through the water easily until it came to rest against Evazee's with a gentle bump. The other two priests were also awake, shaking their heads as if to try to clear away the fuzz. They moved across to the boy and poked him. His body lay lifeless between them.

Zulu motioned to Zee to sit dead still.

The three priests staggered to their feet and resumed their chanting and swaying with their arms looped roughly around each other's shoulders, dancing around their fallen apprentice. Their eyes were shut and their chants boomed out in a deep baritone that echoed in Evazee's ears.

It was time to leave. Zulu motioned to Evazee to go first. She sat frozen in shock at what she'd just seen, and he had to nudge her three times to get her attention. Shaking herself, she pushed the image of the little boy's body aside and resumed her awkward style of non-paddling. She felt about as elegant as an elephant in a tutu. Zulu manoeuvred his boat behind Evazee in complete silence. Only the ripples drifting past her told her that he was close. It felt like two lifetimes passed trying to reach the bank of trees.

They were nearly there when someone from behind shouted, "*Zulumange!*"

Evazee swung around and saw panic in Zulu's eyes. The three priests stood on the edge of the boardwalk, dark skin gleaming purple as if it had been injected into their veins.

"We're seen. Move!"

They gave up trying to hide the signs of their passing and grabbed at any reed to propel themselves away from the menacing priests who bellowed from behind.

"*Zulumange* stop! Get back here!" Their voices were deep and amplified, filling Evazee's head.

Something whizzed down from the sky and clipped her ear before landing in the water with a *plop*. "Ow!" Evazee didn't stop to cover her ears. More stones pelted down from the sky.

"They're waking the sandworms. Faster!"

More stones rained down at them from behind. Each one that sank into water sent out rippling circles. If there was anything alive down there, these stones were bound to bring it out of its rest. Another hit the water just next to her raft and instantly a small whirlpool the size of a dinner plate spun open. In the space of a blink, it had doubled its size. Evazee felt the tug of it on her makeshift raft. "Zulu, help!"

She got caught up in the current and felt her bark begin to turn in a slow circle. Zulu turned back, saw her, and shouted, "Get on mine! That raft is going down."

He stood, wobbling, and grabbed her hand to help her across. As her feet left the bark, it tipped upright, twirled and disappeared, swallowed down into the noisy throat of the whirlpool. Evazee swung wildly, struggling to balance on his piece of wood. Zulu held her with one arm, and with the other, he swung them around and pulled them toward the line of trees.

A second whirlpool started up on the left. Evazee shouted, "Look out!"

Zulu gritted his teeth and pulled on the reeds to get away. Their raft dipped into the water under the weight of both of them. Zulu's muscles bulged with the effort. They reached the cover of the overhanging trees, but the land was still ahead. The bark vibrated beneath their feet. The whirlpool was sucking them in. A layer of sweat beaded on Zulu's forehead, but no matter how hard he pulled, they were going backwards.

They were stuck in the spinning current along the edge of the whirlpool, held there by Zulu's muscles and the sheer force of his will. Evazee glanced back into the vortex, saw sharp teeth and shrieked. If Zulu let go, they would plummet straight into the gaping mouth of a sandworm with its three rings of gnashing teeth. Zulu's hands slipped, and they jerked closer.

"I can't hold it. Look up. Vines. Grab one." Zulu's neck muscles bulged with strain.

Evazee found a vine and jumped to grab it. She missed and jumped again. Her fingers wrapped around the cold tendril as the bark bucked and jerked. Zulu leapt, too, and they hung together.

Their raft tilted wildly and spun toward the sand worm's gaping maw. The sand worm made short work of the raft, chewing through it with the ferocity of a chainsaw. The stench of rotten things dredged up from the riverbed washed over them. This worm smelled rotten all the way through.

Evazee's hands were slipping. Zulu moved as if the vine were monkey bars, swinging one hand forward at a time, knotted muscles gleaming in the purple glow. Evazee doubted her hands would hold her body weight. One end of her vine snapped, and she dropped. Her feet hung inches away from the worm's mouth.

"Swing!" Zulu had made it to solid ground.

Evazee tucked her feet up underneath her and then shot them out, leaning back the way she used to do on the rope swing at home. Back and forth, she tilted and leaned. Each swing brought her closer to Zulu and then out over the monstrous mouth that seemed to track her movements. She kicked hard and flew.

Zulu caught her at the highest point. "Let go of the vine. I've got you."

"I can't. My hands are stuck." She stared at the vine. She gripped it so tight, her fingers had locked in position as though frozen stiff. She tried to pry them open with her teeth, but they were stuck.

Zulu wasted no time. He found a sharp rock and severed the vine. "Bring it with you then."

Together they turned and ran.

~*~

Baldy returned from the guardhouse with a silver device in his hand. It was shaped like a gun but with less sharp angles and more curves. The tip was a round glass dome the size of Kai's thumb nail. "You've been cleared for entry. I need to make it official."

Kai didn't like the look of the silver thing. "What is that?"

Baldy lifted Kai's sleeve and aimed the dome at his upper arm. "What? This thing? It's just a tagger. It won't hurt."

Kai pulled away. "I'm not scared of pain. I just want to know what it does before I let you do it. We won't be here for long. Why do we need to be tagged?"

Zap shuffled in behind Kai. "I'm scared of pain."

Ruaan folded his hands across his belly. "I don't care about pain and I don't care if you brand me, tag me, whatever. All I want to know is will we get food?"

Baldy sighed. "Guys, I can understand your wariness. If I don't do this, you won't be allowed into the city. Everyone in the city is tagged." He turned to Ruaan. "You will get food."

Ruaan didn't hesitate. He stepped forward and lifted his sleeve, shoving his arm under Baldy's nose. Baldy placed the glass dome on his upper arm.

"Hold very still until I say you can move." He pressed the trigger and purple sparks flew between the tagger and Ruaan's upper arm. Ruaan flinched but didn't pull away.

The skin on his upper arm glowed purple, flashed in dazzling brilliance and faded. Ruaan swung his arm back and forth. "It's all good. I can't feel a thing. Let's go. I want lunch."

Kai wasn't entirely convinced. He pulled up Ruaan's sleeve and ran his fingertips across the branded skin. The circle was slightly raised and warm to the touch, the surface a tiny bit glassy, but otherwise it looked normal.

Baldy held out the gun. "I'm not smart enough to explain the science behind it. My job is my job. I do, however, have to get back to the borders. So, who is next?"

Zap chewed his lip. He pointed at Kai with a nervous grin. Baldy shrugged and lifted Kai's shirt for the second time, pulled the trigger, and sparks flew once more. Zap cringed as he watched.

Kai couldn't resist. He doubled over, clutching his arm and bellowing. Blood drained from Zap's face and he looked ready to pass out. Kai straightened up and slapped him on the back. "Just kidding, man. It's fine."

That wasn't completely true. Kai's arm felt odd, heavy—but not in any way that he could explain. He'd decided that if Bree were here in this city and getting this bizarre tag-thing was the only way in, then he'd get tagged and be done with it. He caught Ruaan's eye and motioned toward Zap. They moved in, grabbed his arm and presented him to Baldy.

Seconds later, it was all over. Except for Zap's hurt feelings. Those would probably take a good bit longer to come right.

~*~

Evazee pushed through the overgrown path, trying to keep up with Zulu.

"Zulu, slow down a bit. Those worms. What on earth?"

"Ordinary worms that live in the riverbed sand.

They've mutated from years of living in mushroom infused watery sand."

"What is *Zulumange*? Why were the priests shouting that at us?"

"How are your hands? Still stuck?"

"You're avoiding my question. It's your name, isn't it? Those people know you. Was that your village?"

Zulu shrugged as he held aside a low branch for her to pass under.

"Why did you run away? Don't look at me like that. It's not hard to put two and two together. How else would you have known about the blue water? I won't even mention how much you look like those guys."

"You won't understand. It's messy."

"I need to think about something other than the fact that I may never use my hands again, so go right ahead. Try me."

"Benan is my village. I am the chief's son. I was in training to be the next high priest. You need to see to do that job, and I can."

Zee wanted to ask what he meant, but now that he was finally talking, she didn't want to interrupt in case he dried up. So, she bit her tongue and held on, hoping for more answers and less mystery.

"Some...things...happened and I came to see that the power they worship in that village is dark. It made me"—he scratched his head, trying to find the right word"—unsettled. There are many things they made me do. Dark things, wicked things."

"Like the boy."

"Yebo. I exiled myself to find a better way, to find light."

"Have you?"

"I found light with Beaver and Shrimp. But when you came, it was like I'd been in night for my whole life and when you came the sunrise filled me up and swallowed me whole at the same time."

"Wow, is that good or bad? I can't really tell."

"My heart told me to stay with you. We are close now."

Evazee knew there was something wrong the moment they stepped through the trees where they'd left Elden and Peta. Elden was pacing, wringing his hands.

"Where's Peta?" Alarm prickled down Evazee's spine. The little girl was nowhere to be seen. "Has she gone to the loo? I have medicine for her legs."

Elden stopped pacing, his features contorting. "There were drums, so many drums. I tried to stop her, but..."

"What are you talking about? Stop fooling around. Where is she?"

Zulu was down, studying the ground. "Many feet passed through this way. Did small one go with them?"

Elden shut his eyes and nodded. "I couldn't stop her. I'm sorry. I've never seen or heard anything like that."

Evazee gasped. A scratch ran down Elden's cheek and it bled enough that his collar was red. "What scratched you?"

"Like I said, I tried to get her back. They were too strong for me, there were too many. I can't rest until we've found her. First Bree and now Peta." Elden's face looked ashen in the pale lamplight.

"Zulu, can you track them?"

The whites of Zulu's eyes had turned purple and he was already examining the bushes and leaves. "*Yebo.*" Still bent over, he followed the trail in between the trees.

Evazee's heart nearly stopped when she saw the colour of his eyes. Following him didn't seem like the best idea any more, not after what she'd seen in the village. Elden took Evazee's hand. His fingers trembled, and his palms were clammy, but she let him lead her back into the forest.

Zulu followed the trail until he was almost out of sight. He turned around to wait for them, his eyes glowing luminous in the dark. Evazee clung to Elden's hand, but Elden pulled her along to catch up. Evazee understood his desperation to make up for his mistake, but she couldn't help the dread rising in her belly at the thought of trusting Zulu's purple eyes.

~*~

"Gentlemen, welcome to *Rei Lex*, the city of stone. This is as far as I go. When you get across, present your arm tag to the light scanner on the right-hand side. Someone will be along to help you." The gates to the bridge swung open, and Baldy waved them through. The light on the other side of the arched gateway was brighter still than what was on the road. Water shimmered beneath the bridge, reflecting the soft light that glowed from within the stones of the walls of the city. The water reminded Kai of the water from the Healing Stream, though here it was contained. The sight was breath-taking.

The gates swung shut behind them with a clang

that made Zap jump and squeak in fright. The bridge ran straight from the road that surrounded the city, to a stone archway built into the wall on one side. It was built straight and smooth and carried an age in each stone that hinted at just how long the city had been there. Kai stuck to the middle of the bridge. Two paces either way would take him to the edge, and no railings ran down the side of the bridge. He didn't need to go close to know that the drop was sheer and deep.

Ruaan wasted no time admiring the view. He led the way, growls coming from his belly as if he'd tucked a wild animal under his shirt. Kai followed him with eyes trained on Ruaan's back, walking in his steps, determined not to even look to the sides. Zap walked in a zig-zag, peering over one side and then walking over to the other side to peer over the edge. Each time he got to the drop, he whistled and uttered inane comments. "If you fall off here, you're history. It's so far down, not even water will stop you getting creamed. Maybe they throw their enemies in here. Do you think there are mermaids?"

Mermaids were too much for Kai. "Stop it! Get over here."

They made it across to a sealed stone doorway. Zap rapped on the door with his knuckles. "Helloooo. Now what?"

"Wait a moment." Kai ran his fingers up the side of the doorframe. He found a small knob and pushed it. A beam lit up and Kai lined it up with the top of his shoulder. The door beeped and opened with a swish. Kai walked through. The interior was cool and lit by the glow from the walls. No sooner had he stepped through when the door shut behind him and the lights dimmed. He thought about banging his fists against the door, but both of the others had been tagged and should get in as easily as he had.

The room he stepped into was small, not much bigger than a shower cubicle. It had holes drilled at regular intervals throughout the floor, the walls, and the ceiling. Liquid bubbled out of the holes and began to fill the chamber. The liquid quickly moved past hip height before Kai reacted. He turned and banged on the door so hard his palms stung. "Open the door! It's a trap!"

The water kept rising, past his chest, up his neck. Kai gulped a deep breath just as it closed over his head. *Don't panic. Don't panic. Don't...*

Too late.

He thrashed around wildly, thumping his hands onto the walls, the ceiling. The water flashed an intense blue.

This is my last breath.

A shift in the current spun him around.

Again.

And again.

He twirled like a ballet dancer. A shaft of light shot up from below his feet, and he spun faster until his head felt detached from his limbs. He moved into the centre of the light and dropped instantly.

Flushed. He'd been flushed.

Kai braced himself for impact but the landing never came. He fell into a chamber of clouds. Not real clouds. Those would be wet, and they wouldn't hold him up. These were like the kind you see in movies, the ones that hold up chubby angels and their harps. Sunlit clouds in shades of blue and purple. He floated weightless. Looking around to get his bearings, he realized that his clothes were gone. The shock of it sent him plummeting.

The drop was short-lived, and he landed with a dull thud on something cold, hard enough to knock the wind out. Kai lay on his back on the cold hard stone, willing air into his lungs. Through the stars dancing around in Kai's vision, he thought he saw snowflakes drifting gently down from the roof. They settled on him and into his skin, landing in layers that built up on his skin. The cold metal strip beneath him jerked into motion, and he clung to it as it moved him along like a giant conveyor belt.

Swish. A breath of fresh air blew in, shifting some of the clouds so he could see. He was being pulled toward the centre of a perfectly round opening. Kai's limbs felt heavy and useless, and he surrendered to the strange process. The desire to fight it had left him at the same time as he'd discovered his clothes were gone. He was covered, for now at least, in layers of snowflakes. But who was he to argue?

He passed through the hole and heard it shut behind him. The tube he travelled down seemed lit by a dozen criss-crossing suns that moved in a pattern as if they were weaving light. The rays warmed his skin. The snowflake layers began to melt, but not the way ice does. They melted into each other, forming a single, cohesive layer that covered his body in a seamless garment. The conveyor belt took him through the passage of suns and delivered him through the next hole.

14

Zulu led on through the overgrown forest. Evazee lost track of the time as they stumbled over fallen trees, battled lithe branches, and fought off tangled, hanging vines. Her thighs burned with the effort of keeping up with Zulu. Elden himself pushed hard as one possessed. They paused for brief moments while Zulu hunted for the trail, but it didn't take long, and he was off again. Elden clutched Evazee's hand, and she didn't pull away.

A faint vibration trembled through the ground beneath the feet, causing Zulu to stop and listen, his head tilted to one side like an exotic bald bird. "Not far now." He grinned at them.

Evazee grabbed Elden's arm and hauled him down to her level. "I'm a bit worried about following him blindly. Do you know where he's going? You must know this area."

"Actually, I don't. But you seemed to like this guy. Why the sudden mistrust?"

"I discovered some things I didn't know. Also, his eyes are purple. That can't be good."

"But girls love purple. Don't they?" Elden's forehead crumpled and he shrugged.

"Elden! What are you saying? Not eyes. How is that normal?"

"I don't know. I've been living in simulations for so long now, it's all a blur." He squeezed her arm. "We'd better go. He's nearly too far ahead. We don't want to lose him."

Evazee waved him on, resisting the urge to kick a tree. She followed as he bolted ahead, her feet feeling heavier with every step. A deep drum beat thrummed through the ground beneath their feet, followed by another and yet another.

The vibrations rolled up through the soles of her feet and turned her stomach. Each beat seemed to seep deeper into her bones. The music called, it sang her name. The fine hairs on Evazee's neck rose. This was not possible. Zulu halted. Elden was just a step behind him. They were examining the way ahead, cautious. Curiosity overwhelmed Evazee. She pushed past them both to try and get closer to the music, to whoever was calling her.

As she passed Zulu, the rhythm changed, picking up speed and growing in complexity. She felt the rhythm all through her body, and it made her happy. She wanted to dance but knew that she wouldn't have moves good enough for this music. Her heart sank at the thought. Someone was calling her name. With it came delicious warmth in her insides. Memories of sleeping in on school holidays flooded through her as a sense of well-being. Soft duvet, no rush, no demands. Waking up to hot chocolate and her favourite book.

The forest path opened out on a clearing the size of a soccer field. Lights bobbed and weaved in the trees. She felt a bit tipsy, and the lights danced just for her. There it was again. Her name on the lips of a stranger. It didn't scare her; it felt right and good.

The lights blurred and spun, and she found herself

twirling. Spinning. Dancing. Doing those moves she didn't think she could. She closed her eyes and surrendered. The ground tipped below her, every step took her down. Hands reached for her, welcoming, guiding, sweeping her along.

So many hands.

~*~

Kai sat on the conveyor belt in his new beige clothes. He pulled at his shirt, impressed that it had been made by snowflakes. Pity about the beige. The fabric was unlike anything he'd every worn before. It had the soft coolness of cotton but with a slight stretch to it that made it fit snugger than his clothes normally did. Perfect for such a skinny body. *Not.*

The room was tiny. If he turned with his arms stretched out, his fingertips would brush the walls on each side. All four of them looked identical except for the wall he'd come through that had a hole large enough for him. Kai's belly flipped. There was no door. He stood up to investigate whether he could crawl out on the conveyor belt, but it retracted and the hole in the wall closed up as if it had never been there.

This was not good.

At least it wasn't dark, and the stones still glowed with inner light. Kai breathed deep, trying not to sweat. There had to be a switch that would get him out of this room. He stepped close to the wall in front of him and reached out to run his fingers along each concrete line, each bump, looking for irregularities, anything that might give in to a firm push.

The moment all Kai's fingers connected with the

wall, the surface changed beneath his fingertips, shifting state from stone to smooth, cold glass. He blinked and found himself on stage with a guitar in his hands. The crowds pressed up against the edge of the platform, calling his name.

His old friend. The strings felt alive as he tapped out harmonics and tuned the instrument. With each sound he made, the crowd clapped and cheered.

Ready at last, he allowed himself to look at his audience. The crowd that gathered stretched off into the distance in all directions, a living sea of screaming fans. Kai grinned at the sight before shifting his focus to his instrument, his music. His fingers flew across the strings and frets, drawing out a melody unlike anything he'd ever played before. The crowd went wild.

The familiar thrill bubbled through him. The distinct sense of rightness at doing what he'd been created for. The song tore from him, pulsing with life. Blood pounded through his temples as he built towards the crescendo.

A breath away from the high point, everything froze. A voice spoke to him from inside the chamber. Or was it in his head? A woman's voice, low and soothing.

"Are you proud of yourself Kai?"

I don't understand what you're asking.

"It's a simple question. Just answer yes or no. Are you proud of yourself?"

Kai ran his hand along the smooth wooden neck of the instrument that felt so much a part of him. He thought back to the times he'd played his guitar and brought peace where people had been agitated, the rooftop and the darKounds when his music had sent them all back where they came from. Thinking of all those things, he was actually proud of himself.

Yes.

The voice in his head said nothing, but he felt the twisting weight of displeasure, and it confused him. He glanced across the crowds, hoping for something he couldn't put a name to. Redemption, validation. He wasn't sure. They were no longer cheering. Nobody called his name. Their hands came up with pointed fingers, and their faces twisted into scowls.

I'm sorry.

He dropped the guitar and backed away, hands raised to block his face from their rising anger. He tripped over his own feet and smacked his back into the opposite chamber wall. The stage melted away leaving the cold stone wall in its place. Kai was stuck. Again.

He sat for a moment, dazed. This place was messing with his mind. The sooner he found a way out, the better. His head spun, standing was going to be a challenge. He flipped over onto his knees and steadied himself on the wall. Before he could push himself up, the wall rippled, shifted, and he found himself in a bedroom with an orange woollen looped mat on the floor and tie-dyed curtains in autumn shades. *Retro.*

A woman sat on the floor, cradling her arm and crying. She looked familiar, but Kai's attention was drawn to the baby sitting next to her. He sat with his back ironing-board straight. His eyes were fixed on the woman, and his lips quivered as if he wanted to cry with her.

The baby bum-shuffled closer to the woman, reached for her arm but missed. She was crying too much to notice, and Kai could see a burn mark down the soft flesh of the inside of her arm. The baby's face pulled tight in concentration, and he made another grab for the lady's arm. This time he caught it and held on. His tiny six-month-old fingers dug into the flesh of her burned arm and she cried out in pain. In a second, she gasped and pulled her arm away from him. She stared at it in wonder, cheeks still wet with tears. The burn was gone.

A man came running in. His voice was high and angry. "What did he do?"

"It's a miracle! Roland, look! My arm is better. It's a miracle."

"I'm sorry, TrissTessa. This is not right or holy. God doesn't work through babies. I'm going to take him and find out what's wrong with him."

"But, Roland, he did good. You can't take him."

"It's not safe to be around this boy. He could be possessed for all we know. Until we can figure this out, it's not safe to be around him. It's for his own good, too. He can't live like this. Please don't fight me. I love you too much. I'm taking him. I'm going to find someone who can fix him, and then we'll come home. I promise."

The man called Roland picked up the baby as if he were picking up a loaded gun, turned quickly, and left. The one called TrissTessa sat on the floor of her bedroom, tears streaming down her face, too shocked to move.

15

Kai felt the cold floor on his cheek.

He was dimly aware of being back in the small room. The walls were moving, growing taller. No wait. The floor of the chamber was dropping. It came to rest with a jolt.

One of the walls was gone. He blinked against the brightness of the light that flooded the room from the missing wall. Part of him wanted nothing more than to just stay on the floor. But if the floor moved and trapped him again...

He couldn't chance it. The cold sweat beaded his forehead and made up his mind. Move while the doorway was an option.

He walked out into an open stone courtyard under a dome of pale blue sky and found Zap, sniffing his armpits. He was dressed in the same beige jumpsuit contraption that Kai wore, but he also had slip-on sandals, whereas Kai was barefoot once again.

"Hey, man. How weird was that?" Zap wouldn't meet his eyes.

Kai felt a surge of anger at what he'd been through, followed fast by an overwhelming sense of shame. He shoved it all deep. "I like your clothes."

"Shut up." Zap laughed. The tension eased. "You look pretty good yourself. It's just so you, darling."

"Shut up yourself. Have you seen Ruaan?"

Zap turned and pointed. The wall behind them stretched off in both directions, fitting in ten doorways identical to the ones they'd stepped out of. Only one of the doors remained shut.

Could it be the one holding Ruaan?

"Do you think he's OK?"

Kai shrugged. "We can hope."

"Why are there no people?"

"Maybe they've been eaten, and we're next."

"Um, what?"

"I'm just kidding. Listen. There's something that's been bothering me. Why aren't you freaked out by all this? You and Ruaan seem to be taking it all so well. I'm used to it from my accident, but you guys?"

Zap seemed relieved not to be on some big creature's menu. "Affinity training. We lived in simulations all the time. This is completely normal. I mean, each simulation was different, some weirder than this even. I suppose it's all just what you're used to."

"I guess so." Kai walked to the door. He hoped Ruaan was somewhere behind it. Sitting down, he faced the door.

Zap paced, restless. "So, what now?"

"We wait for Ruaan, and then we decide what."

"Do you think they've fed him?"

"Probably not." Kai couldn't shake the shame from what he'd seen in the chamber. It had sunk into his bones, written itself into his DNA. *Where are you, Tau?* He hauled out the bottle of light from around his neck, grateful it hadn't been incinerated with his clothes. Even though the courtyard was lit from the stones, the pendant pulsed with light. Kai folded his hands around it, wishing he could see Tau one more time. Until Runt found a way to stop the dark Affinity enhancer being pumped throughout the OS, who knew how long they'd be cut off from all things good.

Ruaan's floor landed without warning. He stormed out, looking as though he'd swallowed a thundercloud, and it had given him indigestion. "Whose stupid idea was it to come to this place?" He towered over Kai with his fists lifted and ready.

Zap stepped in and grabbed his wrists. "Calm down, man. It sucked for me, too."

Ruaan's nostrils flared. "What are you talking about? You know nothing."

"Gentlemen, please join us for replenishing." As quiet as a spider, a girl their age had padded in on silent feet and stood waiting for their attention. She was dressed in the same beige outfit as they were, and her red hair was drawn back in ponytail. Her features were plain, but her skin was pale and flawless, even though she wasn't wearing a scrap of makeup.

Kai got to his feet, keeping a wary eye on Ruaan.

Ruaan faced the girl with his fists still waving.

The girl handed Kai a pair of shoes.

Zap stepped between Ruaan and the girl. "Excuse me, but what is replenishing, and does it involve food?"

The girl laughed and instantly looked prettier. "It does, indeed. Follow me, please."

Maybe this wouldn't be so bad after all.

16

The drumbeat stopped, and Evazee collapsed as if someone had sucked out her spine. The fog that had clouded her mind hovered in and around her brain, and she blinked, trying to make sense of her surroundings. The ceiling arched above her like bleached whale bones, pock-marked and holey.

Evazee ran her fingers along the floor beneath her. The same holey, crusty rock. It felt as if she was in a cave. She rolled onto her side. She wasn't alone. Kids her age slouched along the curved walls, talking to each other. Some sat propped up with their arms looped around their legs. She wasn't the only one on the floor either. The brunette next to her lay flat on her back, rubbing her eyes with the back of her hands as if trying to wake up from a bad dream. A crimson birthmark in the shape of Africa marred the skin down the left side of her neck.

A boy on the other side lay curled in a foetal position with his eyes wide open, unblinking. His eyes flickered but didn't shut. Evazee rolled away from him with a shudder. Why had she left the guys? Where were they?

A deep boom shuddered through the rock beneath her. Liquid heaviness ran through her muscles and her mind grew light. The next drum beat vibrated through her. Drum beats like a drug, slowing her heart, churning through her veins like thick mud. The rhythm picked up, beating in time with her heart. One with her heart. Her mind melted into fuzz. The beat sped up, and her heart soared with it. She rolled over and clambered to her feet. The brunette was on her feet, giggling. She tripped on the holey floor and grabbed onto Evazee to break her fall.

Zee caught her and started laughing, too. Until she spun around and caught sight of the boy still on the floor, still curled up, still staring. Her blood ran cold and she detangled herself from the clutches of the giggling girl.

The rhythm swept them along, deeper into the cave. Evazee no longer felt the giddy elation that the others did. She kept seeing the boy's vacant and lifeless face in her mind. The rhythm drew her deeper in, though all she felt was numb. She bumped into the girl next to her and turned to apologize. The girl didn't seem to have noticed her, but her eyes flickered left and right as if she were reading from an invisible screen. The whites were tinged purple.

~*~

Redhead kept up a running commentary as they walked. Her voice had a musical quality about it, and Kai had to force himself to focus on what she was saying.

"This city is ancient. It existed long before the records we have in our history books. There is order here and peace because of it. We live according to guidelines that keep us safe. Once you are a part of the city, it is best never to leave. Nobody would want to anyway. Safety is within these walls. Don't go outside them, and you'll be just fine. We run patrols into the surrounding areas to pick up anyone who is ready for a new way of life or those who are sick or injured. We bring them here for healing and cleansing. Ah, we are here. Follow me, gentlemen."

Kai, Ruaan, and Zap followed the redhead up a flight of stairs that took them up to the next floor. The replenishing room was long and skinny with a table running the length of it. The way in was through a simple stone arch that stretched high over their heads in clean lines, uncluttered by embellishments. Warm air drifted toward them, carrying aromas that made their mouths water. Many city dwellers sat along the edges of the tables, talking quietly, while those serving food bustled in and out through side doors dotted at regular intervals along the walls. They carried covered plates and tall jugs of liquid.

Zap pulled Kai close. "I just don't understand why they have to call it a replenishing room. It's just a dining hall, right?"

Ruaan pushed them apart. "They can call it a feeding trough if they want to. If they're giving away food, I'm in. You can stay out here and argue names. I don't care."

Their redheaded guide hooked her arm through his, drawing him between the others and through the arched doorway. "Just wait until you see this food. You're going to love it here. We're like one big, happy family."

Kai and Zap stopped arguing and followed. The dining hall—replenishing room—was a long room that made Kai think more of a corridor. All the tables were laid out in one long row that ran the full length of the room. Floor-to-ceiling arched windows took up huge sections of the wall, letting in the soft light from the outside of the building. The room itself was built on one of the higher levels of the city. Kai crossed to the window and looked out over the city. All of it seemed crafted from the same glowing stone. Breath taking.

A sea of people filled the hall, all dressed in the same beige outfit that Kai and his friends wore. They chatted in low voices as they filtered in from the doors that led from different parts of the city. Without any direction, they lined up behind specific chairs and waited. Kai followed the redhead and Ruaan, studying each face they passed.

If Bree was here, he intended to find her.

The redhead leaned closer to Ruaan. "Normally, we don't mix outside of our tier, but replenishing is the one great equal."

"What do you mean by *tier*? Are you telling me there is some sort of hierarchy you live by?" Ruaan had forgotten about his stomach for a whole minute. It had to be a miracle.

"It's just a formality. It doesn't really affect our normal day-to-day life."

"It doesn't sound very big-happy-family-ish to me." Zap turned his head from side to side.

The bright smile stayed glued to the girl's face, and she waved away his concerns with a graceful hand. "Of course it is. Your branding will allow you access to areas allowed for your tier. No more, no less. There are ways of moving up, of course. But that is a hard thing to do. Few ever manage. Ah, let's sit here. There've been some spare places here of late."

Supper was at least as colourful as the picnic

spread Gallagher had laid out for them. Kai stared, trying to decide whether he should eat or not. As before, he wasn't hungry at all, but it felt weird to watch every other person in the room eat without trying some himself. He reached for a long, orange tube that glowed along the edges.

The redhead reached over and took it from him. "Rather, don't eat this one."

"I don't get it. Why do they dish it up if it's not edible?"

"Oh, trust me. It's delicious. But we can't eat it. It's only for third and fourth tiers, not first tiers like us."

"How do you know that it's delicious then?" Zap frowned at her.

Before she could answer, Ruaan smacked his belly and hissed under his breath, "Stop being so rude." He turned his attention back to the plate in front of him.

Kai thought he saw Zap stick out his tongue at Ruaan, but it was too quick for him to be sure.

Kai leaned back to allow a server to place a covered plate on the table before him. The girl's hair was drawn back into a sleek, straight ponytail that hung down her back, and her eyes were downcast. One arm was hidden under her tunic, and she fumbled as she put the heavy plate down with the other hand. Kai caught and righted it before anything could tip out. The girl blushed to the roots of hair. There was something familiar about the curve of her cheek, her jawline.

"Bree?" Kai reached for her hand. Her eyes shot up at the name, and he recognized her fully. She pulled away from him as if his fingers burned, turned, and rushed through the closest serving door, disappearing into the room beyond.

Kai shot up, bumping his chair over. He left it and ran after her, not caring if he was allowed to follow her or not. The room was tiny. And empty. A large serving hatch for a dumb waiter took up most of the space. Bree was nowhere to be seen. Kai swung around, looking for another way out. Nothing. The dumb waiter bobbed slightly, enough to make up his mind. He threw himself onto the serving platform. His weight triggered the downward trip, and he picked up speed as he dropped. He braced for impact, gritted his teeth, and landed with a gentle bump.

Kai rolled off the platform, landing on his feet in an enormous kitchen full of people busy with food preparation. They were all dressed just like him but with skull caps to keep their hair out of the food. *Bree, where are you?* There! The kitchen lay directly beneath the eating room above—a long passage of a room. Bree disappeared through a door on the narrow end of the room, off to the right.

Kai ran, dodging the chefs and helpers as they moved about fetching supplies and prepping food for the city folk. He bumped someone as he ran. He heard loud clattering and a sharp curse behind him, but he didn't stop to see what disaster he'd caused.

He reached the door as it swung shut, threw himself at it and forced his way into the room beyond. Cool blue light sparkled and twinkled from the walls. In the centre of the room, he found a staircase, curling downward into a deep part of the city. After the noise of the kitchen, the room was so quiet he thought he could hear footsteps descending. If it was Bree, the girl ran like a spooked rock rabbit.

Switching tactics, Kai tiptoed down the stairs silently, pausing each time he lost track of the footfall.

He got to the bottom and hid behind a pillar.

Bree sat on the floor with her knees crossed, staring at a tall, rectangular booth. The side facing them was taken up by a high, arched opening mostly hidden behind a curtain of running water that tumbled off the top of the structure. Kai craned his neck enough to see that the next side was identical to the first.

No matter how hard he squinted, it was impossible to see through the water to what was inside the arches. The air seemed to shiver and bend. There was no doubt though...something about the room twisted Kai's belly.

17

Evazee sat in the dark with her back against a rock. Around her were snoring bodies, shapeless lumps breathing loudly as they slept. Being in the dark wasn't her favourite thing, but she was grateful the drums had stopped. She would take the dark over the hypnotic drums any day.

Praying seemed useless, but she shaped the nameless longings of her heart and sent them heavenward anyway. *Jesus, protect Peta. Help us find Bree. Help us to shake off this dark Affinity.* She waited for some sign that her prayers had been heard. Nothing.

She wriggled her toes, feeling the soft canvas of her sneakers. Bending her mind and thoughts, she willed her shoes to be gone. Nothing changed. Maybe Bible verses would help. There was one she memorized when she was little. Something about faith. *Now faith is being confident of what we hope for, certain of what we do not see.* Evazee's heart popped in response to the words.

Just then, someone spoke. Evazee held her breath. She couldn't tell if the voice had been out loud, from someone next to her, or just an echo thrown up by her sight-deprived conscience. She waited. Nothing.

"Awakened One. Come walk with me."

Evazee bit back a laugh. Yip, she was losing it.

Now she was hearing voices in the dark. A small patch of rock began glowing under her feet.

"Come to me. All you need do is follow."

A spike of fear shot through Evazee.

"Don't be scared. Just come."

I'm not scared. I'm just...cautious.

"You're safe here with me."

Evazee's mind spun. She tried to remember what normal life felt like—what safe felt like. Belonging. The feelings eluded her. Another glowing dot lit up on the floor.

~*~

Bree sat cross-legged on the floor, chewing on a fingernail. Every now and then she'd rub the silvery imprint on her palm as if trying to make up her mind. Her shoulders set as if she'd decided, and then she slowly pushed herself to her feet. As she stepped toward the cubicle, a symbol lit up above the archway—a twisted infinity sign. It pulsed as Bree drew closer until Kai couldn't stand it any longer.

"Wait!" He threw himself down the stairs, tripped, and rolled toward her like a human bowling ball, coming to rest at her feet.

"You. What are you doing here?"

"Bree, I've been looking for you. You're alive." Questions fought over his lips, but he swallowed them all and let the sight of her wash over him. He reached for her cheek with fingers that trembled, stopped short of touching. Instead he waved toward the arched booth. "What is this thing?"

"Why are you here?"

"I wasn't meant to leave you in the desert. You were supposed to come back with me. It all went wrong. I thought you were dead."

Bree blinked, her normally responsive features completely calm. Kai didn't know what to make of it.

"Your hair. You straightened it." Her wild auburn mop had been tamed, combed back into a single pony tail that hung straight down her back without a single curl.

"It's just hair." Her eyes dropped to her hand, and she fiddled with her imprint, rubbing at it as if she hoped it would come off.

So many things Kai wanted to ask, but he got the feeling that his questions would be left hanging. Now was not the time for him to whip out the inquisition. He reached for the booth and ran his fingers across the intricate carving in the stone work. "What is this for?"

Bree's nose wrinkled, and she held out her arm. Her silvery imprint was clearly visible. "It's to get rid of this thing."

"Your imprint? Why would you want to do that?"

"It's holding me back."

Kai reached for his own, horrified at the thought of losing them. They weren't much use at the moment thanks to the dark Affinity enhancer, but he hoped it was only a temporary setback. He was quite fond of his silvery marks. Why someone would want to get rid of theirs didn't make sense to him.

He reached for her arm, holding gently and rubbing his thumb over the flat, silvery mark. She kept her eyes on his thumb. He led her to the wall and slid down with his back resting against it, drawing her down with him.

Bree sat but pulled away from his touch. "I

shouldn't be here alone with you."

"Holding you back from what?"

"I have hopes of working in the Temple of Tau. They are very strict there. I can't get in until this thing is dealt with."

"They have a temple for Tau here?" Kai's heart pumped in his chest. If he could get to Tau, Tau would know how to fix all this. He would know how to stop the dark Affinity enhancer, help Bree, and find Evazee and Peta. He could help them with everything.

"Of course there's a temple."

"Could you take me? Will it be open now?"

Bree rested her head on the wall holding them up. "I could take you, but you can't go in. Nobody goes in. It's too sacred. Only the selected ones. That's why I want to get rid of this. Maybe then I could stand a chance of being chosen." She waved over her arm.

The blood drained from Kai's face. Bree must be wrong. The Tau he'd met before would never stop anyone coming close to him. If he could get there himself, they would let him in for sure. Bree had been terrified of the Healing Stream. That would be enough reason for her to convince herself she wasn't allowed in. "I don't understand."

"It's not that complicated. There are tiers, right? The first three are for those who are fresh in from outside. They get split according to whether they are: Contaminated, Broken, or Unlit. Contaminated go through De-Contamination; Broken go through Mending and Unlit need Conversion. The next three tiers are focussed on sorting you out in your mind and spirit. The last three are training for giving out what you've been given."

"And you can't mix with people from other tiers?"

"You make it sound like a bad thing. It's really not. It's for our protection. It helps people not to get confused. That's all."

Kai frowned but chose not to push the issue. He gestured toward the archways. "Have you been in one of these?"

Bree nodded, but her lips remained a tight line. Whatever happened in the arches was not something she was excited to talk about.

~*~

A third rock lit up, a good ten paces farther away than the second. As it lit, the first one faded. So there was a time limit to her response. If Evazee waited much longer, the pathway would be gone. Her heart pounded in her chest as she pushed off the floor and followed the light path. The light itself warmed her after being in the dark for so long. It wasn't tinged purple like the mushroom light, yet it wasn't the crystal blue of the Healing Stream other. It was just ordinary rock colour but lit up from inside. No clues there.

As she walked, the pace of the lights picked up. Whatever was causing the light was fully aware of her movements. A chill slipped down her spine, but she kept following. She was being drawn deeper into the cave like a dog on a leash, and she was allowing it to happen.

The passage was wide and tall. Evazee looked around as she walked, but the glowing floor cast strange shadows on the holey walls, and the play of light made ghoulish faces dance in the rock. She shuddered and focussed on the light spots on the floor. Praying usually calmed her, but her mind was spinning. She couldn't string two prayerful words together. Sweat beaded on her palms, her forehead.

The lights took a sharp turn to the left into a smaller passage with smooth walls of midnight-black shot through with sparkling, diamond-like shards. As she progressed down the passage, Evazee ran her fingers along the wall. The sparkles in the deep, dark surface gave her the impression of being under a starry sky. With each step her hesitance faded, replaced by wonder.

At the end of the passage, she stepped out into a huge circular chamber under a glass dome of real night sky. In the centre of the room glowed a hologram image of earth, taller than Evazee, suspended midway between the floor and the ceiling. A low, circular fountain danced just below the image of earth, filling the room with gentle water noise. The midnight marble walls continued from the passage and circled the vast room, scooping outward in deep shadowed recesses every few paces. Evazee breathed in the beauty of it all as if she'd seen nothing but ugliness for weeks.

A control panel mounted on a pole sat off to one side. Evazee crossed to it, curiosity overcoming her natural hesitance. A single row of flat buttons ran down the right side of the touch screen panel, next to a circular dial in the centre. The temptation to push one and see what happened was overwhelming.

The whispery hiss of a door sliding open made Evazee jump. She dashed across the room and threw herself into one of the recesses, crouching low and wishing she were invisible. Or smaller. Or still back in the bony caves.

A man walked in, whistling softly. His silvery hair was drawn back and his grey eyes glowed softly in the gloom. He moved with casual grace, and in an instant she knew him. Shasta. The pale man who had healed Peta's broken ankle, a healing that had left her moody and sad. Changed.

The hairs stood all along Evazee's arms.

He moved to the hologram and turned it with a wrist flick. He stopped it and tapped. The image shifted and zoomed in, homing in on the outside of the OS. A double tap and the roof and walls receded. Shasta's fingers trailed from room to room. Evazee shoved her hand in her mouth. All through the OS people lay on the floor, passed out or dead—she couldn't be sure. Shasta walked his fingers and zoomed in close. The image pixelated and then cleared. Evazee saw herself tucked up in bed, skin pale with dark circles below her eyes. Shasta traced the line of jaw with the back of his hand. He leaned in close and whispered. Evazee heard every word. Not with her ears, but in her mind.

Her teeth broke skin.

Shasta flicked his fingers, the way one would flick water off their hands, and the image zoomed out. The OS glowed as a green pulsing dot. Another flick, further out. Evazee counted eight pulsing dots. Again, flick. This time there were too many to count. A final zoom took the hologram back to the ball of the earth, awash with flashing green. It seemed the OS was one school of many.

18

Bree's good arm crossed her chest and the smirk on her freckled face was the closest thing to the old Bree he'd seen since finding her. "Read it for yourself. I told you. You can't go in."

Kai resisted the urge to untie her hair and ruffle it. He missed her curls.

They stood before a tall building carved with intricate geometric patterns. A silent lady shuffled along, hunched over and gazing at the ground. Kai scanned the quiet street. Other than the old lady, they were alone.

All the other buildings Kai had seen so far had been simple, purely functional. This one made up for all their plainness. A carved stone plaque declared the building to be *The Temple of Tau* in grand letters. The times of worship were carved underneath in tiny writing. Kai poked at it with a stiff finger. "Surely, they open for services. They must." Kai didn't know much about church, but it made sense that the building would be opened for the faithful. "How else would one do whatever it is that people do during church?"

Bree's nose wrinkled, and she shrugged. "That's what the courtyard is for."

Kai was not convinced. He mounted the broad stairs to the over-sized double doors. He pushed, shoved, and tried the handle. Nothing budged. Bree leaned on the plaque at the bottom of the stairs, her face expressionless, but *I told you so* twinkling in her eyes.

Tau, why is it so hard to get to you?

Determined to find a way in, Kai explored the walls alongside the door. He trailed his fingers along each crack, feeling for something that might spring the doors. He'd been on this side of reality often enough to know secret entrances were nothing strange.

Bree stayed at the bottom of the stairs. "Give it up already. You're not getting in. You're just as stubborn as you were before."

Kai heard her, but he moved on to the wall to keep exploring.

"Kai..."

He stuck his hand into a carved recess just at shoulder height and felt around for anything out of the ordinary. This one was smooth. He clucked his teeth, muttering under his breath.

"Kai! They're coming."

"Just give me a moment."

Bree stamped her foot in frustration and ran up the stairs to grab Kai's arm and yank on it.

"What?" He brushed her off and kept on searching.

"Temple Guards. Trust me. You don't want them to catch you here." Any trace of the Bree he knew from before was gone again, swallowed up by this fear-filled, pale creature who couldn't look him in the eye.

Kai stopped and spun around. "That is the single most ridiculous thing I've ever heard."

"Shocking, I know. Whatever. Please can we leave? I swear I'll leave without you." Her hand rested on his arm, and her fingers burnt his skin.

"Fine. Just give me a moment."

Running footsteps echoed down the street as though a small army headed toward them.

"You're out of moments. You're on your own." Bree took off along the side of the temple, ducking behind the hedge growing along the front of it.

"Hey! You on the stairs. Freeze for scanning."

Out of the corner of his eye, Kai saw a group of soldiers dressed just like the two who'd escorted them to Stone City. The image of Bree's death date carved into her gravestone flashed in his head and made up his mind. There was no time for him to hang around and chinwag to this bunch. He ran after Bree, leaving the temple and his only link to Tau behind.

~*~

Evazee tried to breathe quietly, but her heart raced. Shasta stood with his back to her, rubbing his chin and muttering to himself. A girl that looked to be Evazee's age came in and stood quietly. She bounced on her toes as if the floor were cooking her feet. She must be in a hurry.

A full minute later, Shasta tapped his foot on the floor. The hologram powered down and disappeared. He turned to the girl. "Why are you disturbing me?"

"I'm sorry, but there's a problem with the Resonance Pools. We've tried everything, but we can't get them right."

"Have you got samples?"

"All ready for you, sir."

"Sometimes I wonder why I even bother. It would

be simpler to do it all myself."

The girl looked suitably whipped and followed behind him as he left the room. Evazee waited until she couldn't hear their steps and slipped out of her hiding place. She had to know for sure she wasn't misinterpreting what she'd seen. Hopefully, she was wrong.

Finding the spot Shasta had tapped his foot was easy. It was a raised bump in the floor. She stamped it hard and waited. The hologram of earth appeared as before, flashing many spots of green. Evazee copied the hand gestures he'd used and zoomed in, working her way to finer detail each time. Finally, she got right down to the OS and recognised it by the giant instruments decorating the outside. Her heart pounded. Zooming in meant glimpsing all the things someone else had seen all along.

She spread her fingers, and the view switched to the inside of the building. As she tapped and slid, the view changed, and she revisited the rooms that had been her prison. There was the lounge where she'd stolen fruit. Someone had watched all of it. She felt stripped, exposed.

The instrument panel across from where she stood beeped and flashed. She checked the passage to make sure no one was about to interrupt her little escapade and tiptoed across to it.

The small, square screen was brightly lit with one word that flashed over and over: COMPROMISED.

She flicked her fingers at the hologram and the panel fell silent as she zoomed out, away from the OS. So, their doorway and darKound relocation had caused some trouble. Picking a random spot, she flicked inwards until she'd homed in on another school, one she'd never heard of before. Writing scrolled up across the panel, numbered lists. Most of it made no sense, but two headings stood out: Converts and Coerced. The school she was looking at was made up of 92% Converts and 8% Coerced. Converts sounded good, but coerced?

"Ah you came. I thought I felt you here earlier."

Shasta had come back.

Evazee had been so engrossed in what she'd been reading, she hadn't noticed. She wanted to run, but there was no point now. She recognised his voice as the voice in her head. He appeared to be clothed in the same stuff the walls were covered in, though how one made a coat from star-encrusted black marble was beyond Evazee. His silver hair hung long down his back, but his eyes drew her attention. Pale as dove eggs, they fixed on her. She felt stripped.

Evazee shot her hand behind her back and coughed. If he'd been a split second later, he'd have caught her redhanded. "Why did you call me here?"

"You recognized my voice. That's good." Shasta sauntered across the room, a half-smile playing at the corners of his mouth.

There was an agelessness to his face that intrigued Evazee. Between the dome of sky overhead, the sound of running water, and the deep timbre of his voice, Evazee began to feel a little tipsy. The closer he came, the more the feeling grew. By the time he stood a foot away, she felt quite dizzy. She'd never been drunk before, but this must be what it felt like. Delicious lethargy bubbled through her veins making her limbs heavy and her head light.

Shasta tilted his head, his eyes fixed on her face. "You're not like the others here. There is something about you that I like. I want to show you something." In a smooth move, he slipped behind her and placed his hands on the console, wedging her between the keypad and himself. "I see my map caught your interest."

His breath was cool on her neck, and he smelled of sandalwood. She shivered but couldn't find the strength to pull away from him. Her muscles ignored her. "What is this thing used for?"

He flicked his finger across the dial in the middle and hologram Earth spun. He tapped the screen and it stopped spinning. A bright dot glowed and pulsed. The man pointed at it. "That is where we are now."

Evazee shrugged. A small part of her screamed, waving fists as alarms, but the rest of her felt warm and lazy. "So what? What can you do with it?"

Shasta snorted back a laugh. "Oh, nothing really. It's all just decorative. Here to make the room pretty. Like your hair, so pretty." His fingers ran through her long hair, twirling the ends. Evazee shivered, though not from cold.

"Why are there buttons?"

The man moved away, his gaze focussed on her as he circled. "To show you different things. Go on, push one."

Evazee's curiosity piqued, and she did as the man said. The hologram split down the middle and the top layer peeled back to reveal a network of tunnels that criss-crossed the entire planet in every direction. "What is this? What am I looking at?"

"Oh, my darling, this? This is my favourite part. Some call it the spirit cuttings. I think of them more like quick tunnels. It's all connected."

"Did you make them?"

"Would you be impressed if I said yes?"

A trap. She dodged it with a question. "What are they for?"

"I can be anywhere, anytime. Isn't it perfect?"

Stars danced in her eyes, and she had to lean on the control panel to stop herself from falling.

~*~

Bree had changed in many ways, but the one thing she'd managed to hang onto was her run-away-fast-in-a-crisis speed. Kai pushed hard to keep up with her and put as much ground as possible between himself and the temple guards.

Even that concept messed with his brain. Since when did Tau need guards? The Tau he remembered would fling the gates wide to anyone who chose to come close to him. None of them would be turned away.

Five blocks later, Bree ran into a sunken alcove in a wall, came to a sudden halt, and doubled over, breathing hard. The street was busy with people and noise. Bree glared at him as he came close. "You have to learn to follow the rules. You can't just run around doing your own thing. This isn't a game. What's wrong with you?"

Kai stepped in close to read her eyes. "Do you still paint, Bree? Draw?" She blinked rapidly. He'd hit a nerve.

She frowned at him, anger blossoming on her cheeks. "You're not listening. Stop causing trouble."

"The Bree I remember could turn an ugly old shack into a masterpiece with a few strokes of brush.

When last did you paint?" He spoke softly as he would to a fallen bird.

"No! Obviously, I don't. It's not a good use of one's time."

"Show me your hand."

Bree flinched and pulled away from him. "Leave me alone. I didn't ask for any of this."

"Please, Bree. I'm responsible for whatever happened to you in the desert. I thought it would work, but it didn't. It's been eating me alive. I thought I'd killed you." The words hung in the air between them. Kai turned away, hiding behind his hand.

"Fine. I'll show you. But I'm warning you, if you say anything..."

"I know. I know. You'll rip my throat out and feed me my own intestines. Go right ahead."

"That's not even what I was going to say. That's such a stupid thing to say." Her nose wrinkled, making her freckles kiss.

"Your arm?"

She kept her gaze locked on his and awkwardly pulled back the long sleeve where she hid her hand. "There. My arm. Ta-daa."

Kai braced himself but nothing could have prepared him. The wounds were no longer raw but patched together roughly. Her hand was a mangled claw, fingers curled and stiff, shredded and useless. "Bree, I'm so—"

"Don't." A single word packed with the venom of a broken heart left to fester.

"I can fix this." Kai reached for the bottle around his neck. A few drops would be all she needed.

"Stop it! Haven't you done enough?" She didn't shout. She didn't have to. Her words were barely a whisper but they rammed into Kai with enough force to take his breath away. Bree pulled her hand back into her sleeve, tucked a stray strand of hair behind her ear and walked away.

19

Kai started to follow Bree but changed his mind. His heart burned hot and raw. He turned in the opposite direction and walked back to Tau's temple. He couldn't believe that someone who truly knew Tau would be kept out. Zap and Ruaan had probably finished their food by now, but they'd have to keep themselves busy for a little while longer. Kai needed Tau. Nobody and nothing else would do.

Time worked differently here in the spiritual realm. Kai had no idea how long he'd have to wait until the worship service started, but however long it took, it would be worth the wait. As he got closer to the temple, the crowd around him swelled, all walking in the same direction. He kept walking, hiding his head from a pair of Temple Guards who patrolled on the far side of the road. Being careful was necessary for now, until the mixup had been sorted out.

By the time they reached the temple, Kai had bundled up the tangled mess of emotions and shoved them deep. A grim resolve settled over him. He was going to make this right. Whether Bree ever spoke to him again or not.

He checked the inside of his wrist. The imprint was still there though it had dulled to a grey colour. Watching the faces of the people around him, he expected to feel their buzz of excitement. Surely, they would have hope, yet the people around him didn't seem to have received the memo. Kai sneaked a sideways glance at the girl next to him. Her forehead was creased into many frown lines.

A boy on the far side of her was agitated. His eyes roamed, scanning the crowd. For what or whom, Kai had no idea. They followed the swell of people through to an open-air courtyard, flanked on one side by a raised platform. A set of drums waited unmanned on the platform. There were no other instruments that Kai could see.

Maybe Tau himself would step out. A doorway opened in the wall at the back of the platform. Three women walked out and lined up across the stage, equally spaced from each other. The middle one raised her hands and a hush fell over the assembly.

"Welcome to the Stone City Worship Service. Before we begin, let us take a moment for quiet reflection." She lowered her hands and silence consumed the courtyard.

Kai leaned over the girl next to him. "What are we supposed to be reflecting on?"

"Shh!"

Kai was pretty sure that he wasn't meant to reflect on *shh*. He had to find someone less serious. He turned to the guy on the other side. "What are we meant to be reflecting on?"

"Today's failings, shortcomings, weaknesses." He sighed a bit, and his face creased as if he had toothache. Then he turned his attention back to the woman on the podium.

"Well, that doesn't seem very useful."

"Oh, believe me, it is! It is the single most

important thing you can know. Know yourself."

"But we'll always be weak and fail. Focussing on it is not going to make it go away. I think it will only make it worse."

The guy studied him with one eyebrow lifted. "Are you serious right now?"

"I think so?"

The girl on the other side turned to them both with red spots riding high on her cheeks. "You two need to keep quiet, or I'm going to single you both out for disruption."

Kai pulled on the guys arm and leaned close to whisper, "When do we get to see Tau?"

"What do you mean? To look on the face of Tau would surely mean certain death. Oh, but such a sweet death that would be." His eyes grew misty and lost focus as he stared off into nothingness.

Kai leaned closer to follow his line of sight. Yip, he was truly staring at nothing. This boy was a space cadet. Kai glanced at the others around him and picked a black-haired girl who wasn't staring off into space as if violins were playing inside her head. "Excuse me," Kai whispered. Hopefully, no one else would hear. The girl turned to him, her eyes a violent shade of purple.

"Can you tell me how I could get to see Tau?"

The girl blinked, obviously confused by his question. But then she smiled and pointed to the left. "There is a gallery full of pictures just around that corner. Some real beauts. You should go see."

"No, you don't understand. I need to see him. I need to ask him some things."

"You have nice eyes."

"What?"

"Your eyes are lovely." She turned red and stared

at the floor. "I'm sorry. I'm not supposed to notice things like that anymore. I just can't help myself. I don't know what's wrong with me."

Kai thought he might be going insane. None of the people here were normal. Then again, would he even recognize normal if it slapped him in the face? He was beginning to doubt it. *Tau, where are you?*

Without knowing why, he stepped forward, pushing himself between two others. A few shuffling steps, and he made his way through two more groups of people who muttered something unintelligible about rudeness but didn't stop him. He kept going, threading his way, this way and that. Some of those he pushed past were so deeply caught up in their own contemplation that they didn't notice his passing. Others glared as he jostled his way past.

He was sweating by the time he made it to the front. The swell of bodies moved together as one giant organism, pressing him against the stage. The three women on stage had their eyes closed, heads thrown back, and their arms outstretched.

Tau, I need you.

~*~

Evazee woke to the beating of drums vibrating through her from the rock walls of the bed-hole where she curled up. She had no memory of getting back, and the events of the night before seemed nothing more than an odd dream. Somewhere in this mess, she hoped to find Peta. Had to find her.

There was no room for stretching, so she angled her legs out and dropped to the floor of the underground cavern. Pins and needles numbed her feet, and she gave up trying to stand. She leaned back, shut her eyes, and stretched her body, working life back into her feet. Drumbeats rippled through the cave, and Evazee tried to ignore them. Blocking her ears with her palms, she hummed a tuneless ditty. When she looked again, she'd pushed off the wall and stumbled to obey the drums on her tingly feet. She joined the streams of people shuffling along deeper underground.

It was hard to tell how many of them there were. Evazee struggled to focus on anything else while the drums beat. The crowd poured through a corridor into a wide cavern. The roof arched high above, lit by glowing moss. The light cast by the plant-life shone down eerily, making the faces around her seem ghoulish.

The drumbeat stopped and, as one, they all dropped to the floor. A voice filled her head. "Welcome, Awakened One." Evazee glanced around at the others. Some sat with eyes closed and rapture on their faces. Others huddled over their knees with faces hidden. Each one seemed caught up in their own little world. Evazee couldn't tell if the voice was only in her head or spoken to all of them.

"This is just me and you. Don't worry about the others."

Her stomach turned. Shasta was back in her head. And disturbingly, there was a part of her that relished him being there. She shivered and rubbed her arms, fighting panic.

"Calm yourself. Everything is going to be just fine."

His voice rippled through her. Her cheeks flushed,

and she shuddered. The desire to lose herself and surrender to the pull on her insides was overwhelming.

"Don't fight it, Evazee."

The sound of Shasta speaking her name was double cream chocolate. It slid through her and left a trail of well-being that took her breath away.

"Come. It's time."

As one, the crowd rose and moved deeper into the cave. Eva found herself on her feet shuffling along with them. The girl next to her tripped, and Evazee shot out a hand to stop her falling.

"Thanks." It was the same brunette she'd walked with the day before. There couldn't be two girls with Africa plastered down their necks. Her eyes were bloodshot, and she frowned as though her head was sore.

"Hey, I remember you from yesterday. I'm Ash." She stuck out a hand and grinned, which quickly turned to a grimace as her forehead creased.

"Evazee. Are you OK?"

"I just have this headache. It won't go away, and I keep hearing a voice in my head, talking to me. I don't really mind. It's just that it makes the pain so much worse. Wait." She turned to Evazee with her eyes wide. "I'm not crazy. I'm really not. It's just a voice. It's not real. Right?"

Evazee opened her mouth to answer but nothing came out. *Change the subject.* "Um, I'm sorry about your headache. Do you know where we're going?"

Ash shrugged. She folded into herself. "Sorting, I think."

"I don't understand."

"Oh, don't stress. It's all to help us with our

futures. There are some nice people up ahead, and they help you figure out where you fit in life. That's what the voice said any—" She shut her mouth and sighed so hard her shoulders drooped.

Evazee slowed. "Wait, what if I don't need help? What if I know exactly what I want to do?"

Ash frowned, "That's weird. How could you know that?" She blinked and seemed to dismiss it. "I dunno. Tell them and let them figure it out. Look. We're close to the front now."

Booths were set up all across the tunnel. Behind the booths, Evazee counted four different tunnel openings branching off. Only four people were ahead of them in line. The guys manning the booths wore no shirts, baggy pants with the crotch hanging between their knees, and barefoot running shoes that were moulded around each toe.

Evazee bumped Ash and pointed. "I don't think we should ask these guys for fashion tips."

Ash grinned. "But darling, I've always wanted those pants."

"It's the shoes that do it for me." Evazee shook her head with a snort. She focussed on the girl at the front of the queue. She stepped up to the booth. One of the guys had a scanner pressed to her forehead. His lips moved as he silently read whatever was scrolling up the screen. The other man fiddled with something that looked like a gun. Evazee's heart went cold. The two men conferred briefly. The one with the gun nodded and toyed with the settings.

Without any fuss, the second man held the gun to the girl's arm and pulled the trigger. Evazee expected her to fall down or bleed, but the girl did neither. She passed through the booth, the man escorted her to the second corridor and she disappeared.

Blood rushed past Evazee's eardrums. The line moved quickly and it was her turn next. Ash clasped her hands together and squeezed them.

"Are you nervous?"

Ash shook her head. "No. Maybe? A little." She slumped. "OK, maybe a lot."

The man waved Evazee over. On impulse, she grabbed Ash and whispered, "I hear the voice in my head."

Ash's face lit up. "Are you kidding me?"

The man pulled Evazee forward, and her window for making conversation closed.

~*~

The music washed over Kai, and he fought the overwhelming sense of loss threatening to swallow him up. He remembered being with Tau and feeling as if his insides had been replaced with sunshine. There wasn't a hint of sunshine in any of these people, not if their faces were anything to judge by.

The lady in the middle of the stage dropped her arms and the music cut off. The three women stepped back as a tall gentleman took to the stage from the wings. His face seemed familiar, though Kai couldn't place him.

Silence fell over the room.

"Welcome Seekers." The man spoke in a formal tone. "You are all here for one purpose, and one purpose alone. To become acceptable to the One. The only One. I am here to help you in your quest." The man paused and his eyes swept across the crowd, piercing and intense. He cleared his throat. "Before you can approach Tau, you have to lose yourself. Lose your individual ways and thoughts. Outgrow the need for things to be all about you. Embrace the emptiness that remains when all that is you is burnt up, cast off and destroyed. There is no room in the heart of Tau for those who aren't willing to die. Do you want to be acceptable? Sacrifice. Do you want Tau to love you? You've got to earn it. Nothing comes for free."

His voice droned on and anger burned hot in Kai's chest. This man claimed to know Tau, but he was twisting everything that Kai knew to be true. In between nuggets of truth, most of what this man said didn't fit Kai's experience of Tau in the slightest.

The man paused and dramatically stared into space. "Tau is here, and he is ready to perform a miracle so that you will all believe. Who needs a miracle?"

The crowd went wild. The preacher singled out a young girl who'd been carried in on her friend's back. She was passed forward from hand to hand and deposited onto the stage. Her legs flopped uselessly and she had to lean back on her hands to look up at the preacher, who paid no attention to her. He worked the crowd, pacing from one side of the stage to the other. "Crank up your faith people. You can't expect to see a miracle if you haven't earned it."

Finally, with the crowd buzz at an all-time high, he stopped in front of the girl. Her eyes were stretched wide, and her breath came too fast. The preacher plastered a hand to her head and yelled words at such speed that the words made no sense. Then he got down with his face in hers and shouted, "Get up! Walk!"

He reached down, took her hand, and helped her to her feet. The girl's wobbly legs steadied. With the preacher still holding her hands, she managed to take a step. The crowd went ballistic. A girl in the front row shrieked and fainted. Some congregants bounced up and down, laughing and screaming. Others doubled over, cheeks wet with tears. The preacher let go of both her hands and stepped back. The girl took a few slow steps. Then she increased her speed and began to run.

~*~

A hooded, dark figure melted out from the shadows of an overhanging rock and slipped alongside her. Evazee ignored the person, instead concentrating on not face-planting. The floor was pitted and uneven, causing many to stumble as they followed the drums. Evazee's shoulder stung, and she felt sick to her stomach.

The reading and shooting had been quick. After that, they'd guided her to the left-most tunnel. The light in this tunnel throbbed in a blinding shade of milky white, lit by a roof covered in crystals.

"Here, put these in your ears."

Evazee tried to brush past, but the man in the hood sidestepped to block her. Evazee cast a quick glance around, they were drawing some suspicious looks. "Excuse me, please."

"Stop being stubborn and put these in your ears." He threw back the hood and Evazee's breath caught.

"Elden? What are you doing?" She checked behind to see if they were being watched.

"What does it look like I'm doing? Getting you out

of here. Put these in before the next round of drum beats."

Evazee dubiously eyed the makeshift earplugs. They seemed to be made of chewed-up bark. "I'm not leaving without Peta."

"We found her. Zulu is extracting her as we speak. Earplugs now, please."

Evazee reached for them as another beat shuddered through her from the ground. One dropped, but before it could hit the floor, Elden grabbed and shoved it in her ear. Evazee cringed at the damp coldness but held out her hand for the other.

With her ears blocked, the drumbeats still rumbled through her feet, but she had no desire to follow blindly anymore. There was something far more effective about these plugs than simply using her fingers.

Elden took her hand in his, and she allowed him to drag her along. They stayed with the group, careful to blend in. Elden squinted down each passage they passed. The third opening seemed to be what he'd been looking for. It was low and the walls were rough, dotted with growing clumps of purple mushrooms.

Evazee doubled herself over, following Elden's example. Just when she thought her back might never manage to straighten up again, they reached the hole that led upwards. He boosted her from below, and she scrambled for handholds in the rough rock.

A many-legged creature crawled over her fingers, and she bit her tongue to stop herself screaming. Fresh air washed over her face as they moved higher. With each swallow, the chaos in her mind resolved. She drank it in, longing to think straight again.

Zulu waited at the top to haul her out. His muscles

bulged under the strain of her weight, but after one pull, she lay on her back next to the hole, breathing hard.

She fingered the chewed-up wads poking out of her ears. "Can I take these out now?"

20

"Where is she? Where is Peta?" Evazee stared wide-eyed from Elden to Zulu and back. "You said you would get her out." She turned on Elden. "You said he was getting her out. You can't leave her there."

Zulu shook his head. "Small one is in deep. I couldn't get to her."

"I'm going back." Evazee spun around, ready to march off into the darkness and slide down the tunnel they'd just sweated to climb from.

Elden held on to her shoulders. She struggled against his grip but didn't move an inch.

"Please hear us out."

Spots of colour stained Evazee's cheeks. "No! Let me go! What is wrong with you both? You can't leave her there. She's too small."

"Listen. She's been in Affinity training for months already. She's in no more danger than what she's been in all this time. She's not a threat to them."

An angry tear ran down Evazee's cheeks. "None of that matters. Don't you get it? She's going to think I deserted her. That I betrayed her. Apart from that, I don't know how much time she has left."

Elden drew back. "What are you talking about? Is she sick?"

Evazee scrubbed at her nose with the back of her

hand. "Do you remember the day she fell during training? When she broke her ankle?" Evazee didn't wait for Elden to nod. "We watched Shasta heal her. You were right there with me."

"It was amazing to watch."

"Amazing is not the word I'd choose. We also watched him kill and resurrect a LightSucker. Do you remember what happened after he'd done that?"

Elden sighed.

"You do remember. A few minutes later, the LightSucker flew around the corner and died at our feet. It seems to me that Shasta's healings are a sham. A temporary party trick to impress the gullible. So forgive me if I'm not overly excited at the prospect of leaving her in his care."

"I hadn't thought of it that way. I'm sorry."

Evazee shrugged and collapsed at the base of a tree, all her strength sapped. "I can't leave her there. She's fragile beyond what you can imagine."

"Small one is tougher than you think." Zulu towered over her and crossed his arms over his chest.

"I don't care. I'm not leaving her."

Elden shook his head. "But what about the drums. You can't resist them. If you go back, you risk getting sucked into that whole system all over again. And we just got you out. It would be madness."

"You better believe I'm mad."

"I didn't mean it like that. C'mon. Don't be stubborn."

Evazee crawled on all fours and found the two chewed-up wads of bark. She sat in the dirt and stuffed them back into her ears. Once they were in deep enough to stay put, she thumbs-upped the two guys. "No drums can bother me now. Let's go."

Elden's mouth moved, but she couldn't hear a word.

"What?" She fiddled one out of her ear.

"I said you're shouting."

"Oh. Sorry." She shoved the earplug back in and grinned, pushed herself to her feet, and waved the boys back to where they'd just come from.

For a small girl, Evazee was stubborn enough to make kings weep. Zulu led them to the same opening they'd rescued her out of. Little more than a semi-circular framed hole, their make-shift entrance was designed to let air in and out of the tunnels below, most certainly not people. Elden scrambled through first and stood at the bottom with his arms wide. Evazee scraped her shoulder on the way through. She bit back a yelp. Zulu followed, slipping smoothly through the hole as if he were half Evazee's size.

"I'll go this way." Zulu set off and blended into the shadows so well that in seconds it appeared that he'd vanished.

Evazee clucked her tongue. "How did he not get stuck?"

"He's a strange one." Elden blinked, the whites of his eyes flashing. "Let's go quickly now."

Evazee turned to face the gloomy underground, and Elden took her hand. They followed the passage until it opened into a wide, whale-rib hall similar to the one they gathered in before the sorting. She'd deliberately steered them in the opposite direction from the booths.

Feeling soiled, she rubbed her shoulder. Maybe she wouldn't tell him about the marking just yet. She pulled Elden down so that her mouth met his ear. "I don't know where to start. These tunnels go on forever."

"She can't be too far. Come on."

They casually walked through the open space, blending with the rest of the crowd that seemed to be in no hurry at all. Between the subdued lighting and their efforts at not obviously staring, it was hard to tell how big the hall actually was.

Evazee pulled Elden closer to whisper in his ear. "Nobody is doing anything. They're all just milling around. Isn't that odd?"

Elden squinted into the darkness ahead. "There's something going down up ahead. Let's go check it out." He took her hand, and they moved away from the open space in the centre, blending into the shadows along the edges. Her fingers tingled between his. It was distracting. She was tempted to pull her hand away, but a thread of self-preservation convinced her to just go with it.

They picked their way between the people, scanning the faces for their own little silvery-blonde girl. Elden pulled Evazee in behind a bone. "Careful. These guys look like officials."

The milling mass of people were being divided into groups. Officials moved between the crowd with scanners.

"We can't let them find us. I don't know how we're going to do this."

Zulu appeared next to them with Peta clinging to his neck. "Let's go."

"How did you..."

"Shh. No time, move. Scanners coming."

~*~

Above ground, they found a quiet spot to settle.

Evazee knelt next to Peta with one hand on her forehead. "She's burning up."

Elden knelt near Peta's scorched legs. "These wounds have turned nasty. I'm not surprised."

They sheltered in between the roots of an enormous tree, which towered and stretched over them with its generous leaves. Zulu had mushroom light going within seconds of their decision to rest. Evazee hated the purple glow, but she hated the dark even more.

Peta patted Evazee's hand, pulling her close enough to hear a whisper. Her throat was raw and raspy. "Thirsty." The small girl's eyes were bloodshot and tinged purple.

Zulu prodded Evazee with a bony finger. "You have blue water for her legs."

"I do! How could I forget?" Evazee unstrapped the water bottle from around her body.

Zulu grinned at her. "A lot has happened since we took that water."

Evazee unscrewed the lid and bent down to pour some on Peta's legs. Peta grabbed her ankle, pointing weakly toward the bottle. "Thirsty."

"Guys, what do we do? Is it safe to drink this water?"

Zulu shook his head. "Too potent. It might kill her."

Elden shrugged. "The thing is, without water she'll die anyway. This is the only water we have. I say we try it."

Evazee held the bottle to Peta's lips with trembling hands. *Just a drop.* Peta reached up and tipped the bottle toward her mouth with a forcefulness that surprised Evazee. Before Evazee could wrestle the bottle out of her grip, Peta drank deeply down to the last drop. She lay back with a satisfied sigh. Her breathing slowed and settled.

"Oh my word. Come and look at this." Elden's voice was low and normal, but his eyes stretched as wide as an ocean of disbelief.

The damaged skin all down the front of Peta's legs re-attached itself—stringy skin tentacles crossing the raw patches and knitting them back together. Peta slipped into peaceful sleep for the first time since her legs had been burned.

Zulu sat back on his haunches, staring at Peta as if she'd fallen from the sky in a pea pod. "What now?"

Elden stood with his hands on his hips. "Now we wait. While we wait, we can plan."

"We need to find the others, though I don't know where to start. I'm not keen on going back to the graveyard. Not at all." Evazee grimaced.

"They've moved on from there anyway. Zulu, what would you suggest? How do we track our friends?"

Zulu rubbed his chin and held up a finger. Without a word, he withdrew a few paces into the forest.

Elden pointed at the empty space where Zulu used to be. "And now?"

"Who knows? He'll be back. We can't really do anything while this one is out anyway."

Elden crossed the bare ground between his root and hers. He waited for her nod before sitting. "What happened back there? Why did you follow the drums?"

Evazee stared at nothing, avoiding his eyes. "They were compelling. I followed. Not much more to tell really." She shivered at the thought of Shasta, his voice in her head. Unspoken things hung in the air between them. "You know, I don't really want to talk about this place."

Elden settled back onto the trunk with his hands tucked behind his head. He stretched out his legs, crossed his feet at the ankles, and watched her between half-mast lids. "OK. What's better, sunrise or sunset?"

"That's a daft question."

"Humour me." His eyes twinkled and a lazy smile pulled at his lips.

"Fine. Rise."

"Ah yes, the eternal optimist. Just as I thought. You look for new possibilities, the whole brand-new-day thing."

"No. Actually I like the colours. What's got into you?"

"Movies or books?"

"Books. Where are you going with this?"

"That's two points for me, I was right again. Old school. I like it. I bet you like softcover, not hard?"

"Well, yes. But what if I was lying? Hmm?"

"Then I still get points because you cheated."

"My turn. Why were you working at the OS? You don't strike me as someone with wicked intentions."

"Whoa. I thought we were small-talking."

Tension rippled through his shoulders. She'd struck a nerve.

He sat up and fiddled with his shoelaces. "Do you trust me?"

"Now, that is cheating. You can't answer a question with another question. No ways."

"Do you?" His voice dropped so low, Evazee wasn't sure she'd heard right.

"I don't see what that has to do with why you got involved with such a dodgy operation."

He shrugged and drew breath to speak as Peta stirred and rolled on her side. Her eyes shot open. Purple had been replaced by glowing blue, which flashed once and then turned white.

"I can see them. I see streets of stone, I see a field of glass, impassable mist. It's impossible to get to them." She sat up and her forehead creased. "Where are we, Zee?"

Evazee nearly tripped over her feet to get to the girl. "Who do you see?"

"The boys. The one with spiky black hair, the redhead and the one with hair like mine." She paused and glanced around at their surroundings. "Where are we?"

"How much do you remember?"

"I feel like I've been dreaming. I don't know what was real and what wasn't." Peta ran her hands down the front of her legs and smiled at the smooth skin. "That part must have been a nightmare." She got to her feet and stretched her arms wide, making her back click twice. "I'm awake now." She spun in a slow circle, drinking in the sights all around. "It is so pretty here. I don't ever want to leave. Can we stay? Please?" She ran to Evazee and hugged her.

Over the top of Peta's head, Evazee caught Elden's gaze. *What is going on with this girl?*

Elden shrugged, looking as puzzled as Evazee felt.

Zulu came back and leaned close to Peta, his eyes bright. "The darkness has left this little one. She is full of light now. Tell us, small one, what do you see when you look at me?"

Peta squinted at him with her head tilted off to one side. "I see a crown floating above your head, but it keeps disappearing and coming back. I see you split in half and the two halves are playing a game of Tug o' War. I see your heart, all golden and strong. I see..." she faltered, hesitated. "That's all I see. Nothing else." She turned away from him and sat with her back toward him, her face suddenly sad.

Elden's head swung from Zulu to Peta and back again. "How do you see all that stuff? I just see a big old slab of Zulu."

Evazee sucked in air and pushed the girl at arms' length to study her. "Oh my word. Drinking the water from the Healing Stream. It has activated her light Affinity. Look! She's lighting up."

Pale golden light began to blossom beneath Peta's skin, tracing curly patterns along her legs and arms, winding up her throat and making her face glow.

Evazee frowned. "It doesn't make sense though. Why is she lit up, and I'm not?"

Elden shrugged. He was focussed on grinding glowing mushroom into the ground to make the tread of his sneakers glow. "She isn't limited by the strong negative Affinity serum the way the rest of us are."

"Wait, what?" Hairs stood up on the nape of Evazee's neck. "Negative Affinity serum. What are you talking about?"

Elden froze, hunched over with his foot propped up on his knee. He kept his gaze fixed on the sole of his shoe.

"Answer me, Elden. What negative serum?"

He crouched down and fidgeted with his shoelace, "It's just a theory. Could have leaked from the lab.

Something like that could have caused us all to be stuck here." He coughed and rubbed the back of his neck.

Evazee squinted at Elden through slit eyes.

Zulu didn't look happy at all. He circled Peta, keeping the girl at arms' length, "This is bad. How do you know it won't do bad things to her? Sometimes the bad thing only kicks in later."

Peta giggled and held out her glowing arms to hug Zulu. He backed away so fast, he tripped over a log and landed in a bush.

Evazee frowned at Elden and turned away to study Peta, who glowed brighter. "We need more water from the Healing Stream. Zulu, how do we do that? What about your village? Can we go back?"

He was already shaking his head before the words had left her lips. "I can't go back. It was too close last time. They nearly caught me. I won't go back."

"Maybe they'll realize that they can't force you to believe what they do. You can show them a better way."

"But I don't have the answer that I'm seeking yet. I can't face them until I can prove what my heart feels."

Evazee pointed toward Peta with a smirk. "Are you telling me she doesn't qualify as a miracle?"

Zulu shook his head. Peta grinned at him and a shudder passed through him. "Maybe, maybe not."

"Peta, do you know where to find the Healing Stream? Can you see it?"

The girl picked flowers that none of them could see. She looked up and her eyes lost focus. "The Healing Stream is far-far. But I feel there are pools close by." Her head tilted. "Not one pool, but many."

"Could you take us to them?"

Elden folded his arms across his chest. "This is madness. Pools of what? How can you know that what she's seeing is real?"

"Listen. Right now, she's the only one who's not still under the influence of the dark Affinity enhancer being pumped into our rooms. So I think I would rather listen to her than to anyone else. Besides, we've got to get away from here before the drums start playing."

~*~

There was no reason to believe that the healing was anything less than it appeared to be, yet it left Kai cold. Even that felt ugly. What if he was just sour because his own ability had left? Tau's miracles were worth celebrating. All around him, people cheered and screamed, but he turned his back on them to watch the people on stage. The three women clapped, but the man stood with a finger to his ear, eyes narrowed. Kai wished his Affinity was working. He felt so blind without it.

The man on stage switched to full-on performance mode. He walked to the front of the stage with his arms outstretched and a smile that showed all his teeth.

"Do you see the power of thinking right? Can you see that there is nothing that would be impossible for you?" He was right on the edge of the stage now, projecting all the way to back of the open courtyard.

Kai felt for Runt's tiny bottle of water still hanging around his neck. He wanted his Affinity back. He wanted to be able to see, to know what was broken and what was whole. It was such a small amount of Healing Stream water, though. Should he drink it or use it as eye drops? Besides, what if he needed it again like he had in the spirit cuttings? Using it was a silly thought, and he dismissed it.

Kai dropped his gaze and slipped along the edge of the stage. He needed to be invisible, stay anonymous, fly under the radar.

And sneak backstage.

He stepped on a blonde girl's toes, and she hugged him and laughed. He squeezed between a big belly and a guy who stood doubled over. Laughing or crying? Kai couldn't tell which. He didn't stop to find out but pressed on toward the corner of the stage.

The preacher perched on the edge of the stage, staring up into nothingness. His voice dropped to a whisper. "I can see it. It's coming down. Can you see it? Can you feel it?" He stretched out his hand. "Now!" His hand dropped, and an explosion of sparkly glitter fell on the upturned faces of the worshippers in the middle of the room.

Kai grabbed the moment, bolted upstairs, and slipped behind the curtain. He stood backstage in the dark and felt like his heart might explode. This was one of the worst ideas he'd had all day.

~*~

Peta hummed as she skipped along ahead of them. She led without a moment's hesitation. The light that she gave off was just enough for them to see by. The path they followed led along a cliff face.

Zulu walked with Peta, slipping in behind her as

they reached the narrow path. Evazee followed the two of them, and Elden walked at the end. Elden was quiet, the same way a stormy sky is quiet before the lightning and thunder starts.

"You can't sulk the whole way, Elden."

"You think I'm sulking? You have no clue, do you?" He hissed under his breath.

"Tell me what's wrong. You know you can be honest with me."

"Honesty. You want honesty." Elden tripped on a rock, and the stumble seemed to shake his words loose. "My sister is here somewhere, probably dying, and all we do is pick the youngest to lead us on a quest for holy water. Why am I the only one who thinks this is madness?"

Evazee halted. Her mind ran wild with words, phrases, sentences. None of them glowed, none of them made it out of her mouth. She placed a finger in the middle of his chest and glared at him.

Elden squinted at the finger and frowned at her scrunched-up face. "You're not saying anything. What's up with that?"

Evazee's nostrils flared with the effort of bottling all the things she wanted to say. It was so much easier when the right ones glowed.

"Are you trying to be mysterious? It's not working."

Evazee stamped her foot in frustration. All the floating words dropped like dead birds and tumbled out. "I can't help thinking that you're the reason we're stumbling about in the darkness. Somebody pulled a stupid stunt with the dark Affinity serum, and I think it was you. Did you think that would work? You call this mad." She waved a hand over their group, "What do you call it when you bring a whole bunch of us here with no way of getting back. And not just us, but a broken child, too. She's vulnerable. Did you think twice before dragging her into this mess? Why not leave her at home? You're the reason why we can't pray and ask for help. I'm doing the one thing that I think will help. Not only us, but help you find your sister. If that's mad then so be it." She poked him once in the chest, spun on her heel, and ran to catch up with Zulu and Peta.

21

Kai tucked himself into the soft folds of the curtain for a moment, breathing slowly to stop the black spots dancing in his eyes. The light was dim backstage, but he could see enough by spilled stage light to make out a narrow staircase leading up and down close to where he stood. Indecision froze him.

On impulse, he reached for the bottle of Healing Stream water that hung around his neck, opened it, and drank a drop. He hesitated for a moment and then downed it all. He blinked twice, three times. No difference. That was a waste.

He had no idea what he was looking for, just an overwhelming conviction that this whole service was a sham. *Don't think too deeply, just move. Upwards.* He took the stairs two at a time, hunkering down as he got closer to the top. He crouched with his back pressed up against the wall. The noise from the gathering below filtered through to backstage. Kai could hear everything as well as if he were in the audience. Risking a peep, he glimpsed an open door to a control room manned by five people. They stared at huge screens of what was going on below, conferring in quiet voices. Four of the screens were trained on the people with a central one showing what was happening on stage.

Kai blinked. When he opened his eyes, all five people at the controls wore glowing helmets of green. He blinked again, and the helmets were gone. Could this be his Affinity coming back?

He had to get closer. He waited until all those in the control booth were focussed on the furthest screen, pointing and rubbing their chins. Kai slipped off the stairs and tucked himself just outside the control room door where he could see and hear.

"We're losing this section at the back. 7A. Can you see?"

"Another miracle? More glitter?"

"No, too soon."

"Maybe a word of knowing? What about that girl? The brunette." One of the operators poked the screen with a chubby finger. "I know her. She's about to move up a tier but hasn't told anybody yet."

"And she's right in the middle of the section we're losing. Perfect. Do it!"

One of the operators reached for a microphone. "Stage, you're losing section 7A. There's a brunette third seat from the right, second row. She's about to move up a tier. Now is a good time for a knowing."

Kai watched the middle screen. The preacher pointed to the section they'd singled out. He squeezed his temples with his fingertips, eyes shut and lips moving wordlessly. A glimmer of green shot around his head, quickly branching off and spreading until his whole cranium was circled in pulsing light. For a moment, Kai's vision flickered, and the preacher stood before the audience, hollow but filled with swirling darkness, shot through with slivers of glowing green. In a blink, he was back to normal.

The preacher's head shot up, and he pointed

again. "The girl with brown hair. You've got your hand to your chest. Yes, you! I sense great change coming your way. You are excited, but you are nervous as well. And ..." he paused, with his head tilted to one side, "you are heart sore. You don't want to leave your friends behind."

The camera had zoomed in on the girl they'd picked out. Tears streamed down her face, and she nodded with her hands clasped to her chest. The preacher's voice dropped low, full of authority, "I say to you, do not fear. Embrace your new day. Embrace your promotion. You have earned it. By the sweat of your brow, you'll be moving up. It's a new day for you. Throw off anything holding you back." The preacher's voice was building in intensity. "Cut off the doubters and those who would see you held back by their own insecurities." His voice roared through the air, "Today is your day!" The crowd erupted in cheering and clapping.

It turned Kai's stomach. He clapped his hands to his ears and shut his eyes. He didn't want to see such a sham, didn't want to hear the lies. When he opened his eyes, a girl stood in front of him with her hands on her hips. He recognised her as the one that had miraculously been given her ability to walk back. Her entire chest was covered be a breastplate of dirty green, glowing light. Sweat beaded on her forehead from the laps she'd run around the gathering.

"Excuse me. What are you doing here? Do I need to report you?"

Kai said nothing.

Suspicion grew in her narrowed eyes.

She leaned toward the open doorway, not taking her eyes off Kai for a second. "Guys, we have a problem."

~*~

Kai threw himself down the stairs, hesitated for a moment behind the stage curtains, heard footsteps, and ran out onto the stage. The preacher blinked at him, his face changing as the men upstairs yelled into his earphones. Kai leapt off the stage, shoving people out the way as he came down and hit the ground running.

He ducked through the crowd, out onto the street, not stopping or looking over his shoulder to see if he was being chased. The streets were busier now than when he'd first walked them, but he managed to find his way back to the dining hall, now deserted. Ruaan and Zap sat by a window and talked in low voices. They looked up as he ran to them.

"Kai! Where have you been, man?" Zap punched his arm as he got close. "We've just been arguing whether to go look for you or what."

"I wouldn't call it arguing exactly." Ruaan scratched his head. "What's going on? You look stressed out."

"You missed such great food. Whoa." Zap rubbed his belly. Ruaan's eyelids drooped.

Kai leaned out the window to see if anyone followed him. The people walking below all ambled along harmlessly. "Do we have somewhere to stay yet?"

"Oh yeah, that nice girl showed us our rooms. We've all got our own, but they're right next to each other. Come on. We'll show you." Zap led the way out of the dining room, down a broad, carved staircase. Ruaan fell in behind the other two, yawning and stretching. A short way down the street, Zap took them through a carved arch with no doors, up a stone staircase that twisted upwards in regular bends. The rooms they'd been given were on the top floor of a stone building that seemed to be carved out of a single rock five stories high. By the time they'd climbed five flights of stairs, Kai's legs were shaking. He pulled the other two into his room and shut the door. There was barely space for anything but the bed.

"Um, I don't know if you remember, but I did say we each got our own room?" Zap backed into the corner of the tiny space looking twitchy.

"I want to hear where he's been. He can't exactly tell us through the walls, you know." Ruaan sat on the bed gingerly, his knees poking up nearly as high as his shoulders. "Wow, this is a bit extreme."

Kai turned towards them, "Guys, I found Bree."

"That's brilliant! How is she? Why didn't you bring her?" Zap looked ready to tap him on the head to see if his brain was still working.

"She's... different. It's like a huge part of her has been shut down. Stolen, even. She doesn't want to be rescued, but being here isn't helping her. She needs a different environment, but she won't believe me if I say that to her. It's so horrible. I don't even know what to make of it. She wants nothing to do with me."

Ruaan stretched himself out on the bed, tucking both hands behind his head. His feet poked off the end of the bed like flagpoles. "What did you do to make this girl so angry at you?"

"The last time he left this place to go home, he left Bree in the desert outside the Darklands surrounded by darKounds." Zap spoke before Kai could.

"You make it sound like I did it on purpose. I was trying to take her home, away from here. I was so sure it would work, but it didn't. Now she's injured, all bent out of shape, and won't listen to me." He sank onto the bed next to Ruaan's long legs and buried his face in his hands. "The thing is her dad was taken by darKounds years ago. She's had trouble trusting anybody since then."

Ruaan stared at the ceiling, crossing his feet, "Bree's not the only one with dad issues. She can't hide behind that her whole life. My grandma raised me because my parents supposedly died on a missionary trip to Africa. What actually happened is that they were druggies. Both of them. They took to the streets to support their habit." He spoke matter-of-factly without a hint of emotion. "Grandma did what she could, but no one is immortal. When she died, St Greg's got me." He sniffed and rubbed his nose. He pointed at it, "Allergies. I'm not crying."

Zap was still propped up in the corner. He slid down until he sat with his knees drawn up. That's one crazy story, man."

Ruaan shrugged. "Believe me or not. I don't really care." He shut his eyes. "This bed is so comfy."

Kai watched his breathing change. In less than ten seconds, Ruaan was deeply asleep. "How does he do that?"

Zap chuckled. "And on your bed, too. No sleep for you tonight. Not that night ever seems to fall in this place." His chuckle dried up in his throat. "Apparently, tomorrow we're being tested."

"Tested. For what?"

"Aptitude or something. Beats me. Apparently, all

newcomers to the city have to be. I don't know, Kai. I'm not feeling it."

"I don't like the sound of it either. We don't have time for all this nonsense. Your death date is being carved right now if that gravestone is right."

Zap paled. "I'd forgotten all about that. Ah, that stinks."

Kai tapped his fingers on the bed, thoughts snagging and unable to move through his mind. "According to the gravestones, Bree's dad isn't dead yet. What if we could track him down?"

"And then what? How is that going to stop me from dying?"

"Not you, twit. If we find Bree's dad, maybe it would free Bree from this bizarre journey she's on."

"I hate to be the one to remind you, but finding people isn't exactly your strong point. Losing them, now, there's a skill you've perfected. Heck, you don't even have to be tested tomorrow. We can just tell them what your gift is."

~*~

Ruaan had snored throughout Kai's slow count to one hundred and thirty-two. Kai was two doors down and still heard Ruaan as if the walls were made of paper. Sleeping was a waste of time.

The archway where he'd found Bree intrigued him. He'd rather go investigate that than lie here thinking of ways to shut up Ruaan. Few people moved on the streets of the city, though the light stayed at the same level of brightness. All in all, it was a strange setup. Kai and his friends didn't have anyone watching them or tracking their movements. They seemed free to come and go as they pleased. *Seemed.*

Finding his was back was trickier than he thought it would be. A few wrong turns and some dead-ends later, he found his way to the room where he'd spoken to Bree, the small room with the testing arch. In this bright city, finding a room full of shadows and dimness seemed odd. Especially when the purpose of the room was to make you more suited to the light. The archway itself brooded over the room with a heavy malevolence. The untamed music of running water usually soothed Kai, but this water tumbled off the stone to hit the ground, just as doomed lemmings would fall off a cliff.

Kai faced the arch now, and his belly pinched. His imprint flashed silvery in the gloom. He touched it and a swell of music rose within him, a living torrent building and growing. His hands itched for his guitar.

A flash of heat washed over him, and he glimpsed the instrument he longed for deep inside the archway facing the entrance door. It pulled at him, drawing him closer. And yet he wanted to see into the other three arches as well. The two desires tugged at him.

Curiosity won.

Five small steps and he was around the corner. Soft emerald light flooded from the opening, played across the tiles of the floor, and spread longing through Kai's heart, stealing his breath. He barely dared to look into the glowing opening, yet he couldn't resist a peep. No sun-drenched forest or carved emerald, it was simply an uprooted plant.

The spell broke. Hands on his hips, Kai frowned at the arch. It was the same green one that compelled him to replant the last time he was trapped here. That had caused so much trouble. His hands itched just looking at it.

Kai scrambled to get away. The next archway seemed closed up at first. Kai reached out to feel and almost fell in as he leaned and rested on nothing. A narrow gap between two solid rock faces led away from the opening, the space between the two walls utterly dark further in. It also seemed to narrow towards the back. Kai shuddered and moved on.

The next opening blazed in fiery shades of red and orange. Blood rushed through Kai's ears, and he knew what he was going to see without having to look. He looked anyway and regretted it instantly. The desert outside the Darklands. The desert where he'd lost Bree, left her at the mercy of darKounds.

What if this was his chance to go back and change what had happened? He paced, rubbing the back of his neck. But it was just a thought. He might step into the archway and get stuck in the desert and die there.

Or he might be able to save Bree.

He stepped toward the opening. The heat intensified, flickering out of the archway—an invisible, tangible thing, close enough to scorch his skin. Another step, and he'd be consumed. Someone screamed from inside the arch. Bree! This had to be it. He could go back and make it right.

Footsteps outside the door. Someone was coming. He slipped into the shadow to the right of the doorway. He crouched down, hardly breathing.

Bree walked past him, shut the door behind her, and glanced around the room quickly—missing him completely. She threw off her heavy cloak and strode determinedly toward the arches. Kai's Affinity kicked in, and Bree's arm lit up. Kai instantly regretted drinking the last bit of Healing Stream water. It might have been enough to restore Bree's shredded hand. The only other option was to get her to the Healing Stream.

Bree circled the four arches. She stopped in front of the one where Kai had seen the desert. No light reflected on her face. Her hands trembled, but she squeezed them together and stepped through.

~*~

Peta climbed the short hill and glanced back, her eyes sparkling. "We're here. We're at the pools."

Evazee forced herself to climb the last rise. Everything seemed to take so much more effort. She made it to the top and gasped. A rolling field of undulating hills spread away from her feet, punctuated by pools of water. None of the pools reflected what was above, but each seemed lit by their own internal play of lights that cycled through a range of colours, throwing up a living tower of dancing light that stretched high toward the sky.

Zulu knelt in reverential silence. Peta found Evazee's hand and pulled her toward a free-standing rock. "Come see. Here are rules."

"Rules? That's weird." Evazee allowed herself to be dragged along, curious to see what rules one would apply to a place this beautiful. Somehow *do not bomb-drop* and *no diving* would seem completely irrelevant.

The rules were carved into the rock, words chiselled carefully into the hard surface. As she read them, Evazee realized they were more instructions than rules.

Welcome Seeker,

to the Pools of Resonance.
What you see may be, or may not.
One alone can set you free.
Look, don't touch,

Evazee read it through once and then again. "There's a section all chiselled off after 'touch.' Somebody must have made a mess. I guess it's hard to rub out a mistake when you're carving in stone." She grinned at Peta, who giggled at her joke. "I don't know what to make of this. I'm not sure I understand the point of it all."

Zulu padded over on silent feet. "Where's Elden?"

Evazee swung around, but realized she hadn't seen Elden since their argument. "Well, that's just perfect. You know what? He's a big boy. Maybe he needs some space. I'm sure he'll join us when he's ready. Let's have a look at these pools."

Peta stared into the distance, her brow creased in concentration. She shrugged and skipped toward the pools. Zulu followed her. He seemed to have taken it on himself to be the girl's protector. Evazee couldn't believe anything bad could be lurking in such a beautiful place, but by now, she knew that looks could be deceiving. Still, leaving Peta with Zulu for a few minutes should be OK.

Evazee drifted in between the pools, letting her feet take her. After all the darkness, this much light and beauty spread a feast for her soul. Her imprint pulsed gently in time with the dancing light beams as they washed over her in waves of light-colour.

She recited the instructions in her head and her heart pinched at the very last line. If this was water from the Healing Stream, it could reverse the effects of the dark Affinity enhancer they were all affected by.

Evazee couldn't imagine how great that would feel, but now she had to argue with herself about trying the water or not.

The pools varied in size, some as big as the soccer field at school, others no bigger than a *Koi* pond. One of the smaller ones shone a constant blue light that caught Evazee's attention. She knelt down next to the edge of the water, leaned on her hands so that she didn't do anything silly like fall in, and closed her eyes. Why was this so hard? She braced herself, took a deep breath and stared into the water.

The colour reflected on her face and made her skin tingle. She breathed it in. The water seemed impossibly deep. It was crystal clear and still, but she couldn't see the bottom. She waited.

A small spider skittered across the surface, causing tiny ripples. Evazee shooed him off and started again. Waiting. The water looked pure and alive. Surely it came from the Healing Stream. She checked to make sure no one watched, dipped her hand in, and brought it up to her mouth. She hesitated a moment before swallowing. It ran down her throat easily and she could have drunk more.

She checked her imprint, nothing. She looked around her, but the light and colours still came from the pools. None of it was from her. So that settled it, then. This was some other water, not what she needed at all.

Her head grew heavy. She shook it and locked her elbows to stay upright. Patterns formed in the water. Swirls of colour that shifted from random patterns to shapes, forms that seemed familiar, but she couldn't quite place.

Jesus, this place reminds me of You.

Evazee thought she saw the water ripple. Maybe the little spider was back. She checked around the edges of the water but couldn't see anything that would have caused ripples. Zulu and Peta chased each other around one of the other pools. Listening to her tiny friend laugh made Evazee's heart sing.

Please keep Kai safe.

The water shifted as if a breeze blew over it. The centre section stilled to a glass-like, smooth surface that spiralled out toward the edges. Soon the whole surface lay flat and still. Blue light darkened to charcoal and a glow burned in the distance.

The longer she stared into the water, the clearer the picture became. A vast desert stretched across the full width of the pool. Fire blazed in the distance, casting a red glow over desert sand dunes. A tiny speck moved along the base of a dune, followed closely by another. A wide circle formed around them. Evazee squinted. Were they camels? She leaned in closer. Not camels. People. She leaned closer still, and a cold flash of recognition passed through her. Kai and Bree. What looked like dark dots surrounded them. Cold chills shot down her spine.

DarKounds.

22

Intense heat slammed into Kai as he stepped through the arch. He ran his fingers over his forehead and cheeks, no blisters. Heat like this would surely cause some damage. Why Bree chose to come back here was a mystery. Kai checked his shoes. His navy trainers were still on his feet. He wouldn't be chasing a girl through a desert with bare feet. Things were looking up from the last visit.

He took a few cautious steps and swung around. Was the way back still there? It wasn't. Kai barked a laugh. Obviously, it wouldn't be that easy. Only one thing made sense. Head to the highest point and get the lay of the land.

The tallest stood closest to him and without much thought, he trudged up the side of it. Dune climbing was hot work, and soon he was drenched as if he'd fallen into a pool. A breeze picked up as he reached the top. Kai turned a slow circle, searching for a clue. Or Bree herself. That would be even better.

Further along the base of the hill, a lone figure stumbled through the sand. It had to be her. Movement caught his eye to the right. A darKound. He knew them so well that just a glimpse of the sleek, blue-black skin pulled tight over ropey muscles sent a shiver through his body. There were more coming over the hill, too.

He had to get to Bree. His long legs took on a life of their own and pinwheeled him downward. It felt as if he might split in half. He tripped on a rock, rolled, and hit the bottom of the dune with sand in his ears, mouth, and everywhere else.

The other walker was just up ahead. Kai coughed, rolled onto all fours, and pushed himself to standing, hoping his wobbly legs would support him.

Grim thoughts built on the edges of his mind. That meant the darKounds were closer than he'd estimated and were moving in. There was no way he would let Bree get attacked twice. At least while he was still alive.

"Bree! Wait for me!" He didn't wait to see if she'd heard him but took off after her faster than he'd ever sprinted at school.

The thoughts were louder now. DarKounds were closing in. His imprint flashed bright, and in an instant, he knew what to do. A gust of wind blew through, strong enough to knock Bree off her feet. Kai ran to her. He was close enough now to see the green glow on her damaged arm. It had spread to her chest and head. Kai helped her to her feet as another strong wind blew Bree right into his arms. She bounced off his chest.

"What are you doing here? Are you completely mad?" She pulled her hand from his as another gust of wind hit and knocked down both of them. The ribbon that held her hair came undone. As the wind whipped through her hair, it blew the straightness out and brought her curls back.

Kai stared, blinking.

"Kai! Snap out of it. We're surrounded."

They were hemmed in. The circle of darKounds

drew closer with their blue-black skin gleaming, powerful muscles rippling underneath. Kai scrambled to his feet, wishing he could tuck Bree away safely and deal with these creatures alone.

Fiery heat coursed up Kai's arm, his imprint was glowing. With each passing second, the intensity of the burn increased, and with it came a swell of music from deep within. Bree was breathing too fast, panicking. Kai threw an arm around her and tucked her close to his chest. He raised the other arm and opened his mouth. The words came as he did so, a song of defiance, full of the untamed love of Tau. Joy bubbled through him. He closed his eyes and his spirit rose buoyant, light, free. A shudder passed through Bree, and she stiffened.

A thunderclap cracked through the air. Reality smeared and blurred into a whirlwind that sucked them both upwards. The atmosphere around them snapped, and they fell hard onto cold stone. Bree broke her fall on Kai, and he lay there, the wind knocked out of him. They were back in the testing room, facing the desert arch which was now sealed off by a stone door.

FAILED.

The word rang out and bounced off the walls, echoing and re-echoing.

~*~

The image in the water swirled and faded until the pool was back to glowing blue. Evazee sat back on her haunches. What was she meant to do with that picture? She pushed herself up, careful not to touch the water again.

Zulu and Peta had settled next to a pool that shot up sparkling golden rays. Peta sat cross-legged, both hands playing in the glow. She pulled her hands out. They were covered in sparkles. Giggling, she held them out to Zulu. He sat on his haunches, observing but not getting drawn in. He smiled at Peta, but gently brushed her hands aside when she tried to wipe the sparkles onto his cheeks.

Peta's face pinched with concentration. She reached into the rays of light and began moving her hands in deliberate patterns. The sparkles responded to her small fingers and without too much trouble. She'd fashioned a gold crown that floated on the light rays. Reaching in with infinite slowness, she took the crown and placed it on Zulu's head. The big man didn't argue or push her away. He let her put the crown on his head and then sat up to kingly straightness. Peta clapped her hands in delight.

Evazee didn't want to disturb them, but Zulu was ever alert and stood as she got to them. His fragile crown dissipated leaving nothing but a faint dusting of gold on his forehead.

"Have you seen enough?" Zulu swept an arm across the field of pools as if he owned it all. Peta sat at his feet, juggling three balls of sparkles that she'd fashioned from the light rays.

Evazee shrugged. "I don't know that I want to see anything else."

Zulu patted his chest. "Heart says one more."

Peta looked up from her light juggling and nodded. "I want to stay here."

Evazee crossed her arms. She couldn't help feeling conned. "OK, fine. You two should really try another pool yourselves."

Peta dropped her three balls. They landed on the ground and vanished in a glittery puff. "But I like this one."

~*~

Bree pushed away from Kai and lay on her back as a single tear ran down her temple. Kai rolled onto his side and brushed her tear away. He reached for one of her curls. Her hair was silky between his fingers. "We didn't die."

Bree stared at the ceiling. "But we failed. That's worse."

Kai checked his imprint. It was no longer just silver, but the edges were tarnished, an ugly shade of coppery yellow. "I want your arm to be healed."

Bree sat up and glared at him, "So that's what all this is about. Making you a hero. No, thank you."

"It's not for me, Bree. I don't want to see you going through life unable to do the things you love the most. That's not living."

"For your information, I am more satisfied now than I've ever been." She sat up and looped her arms around her knees.

"But you're not happy."

"I don't care about happiness. I want nothing more to do with that stuff. Happiness, hope. I spent years hoping things would change, hoping it would get better. What a joke."

"What about Elden?"

"What about Elden?"

"He's dead worried about you."

"Not true. He just wants me recruited. I won't do

it."

"Maybe you don't know your brother as well as you think you do."

The door swung open and Zap peeked inside. "We've been looking for you everywhere. Come on. They're taking us to the pools."

~*~

The walk from Stone City to the pools left Kai sweating.

"Before you go in, a word of warning. Don't touch the water. It's right here in the rules." Their guide tapped on a raised rock with words carved into the surface. He was a skinny fellow, all bones and hollows with teeth that grew whichever way they pleased. He looked to be about the same age as them, but he acted and spoke like a granddad.

Kai pushed past Ruaan and Zap to get to the rock. The words had been painstakingly chiselled into the hard surface.

Welcome Seeker,
to the Pools of Resonance.
What you see may be, or may not.
One alone can set you free.
Look, don't touch,

"There's a bit scratched out at the end here. Do you know what it said?"

Guide-boy shook his head. "If we needed to know, they would have left it. Couldn't have been important."

Kai didn't agree, but decided against arguing. There was something about the place that gave him butterflies in his belly.

"Make good use of your time here. I'll return later to take you back to the city."

Kai waved him off absently. For the first time since waking up in this place, he felt a bubbling lightness inside.

Ruaan stood, scratching his head. "Now what?"

Zap clipped him on the shoulder. "We go swimming, that's what."

"Weren't the two of you listening at all? We can only look into this water, we can't touch it. So, I guess we pick a pool and have a look. Hard to choose, there are so many."

Pools dotted the landscape like a toddler's plastic baubles thrown carelessly. The range of colours cycled through the entire rainbow. It was breath taking.

Kai stepped onto the spongy grass path and relished the feeling of sinking into its softness. He breathed deeply. Even the air was different here. His lungs tingled. Zap pulled Ruaan toward a purple and emerald pool. Ruaan dug in his heels and did his best to resist getting any closer to the water, but Zap managed to drag him closer anyway.

Tucked behind a handful of pools, sat a small one the size of a modest coffee table. Kai watched the colours cycle through all the sky-shades from sunrise to sunset. He settled down in front of the water, not sure what to expect. The water turned chaotic and choppy, bubbling and hissing. Violent purple and green flashes clashed and fought. Deep from within the centre of the chaos came a dark shadow, sliding and oozing, forming a path. No sooner had it flattened out when he heard the howling. First one shadow low and compact, running. A darKound. Followed by another, and then more until the entire surface of the water teemed with gaping mouths and dripping fangs. Kai fell back and hit his head on the ground. Pain sliced through his head, but it was preferable to what he'd just seen.

Kai scrambled to his feet and let them take him. He found himself drawn to a pool that sent up a steady beam of white light. He settled down at the edge and wondered what to do next. Leaning over the water, he let the glow wash over him. *Tau, where are you?*

The pool rippled once then cleared to a flat glassy surface.

Come on in.

Kai knew that voice. The water rippled once again, almost parting to make room for him.

Um, I'm not supposed to do that.

Deep laughter bubbled through Kai, and he felt the open invitation as clear as if he held a card in his hands. He sucked air into his lungs and slipped into the pool headfirst. This was unlike any water he'd been in before. There was a moment of chill as he passed the surface, but after that, it was like drifting through feathery duvet-clouds.

Tau appeared next to him, floating flat on his back with his bare feet crossed and his hands behind his head. Kai was struck by the absurdity of it all and laughed. Tau turned toward Kai with a grin.

Happiness rippled through Kai. "Where have you been? I've been looking for you!"

"I know. I've been close. I always am, even if you can't feel me."

They floated close enough for Tau to reach out a hand to Kai. "Let me see your mark."

Shame washed over Kai. He knew it was tarnished

from trying to save Bree. Shutting his eyes, he held out his arm. Tau ran his fingers over Kai's markings and they flashed hot and then icy. With a final pop, Tau let go and the icy heat left. Kai dared open his eyes long enough to see his imprint had been restored. Another wave of happiness washed over him.

"That's brilliant. Can't you come back with me? Bree needs you."

"I've had my eye on that one. It is nearly her time."

"Why does that sound like a no? Ugh. Never mind. How do we get back?"

"There are things you need to do here before you go back."

Kai waited. Surely, Tau would explain what he meant. They were still floating in mid-air, and golden light surrounded them. It seeped into his pores, warming him. He couldn't wait any more. "Are you going to tell me what those things are?"

Tau turned his body upright, and it gave the illusion that he stood on a cloud. "You know already. You don't have much time."

"I don't think you were watching as closely as you thought. This has been one long mess up."

Tau nodded, thoughtful. "Don't lose your courage. Keep moving. There is much more at stake here than what you know." He took a deep breath and his cheeks puffed out as he blew toward Kai. Cool air washed over him, raising gooseflesh down his arms.

Tau paused for a moment, frowning. "One more thing. Your suspicion that Bree needs her dad? That's a good place to start." As the words left his lips, his form grew hazy and indistinct.

"I know that. Wait! Don't go. Where do I find him?

I'm not ready for all of this. I still have questions." But Tau was gone, and the wind that had started in his lungs took on a life of its own. Kai was lifted, tumbling head over heels until he could see the round edges of the pool above. One last gust deposited him on the grassy bank. He lay there for a moment, savouring all that it was to be with Tau. He reached down and patted his jumpsuit. It was dry. So was his hair. Maybe he'd dreamt it all.

23

The light extinguished, and Evazee fell back. It was as if something had her head in a death-grip but decided that she wasn't worth eating. Her eyes filmed over, and she blinked rapidly to clear her vision. Someone had called her name, and she could have sworn she'd seen Kai. She blinked again and shook her head to clear the strange fog in her mind. She needed to think clearly.

"Zee! Is that really you?"

Somebody had called her, she hadn't imagined it. The boy that came running looked too tall, too thin. But there was no mistaking that face. She lay back on the grassy path that meandered between the pools, watching him as he ran toward her.

Was this part of the vision from the pool?

Then the vision bent down and folded her into a hug that seemed to last forever. Evazee breathed in the smell of him. "Are you really here? Or is this some weird thing my brain is cooking up for me?"

He laughed and hugged her, but she didn't hug him back. He backed off and waved a hand in front of her face, frowning. "Are you drugged, Zee?"

Evazee couldn't believe what she was hearing. She pushed herself to her feet and turned on him. "How is it possible that even visions of you annoy me so much I could cry? How, I ask you? And what is that awful jumpsuit you're wearing?"

"I promise I'm not a vision. They brought us here for testing, but I found Tau instead. So their plans aren't working too well on me. I was killing time, hoping to fake it, but now you're here, and it's all worthwhile. I've been so worried about you. How are you? What have you been doing? Have you figured out how we're supposed to get home?"

"Who are *they* and why are you wearing that thing?"

"Oh, and we found Bree. Zee, I don't know what to do. She's changed, nothing like she used to be. She wears her hair straight and doesn't paint anymore." Kai seemed to run out of words, though the creases in his face spoke of his deep worry.

Evazee took his face in her hands, lining up with his eyes. He looked real. He sure felt real, too. This vision was overwhelming. There was no way of knowing whether he told her truth or lies, though. "Kai, who are they?"

"We've been at Stone City. You know the light we saw from the graveyard? Well, we found it. It's just back this way."

Zulu and Peta were sitting cross-legged next to a pool that cycled through hues of pink, purple, and a shade of turquoise so pretty it made Evazee's heart pop. Peta was telling Zulu a story, a funny one by the loud guffaws coming from Zulu.

"What kind of place is it? So far, we haven't found anywhere safe. I keep waiting for bad things to happen."

"There's no simple answer to that. It's beautiful and organised. The people are kind. Except that one soldier who took his job too seriously. It all seems to work. They live in light, not darkness." Kai traced his finger in the sand along the edge of the pool. "It's so weird. We had to go through all sorts of obstacles to get to Stone City and yet if we'd come this way, we could have walked straight in."

"What are you not telling me?"

"What do you mean?"

"C'mon, Kai. I know you by now. What's it about this place that doesn't sit well with you?"

"I can't put my finger on it. I guess the way Bree has changed has me somewhat rattled. It's not a city full of people who celebrate differences. They seem to want everyone to fit the same mould."

"Is that such a bad thing?"

"That's what I'm struggling to figure out. What do you think?"

Evazee didn't answer. She felt an overwhelming urge to dive into the pool in front of her. She needed answers. Maybe this walking, talking vision of Kai was her answer.

"Come. You can get a good view of the city from just up that rise. Maybe you'll get a gut-feel of the place." He helped her to her feet, and she dusted grass off her pants. The path narrowed, and she slipped in behind him.

Kai turned back. "It's right up—" He bounced off an invisible barrier, snapping backwards into her. They both stumbled and fell. "What the heck?" Kai helped her to her feet, and his hand shot out, apparently reaching for the invisible wall he'd just bounced off. "This barrier seems to stretch across the path. I can't reach the top either."

Zap and Ruaan slipped out of the bushes on the

other side of the barrier, panic all over their faces. Zap shook his head and ran a thumb across his throat. Ruaan had both hands up, palms facing Kai. They ran straight through a barrier that Kai couldn't stick a pinky finger through.

Zap's eyes darted to the sides. "Run, Kai, they're coming for you." He stopped dead as his gaze settled on Evazee. "Is she for real? Or some sort of mental simulation?"

"Real. You can hug her. But maybe not now." Kai shook his head. "I need to get back to the other side. I need to get to Bree." He turned back to the invisible barrier and smacked his hands against it. They bounced back, stinging. "You try, Zap."

Puzzlement played over Zap's features. He turned and walked back the way he'd come, bounced, and fell on his rear. "What is that thing?"

"So, it's not just me."

Ruaan tried, too, and walked through the barrier as if it weren't there, spun around, and came back. "I don't know what you guys are talking about."

Bodies flashed by, running through the trees. Evazee leaned in close and felt the blood drain from her face. *Run Kai. They are coming for you.* "They seem kind of desperate to catch you. Should we go?"

A group burst around an enormous bush on the far side of the pools. They ran swiftly, some carried guns.

"Kai, run. Now! Go!"

They turned together and took off. Kai's hands were suddenly on her back, pushing her in front of him.

They picked their way between the pools and the other visitors who glared at them for running.

"Why are they after you?"

"I busted a fake healing meeting." Kai gasped for air as he ran. "I know how they trick people. They saw me."

They made it over the top of a small hill. Evazee shaded her eyes and searched for Zulu and Peta. There. She grabbed Kai's arm and pulled. They barrelled downhill at full speed and slid to a stop at the edge of a pool. Peta jumped to her feet with a shriek.

Evazee threw an arm around Peta and steadied herself on Zulu's shoulder. "Zulu! We need to leave. Quick!" Her hand waved between the boys, "Kai, meet Zulu."

"Zulu, Kai." Evazee doubled over, catching her breath from the run.

Zulu rose to his impressive tallness. "They will not follow beyond where the pool light ends. Come. We must run." He reached down and lifted Peta onto his back. "Hold tight, small one."

"Whoa! Who is he?" Zap grabbed Kai's arm and pulled him close. "What's up with the big guy? When did we get him?"

Evazee answered over her shoulder. "You can trust him. I think. We have to go."

Zulu gathered them together and they ran, single file between the pools. They reached the edge of the light. Evazee steeled herself and stepped into the darkness. It seemed darker than she remembered. They melted into the shadow and switched from running to a fast walk that gave them enough time to navigate without tripping.

Evazee risked a glance backwards. Their pursuers stood within the edge of the glowing light and shook their fists at the darkness. Just as Zulu had predicted, they wouldn't go any further. For the first time, she felt grateful for the dark.

Kai manoeuvred next to Evazee

"Are you grinning at me?"

Kai cleared his throat. "You can't blame me. Finding you and Peta? It's just the kind of miracle I need."

Zulu halted, and Peta slid off his back. "We stop here. Make plans. Yes?" He didn't wait for anyone to agree, but went about kicking purple mushrooms until they sat in a glowing circle that gave off enough light to see each other's faces.

Evazee eased herself down onto a fallen tree trunk and stretched her legs out in front of her. "How did you get to be on our side of the barrier?"

"I don't know. I just walked through. There was nothing there. But you saw what happened when I tried to go back."

"They must have a selective one-way filtered barrier of sorts."

"So what you're saying is that we failed to make the grade?"

Evazee shrugged. "Draw your own conclusions. I'm just calling it as I see it."

"Well, that's not very nice."

"Oh, stop frowning, we have bigger issues. You know the OS problem that we solved? Well, that was just one small anthill in a world-wide network of anthills and tunnels."

"What are you saying? More schools?"

"An entire global network of schools and some sort of underground tunnel system to connect them all."

"It's not possible. How do you know?"

"I found a map thing."

"You found a map. Where? Did you bring it? Let me see."

"I said a map thing. Not exactly something I could stuff in my back pocket. And before you ask me to take you to it, it's right in the heart of where I've just escaped from. I don't really want to go back."

Kai settled onto the tree trunk next to Evazee. "I feel like I'm completely blind. I was clueless last time I was stuck here, so this time I should be a little wiser, you know? But everything is different. I haven't seen a single darKound or LightSucker. Tau is mostly gone. I just don't get it."

Evazee rubbed her temples with the heels of her hands. "The way I see it, our most important mission is to find the Healing Stream. With that, we can break the power of the negative Affinity serum and—"

"Wait! You know about that? How?"

"Not know, exactly. I suspect. What do you know?"

"I had a chat with Runt. Don't ask how. Anyway, she told me that everybody back at the OS is completely knocked out. When I find out who did this..."

"The question is what do we do now?" Evazee shivered and rubbed her arms.

Peta settled herself next to Evazee. She rested her head on Evazee's thigh and almost immediately, her breathing slowed.

Evazee stroked her silvery fair hair, and Peta smiled in her sleep. "If we can find the Healing Stream, the water will reverse the effects of the serum." She glanced over to Zulu, who examined something at the base of a tree a good distance away from them. She leaned close to Kai and whispered, "His village has a supply of Healing Stream water. He won't go back, but it might be our only option."

"How can you be so sure that it will work?"

Evazee smiled gently at the young girl on her lap. Peta's mouth was wide open, and she snored softly. "This one. This is how I know."

"I still think your map thing needs to be our starting point."

Evazee rolled her eyes. "You don't know what level of stupidity that would be. I can't believe you'd actually consider it."

"You won't tell me anything, so how can you expect me to make good choices?"

"I suppose I thought you'd use your common sense."

"Ouch." Kai pulled back as if she'd slapped his face with her words. "The thing is, Zap, my friend Pete, he doesn't have time for us to mess around. His death date is being carved right now. Who knows, it might even be finished. Not to mention Bree and her grave. We need a map."

"I know. I was there. Remember?"

"Then you should understand."

Evazee struggled against the words on her tongue. Again, nothing lit up or glowed. It was just her and her bad people skills. She should tell Kai about Shasta. She should. But every time she thought back to his breath on her neck, how close he stood to show her the map, she knew she couldn't talk about it without giving away the fact that she had enjoyed being alone with him. And yet she hated everything he stood for. The battle inside her showed up as two hot spots riding high on her cheeks.

"What is going on with your face? What are you thinking?" Kai's left eyebrow rode high.

"Nothing, I'm just feeling the heat." Evazee fanned her face with her hand, avoiding Kai's eyes.

"That's odd. I'm not feeling hot. In fact, it's quite cool here under the trees."

"Well, boys and girls are different, you know." She turned her back on him, shifting Peta to a more comfortable position. Maybe he'd get the hint and go away.

~*~

"I'm still here, you know." Kai rubbed his temples. The stubbornness of this girl gave him a headache.

A deep boom shuddered through the ground beneath their feet. Evazee jumped up, her eyes stretched wide. Peta slipped, banged her head on the tree trunk, and cried out.

Kai slid over to Peta and pulled her closer. "Evazee, what's going on?"

A double drum beat rippled through the ground. Evazee shut her eyes. She was swaying on her feet. A sudden quiver ran through her body.

Zulu stood, rooted. "Not this again." His muscles bunched beneath his dark skin.

As the next drumbeat rolled, Evazee stumbled through the trees and began to follow a path that led downhill from where they stood. She was picking up speed.

Peta's cheeks were wet with tears, but she made no noise. Zulu took off like a cheetah after his prey. Kai wasn't planning on losing Evazee again. "Guys, follow!"

Zap looked up. "Cheetah indeed." He roused Ruaan with a shove to his shoulder. "Come on, sleeping beauty. There's some trouble going down."

Ruaan rubbed his eyes and stretched, blinked twice, and squinted off into the distance. "I see them. Follow me."

Kai shivered at the sight of Ruaan's glowing eyes. He picked up Peta and followed, dashing through the trees, losing ground to his friends. Her slight weight became heavier as he ran, holding her in his arms. More drumbeats followed, picking up the pace, building toward a crescendo. Evazee ran faster than Kai thought possible. She crashed through low-hanging branches and left them swishing wildly.

Zulu halted. He waited for Kai to catch up, "We can't let her get to the underground gate. Once she's in there, we would lose her too quickly. I think there's another entrance close to here. I'm going to stop her."

His eyes flashed purple in the gloom, and Kai's heart shifted. *This is Zulu. You can trust him. I think.*

"No! Wait!" But Evazee and Zulu had both vanished from his sight in the thick undergrowth. Kai stopped running and let Peta slip out of his arms. "Let's keep going. I'm not losing them."

Peta slipped a small hand into his and nodded. Her eyes glowed a luminous blue in the dark. She took off in front of him, running like a spooked rabbit. She dodged, weaved, and dove under low-hanging branches. Kai pushed hard to keep up with her.

The drumbeats took on a regular rhythm, and Kai ran in time to them. They rounded a corner and Peta thumped into a solid object. Zulu. He stood waiting for them, the few lines on his forehead the only indication of his anxiety.

"Where are they? Why did you lose them?"

"Your friends have fallen under the power of the drums."

Kai pushed past Zulu and Peta. "Did they go that way?"

"You can't follow them."

"Who's going to stop me?" Kai paused for a fraction of a second before turning back to the path. *Tau, show me the way.* He saw it then, broken leaves and branches all glowing green, telling the story of many feet passing in the same direction.

Zulu took Peta's hand in his. "If you're going, so are we."

Kai studied Peta, standing so still and unmoved by the rhythm that seduced their friends. He nodded once. "Stay together."

Moving through the forest as quietly as possible, Kai tracked the signs all the way to a broad dip in the landscape. The forest floor ran all the way up to the base of a big rock. The trail ended there.

Zulu whispered from behind. "Keep going. The way will open."

Kai's mind churned through the possibilities. Zulu's plan was the only one if he wanted to see his friends again. He stepped onto the slope, took another step. Nothing exploded or set off an alarm, so he kept going. Kai was about halfway to the rock when the ground beneath his feet tipped downward, opening up a gaping hole in the ground.

Sweat broke out on Kai's forehead. This felt like walking into his own grave and waiting for the shovels of dirt to start piling up. His heart pounded.

Zulu and Peta walked in first, still holding hands.

Kai hesitated at the entrance, pacing. *Stop being such a chicken.* The ground trembled, shaking so hard that he lost his footing, fell, and rolled the rest of the way down the hill. As he lay on his back, he focussed completely on drawing the next breath. Stars danced in his vision, but he knew they weren't real.

The trapdoor slammed shut with a loud creak.

24

Kai scrambled to his feet, holding onto the wall to stop from falling over. He looked around. Was he in a cave? The entire structure was made of something that looked like lacy dinosaur bones, all arched and curved, bleached pale and pockmarked.

Everywhere Kai looked, there were people, who seemed to be milling about, doing their own thing. Throughout the holey bones, there were people curled up in the holes. Each hole seemed to be a bed, or possibly even a bedroom.

Zulu stood to one side. He kept his eyes cast down to the floor, Peta held on to his hand, her eyes wide, taking in all the details. The look on her face was more curious than scared. The drumbeat stopped, and those who'd followed it dropped to the ground like some giant, rehearsed flash mob. Kai dropped to the ground, waving at Zulu and Peta to do the same.

A circular section of the roof detached and dropped toward the floor, filling the air with a sharp hydraulic whine. It stopped short of touching down, low enough for Kai to see that it held a group of people. Unlike those on the floor, the group on the platform stood. One towered head and shoulders above the rest, though whether it was natural tallness or something that boosted him, Kai couldn't tell.

"Your first task is to sort the new intake. New software has been uploaded to your implants to make the process quicker. Let me demonstrate."

The tall one stepped down off the platform and walked across to the closest body on the floor, rolling up his sleeves as he walked. "Observe. The reader is built into your left hand." He clamped his left palm over the person's forehead as though he checked the man's temperature. He held up his right arm toward the platform, as if reading the time on his watch, but there was nothing there. Lines of glowing text appeared, hovering over his skin.

"Once the text appears, your reading is complete, and you can use you left hand to select whether the candidate is more suited to conversion or coercion. Your reading will also show whether they've been through recruiting before. Anyone who shows signs must be quarantined immediately. There is an emergency unit set up to respond to that. Just use your buzzer. Once you've read them, stamp them and move on. We have a lot to get through tonight. Two separate teams will be coming through later to take them to training for one or the other. Any questions?"

Kai swallowed the bile building in the back of his throat. This was Affinity training all over again, but on a mass scale like he'd never encountered.

"Are there likely to be any anomalies, and if so, what do we do with them?"

"That's a good question but not one that you need to be concerned with. The drums have been our most accurate attraction method yet. It may seem primal, basic, but don't be fooled. It has taken a good few years to research the science behind the calling method. It is now used all across the world as an elegant solution that has proven to be more accurate than the old method and it takes a few seconds per candidate, compared to half an hour each like the previous testing. We're on a tight schedule. Move out."

Kai could hardly breathe. His mind ran wild. He searched the crowd for his friends, but in this sea of people, they could be anywhere. If he were invisible, he might stand a chance at tracking them down without attracting any attention to himself. Deep into the cave, right on the far side, he saw a girl moving. It was Evazee. She slipped from deep shadow to deep shadow, avoiding the purple lit-up areas.

Kai squinted in an effort to see where she was heading. Evazee had worked her way around the room and now slipped into a side tunnel. Kai checked the location of the passage Evazee had disappeared down. All the recruiters were busy with people on the floor.

Leaning across, Kai whispered in Zulu's ear, "Keep her safe. Don't let them take her. I'll find you." He waited for the single nod from Zulu, stood up, and blended into the shadows that fell outside the purple light of the broken mushrooms.

~*~

Kai stood outside the passage, wondering for the umpteenth time if it was stupid of him to follow Evazee. But he'd come this far, no point turning back now. The passage was dimly lit, but Kai felt exposed. There might as well be a spotlight on him as he tiptoed along.

His fingers trailed the walls. Smooth, marble-like, the colour of deep midnight speckled with stars, and yet the illusion was not enough to stop him from feeling stifled. The corridor curled and twisted. At least it seemed that he was alone. Soft conversation reached his ears, and he tried to breathe more quietly. The voices came from around the bend. Moving light from around the corner played across the floor at his feet. He sank down onto his haunches, straining to pick up the conversation.

A man spoke and the hairs all down Kai's arms stood up. He knew that voice.

Evazee answered, though her words were too muffled for Kai to make out. She didn't sound scared or threatened. Kai had to see for himself who she was speaking to.

He held his breath and peeped around the corner. Evazee and a man had their backs to the doorway. In front of them floated a holographic map of the world. The man pointed something out to her, and she nodded and giggled. Kai focussed in on the man. His silvery hair hung down his back in a long ponytail. He turned to whisper again in Evazee's ear, and a cold chill ran down Kai's spine.

It was Shasta. And he had Zee eating out of the palm of his hand.

Kai waited until their backs were turned and sneaked down the last stretch of passage. He hid in the sheltered spot just next to the doorway of the room. From here he should be able to pick up what they were saying. He caught Zee mid-sentence.

"Converts and coerced. So those who embrace the lifestyle are your converts, but those who don't?"

"Let me put it this way. We persuade them. Either way they end up doing what we want them to."

"Coercion. So you don't feel that it's wrong?

You're forcing people to do what they don't want to do."

"It's not that invasive. I prefer to think of it as realignment. Let me ask you a question. Would you like to live without your affinity power?"

"I have been for the last while. It's horrible. I get things wrong all the time."

Shasta's face softened. He trailed his fingers through her hair, wrapping a single lock around his thumb. "Exactly. What we do here helps people to never experience that. That isn't a bad thing, right?"

Kai's heart beat so fast and loud, he felt sure they heard it. Anger burned through his veins. Anger at Shasta for being so slimy? Or was he angry at Evazee for falling for it?

Evazee sidled over sideways and looked Shasta in the eye. "What is the big purpose, though? I don't understand. Why bother with all these people?"

Shasta picked at a nail and shrugged. "Let's just say I don't like seeing people lied to. I don't like seeing them misled into believing they are a whole bunch of things that they just aren't."

"Like what?"

"Unique. Special. Loved. Only a handpicked few are all of those things. Most people find their meaning in being part of something bigger than themselves. Higher, loftier, more noble. Most are followers who simply wait for someone to take the lead and sweep them along toward a grand purpose. I provide that purpose. I do the sweeping." He leaned in close, towering over Evazee, his body forming a sheltered space for her to nestle in. "You, my dear, on the other hand, are all of those things and more. And we've only just begun to tap into your full potential." He straightened and stepped back. "But that's enough for one day. You must be feeling tired."

"Wait!" Evazee took a faltering step towards him. "I have another question."

A momentary flash of impatience showed on Shasta's face, but then it was gone. His lifted eyebrow invited her to continue.

"Why is it so different this time? Coming back here, I mean." Evazee was tripping over her words like a nervous school girl. "It's just last time the landscape was different. We were constantly dodging LightSuckers and darKounds. I haven't seen a single one of either of those this time. I don't understand."

Shasta stared at her in silence, a hint of indecision riding his eyebrows. But then he seemed to snap to a decision in an instant. "Let me show you." He turned back to the holographic globe and punched buttons on the key pad. The view changed, and glowing lines appeared, dividing the ball into segments much like a mom would cut up an orange for her kid. Eight segments in all appeared.

"What's that? What are you showing me?"

"Sections. Each has its own purpose. Different training, different tests aimed at different people. The tests in each section are carefully designed to bring about the desired outcome. So far, it's working incredibly well." He touched the floor and earth vanished with a hiss. "Let's get you back to your rest pod. Tomorrow will be a long day for you."

"But I just want—"

Shasta steered her by the elbow, his touch silencing her objection. They were headed straight for the door, Kai panicked. He tucked himself into the corner, shut his eyes and wished he were invisible.

~*~

Evazee wasn't ready to leave. She still had questions to ask. But Shasta had her elbow in a death grip. She wasn't yet secure enough in her standing with him to push. Something moved just outside the doorway. Evazee squinted in the semi-gloom. Kai!

Feigning something in her shoe, she bent down and fiddled. When she stood up, she made sure it was on the other side of Shasta, away from where Kai hid. A flush washed her cheeks. She had to keep Shasta's attention.

"I haven't told you how much I love your eyes." She reached up to tilt Shasta's face toward her.

"You're shaking."

"You are somewhat overwhelming." There was truth in what she said, and there was nothing Evazee could do to stop her fingers trembling. She could only hope he'd mistake her fear for something else. She smiled at him as they walked through the doorway. Her heart pounded loud in her ears. *Keep him focussed.* "So why me? I'm just like any other girl." Evazee kept walking. One foot in front of the other. Keep moving. Away from Kai.

Shasta's gaze roamed over her face, his expression unreadable. "Your gifting is strong, but I fear it has been tarnished by your long use of Light Affinity. I hope that together we can reclaim your former strength. I guess only time will tell." He cupped her cheek, his thumb tracing the line of her cheekbone.

They were far enough down the passage that Shasta wouldn't spot Kai at a casual glance. She had to keep him walking with her to give Kai a chance to get out of the tunnel.

"But that still doesn't tell me why you want to use my talent. "

"Your gift is words, right? You always know just the right thing to say. That's a skill we want our new recruits to learn. Given the right training, you'll be able to fast-track those with the same raw talent, to do what you do. It will be for their good. In fact, everyone around them will benefit." His smile was magnanimous.

His words pooled around Evazee's heart, leaving it marinating in the same good intentions written into her DNA. "I would love that. I'm not sure how to do it, but I can learn."

They reached the end of the tunnel. Evazee panicked. She had to try to give Kai a chance to get out. "Where must I go now?"

Shasta waved her off. "Go find a sleep pod. Don't come back until I call you. Do you understand?" He turned and disappeared back down the passage, trapping Kai inside.

A wave of nausea washed over her.

~*~

Kai wasted no time. The moment Evazee and Shasta were around a bend and out of sight, he tiptoed into the room and crossed to the control panel. The buttons were simple enough, and he pressed and clicked until he found the label: *Stone City*. From there, he trailed his finger in a spiral, circling outwards, searching a larger perimeter with each loop.

His finger butted up against something that wouldn't budge, an invisible barrier that ran from pole to pole. His finger leapfrogged the barrier and carried onto the other side. He zoomed in on the first place on the other side of the barrier. It was TrissTessa's art gallery. Using the familiarity of that place, he quickly located other landmarks, homing in at last on the one thing they were all hoping would bring relief: the Healing Stream.

His Affinity ran like hot liquid through his veins. He pushed buttons on the console as if he'd been doing it his whole life. It seemed instinctive now, not forced or beyond what he knew to be comfortable.

The top layers peeled back, and he hunted for a clue as to what the barrier was made of. Using his thumb and forefinger, he swiped outward and the image zoomed in closer. A few more swipes and Kai's stomach turned. Dividing the two sections was none other than a tall hedge of growing plant-life. A plant that he himself had insisted on replanting the last time he'd been here. It seemed to stretch taller and grow thicker as he stared at it.

There was no way he'd manage to get his troupe to the other side of this thing. Not under, over, or through.

25

Evazee sat opposite the passage to Shasta's room with her knees drawn up, shivering. Her muscles ached from sitting too long, but she couldn't leave until Kai came out. There was no way of tracking time in this place. All she knew was that he'd been gone a long time. Too long.

Why had he been foolish enough to follow her in the first place? When he finally did come out, she was going to yell at him.

Someone was coming.

Evazee hardly dared breathe. It was Shasta, alone. He waved a hand and four soldiers materialized. Evazee hadn't even been aware of them waiting silently in the shadows. They conferred quietly with Shasta, and he sent them away, hurrying as if they were on a mission.

Shasta remained standing there, but his attention seemed caught up elsewhere. His grey eyes glowed, faintly luminous in the half-light.

Evazee studied him, absorbing every detail she normally overlooked: the slant of his jaw, the sprinkling of pepper in the silver hair just over his ears. The man was an enigma.

Where was Kai?

Her imagination complied with a myriad of

possibilities. All of them made Evazee want to cry. Maybe she should go ask Shasta. Her stomach turned at the thought. Being near him was like stepping into a magnetic field strong enough to melt her mind.

Indecision paralyzed her.

~*~

Kai hadn't intended to go exploring. He'd decided to wait a while to make sure he and Shasta didn't bump into each other on his way out, and then he would leave and find his friends. But the sound of footsteps panicked him. He tripped one foot over the other and fell head first into a chute carved out of the same bony substance as the cave walls. He slipped down the worn white surface, clawing at the walls to control his fall but only making his descent faster. Along the way, he twisted around and hit the ground, feet flailing.

He rubbed the tender part of his rear that had broken his fall and wished he had more meat on his bones. The chamber had a perfectly round, dome ceiling. Six pillars that stretched from the floor all the way up through the dome were evenly spaced around the edge of the room. The surface of the walls was divided into rectangular screens that flickered on and off. Hundreds of them.

A circular workstation sat in the centre of the room manned by two operators with earphones. Their backs were to Kai. One guy had flaming red hair. The other man's was as black as Kai's. They scanned the images constantly, stopping to confer in hushed voices. With a few clicks, the redhead zoomed in on a place Kai didn't recognize, while the other man wrote notes.

Kai sank down low, trying to make sure his bones didn't creak. He slipped in behind a pillar and studied the screen in front of him. Most of the images made no sense. A sparkling expanse of rocky ground, dotted with small mounds. A village on stilts lit in purple mushroom light. The more he looked, the more he recognized. Tau's temple, the graveyard where they'd first arrived, the streets of Stone City. Even the testing arches that he'd gone to with Bree.

The operators were focussed, completely absorbed in what they were doing. Kai tiptoed across to the next pillar. Images washed over him, turning his stomach. These were not from this visit, but from the time the bus hit him. Bree's empty shack. The slums outside the OS. The desert where he'd lost Bree. *Lost her in more ways than one.* It all gave him a watery feeling in his belly. Every inch of this place was under surveillance. Everything that moved or breathed was under careful scrutiny.

A wave of dizziness sucked air from his lungs and he hung onto the pillar to stop himself from toppling over. Now the operators were arguing. As their excitement grew, their voices grew louder, too.

Kai risked a glance. The screen causing all the upheaval was milky white.

"I'm telling you now, that is something we need to investigate." The redhead who sat closest to Kai was also red in the face and spoke with such force that spit flew.

"And I'm telling you that it's a monitor malfunction. We need to get Technical in to see to it."

Green glowed around both of the operator's heads, but there wasn't even a smidge of green on the monitor. It was in perfect working order. Redhead had his vote.

"Have a look around. Every single screen is working. Why would that one continually fail? Only that one? You can't answer me, can you? Besides, look carefully. That is not a broken screen. That is a shield. Someone is hiding something." The redhead spoke slowly.

"That's rubbish and you know it. We see everything."

"He sees everything."

"It's the same thing, really. Come on. There are three more sections to get through before our shift ends. Flag the area and come back to it."

"I don't agree. I'm going to check it out quick. I'll use the spirit cuttings and be back before you miss me."

"You're just lazy. You know that?"

Red patted his pockets. "I've left my navigator somewhere. Can I use yours?"

Black Hair stared at him as if he'd lost his mind, but he dug into a pocket and handed over a device. Kai squinted as he saw the device change hands. It was the same as the one he'd brought along from Torn's office, the one he'd strapped to his chest and forgotten about.

Red clicked on the milky screen and numbers appeared in the centre of it. He activated the navigator and entered the numbers into the central section before slipping it back into its harness and fastening it around his body.

"I still think you're wasting our time."

"I know. You keep saying so." Red left, and his co-worker muttered under his breath.

Kai forced himself to wait for a full minute before

following. He was just about to slip through the door when Red came back.

"The way is blocked," Red said. "The web is almost right up to the door at the moment. I can't get through without protective gear."

"I won't say I told you so, but I really did."

"You just said it, and anyway, it doesn't mean that the screen's broken. I just couldn't go check it out. I'll try later once the web has moved on."

"Whatever. You can do it on your own time. We need to finish. No more wasting office time."

Red got back into his seat, and they both rolled to the right and started working through the next area.

Kai slipped to the next pillar, staying neatly behind their backs. The images flashing down from this section were all completely foreign—areas he'd never been to. All but one of the screens.

Kai stepped away from the pillar, closer to the screen to get a better look. Brio Talee, the spirit cuttings. The black, oozing web grew before his eyes and pulsed along the bridge where the screen was focussed. It was moving twice as fast as when Kai had been through. What a mess.

Kai slipped back to the section, monitoring where his friends were right now. A girl caught his attention. She was a stranger to him, sleeping curled up in a hollowed-out hole in the rock of the underground cave. Her face contracted in a frown, and she thrashed in her sleep. Whatever she was dreaming was messing with her.

Kai rubbed his eyes to clear them. Was that dark mist coming off her? He shut his eyes tight and opened them wide again, but it was still there. It hovered over her for a brief moment, but then something shifted, and the mist was sucked into the rock. Kai stepped closer, not quite trusting his eyes. The air around her was clean again. Maybe he'd imagined it.

Another image caught his attention. A worship service at Tau's temple. The people were lost in the proceedings, and the preacher had whipped them up into a frenzy. Most of them had their eyes closed, stamping their feet as they shouted out loud. It was there, too. The black mist, pouring off the crowd, oozing out of their pores. It hovered over them in a thick cloud. Two long pipes stretched out over the crowd from the top of the platform. Fans started up and the mist was drawn up into the pipes and sucked away.

What was going on?

Kai checked another screen. It appeared to be a room inside Stone City—Kai recognised the cold walls. A sign on the wall displayed the counselling hours. Beneath it stood a spindly desk with a snooty lady presiding over it. She was dressed in the same cream jumpsuit that they all wore, but she had a way about her that made the jumpsuit look like it was tailored just for her.

A girl Kai's age sat opposite, her feet crossed at her ankles, eyes downcast to her hands on her lap.

There was no sound, but as Kai focussed, he could see the smart lady speaking sternly to the younger one. She didn't dare raise her eyes but kept her head down. Kai watched a single tear roll down her cheek. As it hit her arm, a small puff of dark mist left her and collected over her head like a tarnished halo. Just as he expected, it was sucked up through the air vents in the wall. The dark mist was being harvested.

~*~

Evazee felt the tension might split her in two. She just didn't want to be alone anymore. She didn't want to carry the weight of whatever might be happening to Kai by herself. Sticking to the edges of the crowd, she made her way back to where they'd all entered. Hunting through the crowds, Evazee's heart raced and her mouth went dry. Where were her friends?

A small hand slipped into hers.

"Peta! You found me. I was dead worried I wouldn't find any of you. Where are the others?"

Peta's nose wrinkled, "Zulu is back there where there's no mushroom light. I don't like this place. Can we go now?"

"Take me to him."

Peta sighed, grabbed Evazee's hand, and hauled her along. Off in the distance, officials shouted directions, moving through the crowds and sorting people into groups of who-knows-what.

Peta led her down a side-passage. Part of the wall detached itself, and Evazee bit back a yelp. It was Zulu. He blended into the shadows so well that when he moved, it looked as if the wall itself had come to life. Ruaan and Zap sat in the shadows behind him, blinking like owls. Wads of chewed-up bark stuck out of their ears. Zap grinned at her, pointing to his ears and showing her a thumbs-up

The pressure of the morning weighed down on Evazee, and the words popped out. "I've lost Kai. He's in the main cave. I've been waiting for him to come out, but he hasn't. He should have come out by now. What do we do?"

Zulu scanned the crowd. The officials were getting

closer to their hiding place. The whole open area had gone from a chaotic melee of random drifters to organised groups herded in different directions. If they tried to cross the field now, they would be spotted in seconds.

"I think we may have lost our opportunity to get to him. The way has closed."

"What are you saying?"

"Look for yourself. If we cross now, we'll be scanned and grouped along with them all."

"Well, what do you suggest?"

"I don't know. But we can't stay here. Look."

Soldiers branched off, hunting for stragglers. The tunnel they were in would be checked, and they'd be found.

"We've got to get out of here. Come."

Zulu led the way down the passage that Elden had used to get Evazee out. Evazee's belly pinched at the thought of Elden. It was wrong to have left him behind. She drew the bad feeling around herself like a coat.

Zulu reached the air vent that had taken them to the surface and climbed up to open the lid. He grunted and huffed, trying to budge the flap before slipping back down to the ground.

"They've sealed up the tunnel. We can't get out."

~*~

Kai stayed hidden behind the pillar for what seemed like an eternity. He absorbed the images on the screens, each one landing a punch to his bruised heart. This was all so messed up. He homed in on a screen showing the Resonance Pools. Surely, that was not a wicked place also?

A familiar figure walked across in front of the Resonance Pool, where the camera was focussed. Kai did a double take. Was that Elden? He leaned in closer, almost squinting. The guy on the screen turned briefly, and there was no doubt.

"Elden!"

Silence hung in the room, thick enough to choke on.

The chairs squeaked in tune, as the two guys operating the control panel swivelled and stared at him.

They spoke at the same time. "Who are you?"

"What are you doing here?"

Kai stepped out from behind the pillar, fishing for something appropriate to say. His eyes locked on the greyed-out screen.

"I'm here from maintenance. To see to that screen." He pointed, feeling his ears go hot. He grinned at them, trying to look professional and harmless all at once.

"Nice try. I'm calling security," said the black-haired man.

The redhead motioned for him to put the phone down. "Don't worry. He doesn't look dangerous. I'll walk him out myself."

"Fine. Suit yourself. You just want to get out of working. Leave me here all by myself. As long as you know that you'll be staying on to work late if we don't get through."

Redhead lifted a flap to get out of the circular desk and sauntered over to Kai. He frowned. "I'm not going to handcuff you or anything, so behave yourself. OK?"

Kai shrugged and nodded. "Where are you taking me?"

Up close, the guy looked younger than Kai had originally thought. As he stepped closer, Kai's Affinity kicked in so strongly that it caught his breath. Red lit up like he'd fallen into a vat of radioactive sludge.

"Come on. This way." He led Kai back to the section of the room where Kai had been hiding out. He touched the wall between two screens, and a rectangular portion of the wall shifted forward and slid sideways to reveal a staircase leading downwards. "We have a holding room. Someone's going to have to figure out what to do with you. But it's not going to be me."

Kai followed, examining the guy's green-lit head and chest. They'd reached the middle step when the doorway above shut once more with a whoosh and a click.

"Tell me, is it true that you aren't here because of your loyalty to Shasta, but your reason for signing up was more of a, let's say... personal reason?"

The effect of his words on his captor was astounding. The poor boy nearly choked on his tongue.

"What are you saying? Why would you say that?"

"Wait...give me a moment." Kai felt for the knowing. An image flashed through him. A small boy riding high on a strong man's shoulders. The feeling between them was so foreign to Kai that he knew it could only be one thing. Family. "You're looking for your dad, aren't you?"

Red's face morphed from red to death-white. "How did you know that? You can't breathe a word. You can't even think it around Shasta. He'll know. Why are you here, anyway?"

"It's a long story. I don't want to bore you."
"Oh, don't worry. Boring is my middle name."

26

By the time Red ushered Kai into the holding room, they were chatting like old friends at a school reunion. It didn't take much to get Red talking, though it seemed it would take some low-grade miracle to get him to stop.

The holding room was little more than another small cave, a bench for sitting carved out of the same stone that formed the walls. Concealed black light lit the room to a mere shade above complete darkness. Kai had no desire to sit and wait to be rescued in this box of a room. He studied Red, wondering if he could nail the psychology of the guy. He didn't exactly seem like the most confident of people.

Kai settled down on the rock bench, keeping his demeanour relaxed. "I'm listening."

"Things at home were different without Dad. I felt so empty. They recruited from school and I was never really interested, but when my dad got sick, I thought maybe I could help him somehow."

"With the Affinity power that you'd be trained in?"

"Something like that." Red scuffed the floor with his foot. "What's your power?"

"I see things that are broken, and I know how to fix them."

"So that's how you knew about me?"

"Pretty much."

"Makes me feel naked. Whoa. What does it look like?"

"Green. Lots of green. Listen, I overheard your argument about the screens."

"Yeah, we've been working together for ages, but do you think he'll ever believe me about anything? Nope. He always knows better."

"Well, I believe you."

Red pursed his lips, "Did you use your power to look at the screen by any chance?"

"Maybe."

"And?"

"There's nothing wrong with that screen. Absolutely Nothing. You glow greener than that screen. I want to know what's going on."

"Wow, I didn't think I was that bad off." Red crossed his arms over his chest.

Kai could have kicked himself for getting it wrong. More than anything he needed this guy to be on his side. He needed an ally.

"Oh, trust me. You're not. I've seen some real radioactive folk. Lit up like Christmas trees, I tell you."

Red nodded stoically. Disaster seemed to be averted for now at least. "I have to get back upstairs. Otherwise, I'll be working for hours after the end of my shift. Will you be OK here?"

"Just a question. Is there some logic to how the screens are set up?"

"Pretty simple, really. It's all divided up into sections. Each section has a different purpose to fulfil in the Big Plan."

"Shasta's plan?"

"Oh no. This is way bigger than anything he could dream up." Red's eyes rolled as if trying to see the full Big Plan in all its glory. "He's just responsible for one section of it. Basically, the screens on one side show different sections of the real world, while each screen directly opposite shows the spiritual realm. It's pretty easy to see what's going on. I must get back."

"One more. Just quick. That one screen that shows nothing. What is it supposed to be focussed on?"

"We're not sure. The closest we can guess is somewhere on the swamp. Though why anyone would try hide anything there, doesn't make sense." Red shrugged. "Make yourself comfortable. I'll be back just as soon as I can."

"Don't worry about me. Do what you need to." *Trapped in a small place. Perfect.*

Red shut the door, and Kai listened for the second click. But it didn't happen. The door was built to mould seamlessly into the wall of the cave. Someone had gone to a lot of trouble for something so functional. Kai waited a moment and then decided to test his theory. He tried the door handle. It swung down easily and the door opened. He stuck his head out and saw Red halfway down the passage.

"Hey, aren't you going to lock this?"

"No. I trust you." Red waved and disappeared around the corner.

Kai sat down on the bench to think. He may need to destroy Red's trust, but he wasn't ready to do that just yet. He held up his arm, took a deep breath, and allowed Tau's LifeLight to glow inside. Threads of light traced along his arm, but there was no filling inside. Kai had hoped that drinking Healing Stream water would fully restore his resistance to the negative

Affinity serum, but here he was, barely able to light up more than a candle in a blizzard.

Getting Bree safely out of here was looking more impossible by the minute.

~*~

Evazee held onto Peta's hand as the soldier led them toward a testing station. She debated telling him that she'd already been sorted, but then he'd ask all the awkward questions, and she could wind up worse off than she was now.

Evazee wanted to giggle at the soldier's baggy pants and barefoot shoes. She caught a glimpse of Peta copying the soldier's swagger. Evazee bit back a laugh and shook her head.

Peta grinned and seemed on the verge of skipping, but then she sighed and her face turned sad. Obviously, the gravity of the situation was not lost on her.

Evazee squeezed her hand, wishing they could be anywhere but here.

They were led to a soldier with a scanner, who seemed to have been out of bed for too long. Everything about him drooped. Even his ears. Evazee didn't know whether to sympathize or laugh, so she held it all in and faced him with her shoulders thrown back.

"Hello, lovelies. Step closer. This won't take long." He hummed as he set up his equipment. He brought his scanner closer but stopped short of doing anything with it. He tilted his head at Evazee's imprint nestling between her collar bones at the base of her neck. The humming stopped, and he called the other soldier closer. They examined Evazee's mark and then withdrew a few paces to compare notes.

When he came back, his face was grim. "I'm sorry, but we're going to have to split you two up."

~*~

Kai was bored. He'd sat in the room for as long as his busy mind would manage, but he kept seeing the graveyard. Between Bree's grave filling up, Zap's death date being carved, and Bree's dad's date set for a few weeks time, there just wasn't time to sit around and twiddle thumbs.

He let himself out of the room and turned down the passage to the right. This place felt hotel classy, even though it was a cave deep underground in some random section of the spiritual realm. His feet sank into the spongy carpet, and the walls glowed in a mellow shade of dark light.

The passage ended at a door at a t-junction. No signs indicated what lived behind the door, but to Kai, the logical thing was to try the handle. If it opened, he was meant to go in.

He listened to make sure no one was coming, breathed deep, and reached for the knob. The smooth metal turned easily in his hands and stepped through the hole before he could change his mind. He shut the door behind him and turned to see what he'd gotten himself into. He nearly tripped and fell head first into the hole at his feet. He hung on to the doorknob until he'd regained his balance. The walls of the room seemed fashioned from cold metal, polished and smooth. A stairway led down below, straight into the curving arches of Brio Talee. He'd come to another entrance to the spirit cuttings. There was no sign of the web that infected the tunnels elsewhere.

He studied the bridges with his Affinity operating. The structure glowed through and through. He walked down a few steps, listening for anything moving. Silence hung thick in this space between. Hearing nothing move, he grew more confident and climbed the steps until he stood on the bridge that led to the centre ball. There was no sign of the web that had nearly swallowed Zap, just a lot of emptiness surrounding the spindly bridges.

Kai resisted the urge to run and walked the rest of the way to the central ball. *Tau, which one? Why am I here?*

He turned in a slow circle, considering his options. A sliver of gold caught his eye, and he had to turn back to hunt for it. On one of the bridges, the faintest trail of gold ran down the centre. There was no other like that. Not that he could see. With no others showing even the faintest hint of anything other than green, this had to be a good one.

He bent down, tightened his shoe laces, and followed the golden thread.

~*~

Evazee hugged Peta hard and whispered, "It's going to be OK. I will find you."

Peta blinked at her as if Evazee were speaking a foreign language. Then she calmly turned to the soldier. She hauled up her sleeve and aimed her shoulder at the soldier trying to lead her away. "Is it because she's got one of these and I don't? Hmm?"

The soldier halted and bent down to examine the skin on the top of her arm. He rubbed at it with his thumb. "Well, I'll be darned. Give me a moment." He left once more to go find his fellow officer.

Evazee seized the moment and made the decision in less than a heartbeat. "Peta, run." Holding hands, they made a run for it. If they could get to one of the side tunnels, they might just be able to hide and avoid being recaptured. Peta's short legs flew.

"Hey! Stop those two! Catch them! Halt!"

The others waiting in line must have seen them run past but didn't make a move to catch them. The officer himself lumbered after them, red in the face and sweating. Steps away from reaching the side tunnel, the lumbering ox came at them from one side, while his fellow officer cut them off from escape.

"Sorry girls. That won't be happening. Take them downstairs. I don't feel like any more excitement today."

Evazee mouthed "I'm sorry" to Peta. Peta mouthed back something that looked like "we ride." We ride what? She didn't get to ask as they were bundled unceremoniously toward a side passage leading off the opposite wall of the room. The side that would take them deeper underground, not toward the surface.

27

Kai followed the golden thread across a bridge that was too long to see one side from the other. He walked as quietly as he could, shaking his head at himself as he went. It wasn't even logical to think that the black ooze would hear his footsteps and follow him, but that didn't stop him tiptoeing.

The bridge led to a doorway that looked more like the metal doors to an elevator than anything else. He looked for a button or a sensor and found nothing, but the doors drew back as he stepped close anyway. Kai hesitated before stepping through. He had no idea where this door led. He could only trust that it was Tau doing the leading.

He stepped through and blinked against the sunlight pouring in through a glass window. Wooden floor beneath his feet, greenish fog hanging in the air. He spun in a circle taking it all in. He was back in the OS.

Runt!

Waving the green mist away from his face, he found a chair and propped it in between the two lift doors before going to find his little friend.

"Runt!" He cupped his hands by his mouth and called again, louder this time. He ran down the passage, opening doors as he went. His small friend was nowhere on this floor. Everywhere he looked were bodies, passed out. He choked on the chemical taste of the Affinity Enhancer pumping through the building.

Instinct sent him to the kitchen. There on the floor, he found Runt. She had an upside-down kitten stretched out on her lap and a small bowl of water next to her on the floor. Kai watched her for a moment. She was picking fleas off the kitten and drowning them in the dish of water. There were dark rings under her eyes. The sight of them made Kai's heart ache.

"Hey."

She glanced up and immediately went back to flea hunting. Kai sat down on the floor in front of her and crossed his legs. "Are you winning?"

Runt thumbed toward the bowl. At least a dozen flea cadavers floated in the water.

"Looks good. I'm sorry you were left behind. I don't know how that happened. Or why."

She chewed her lip. It was the only sign she'd heard him.

"Elden and I were going to go back to look for Bree. But somehow this mess happened and everyone was taken back. It really is a mess."

The kitten struggled on Runt's lap, but before it could jump off, she re-tucked it firmly between her knees and kept on with her flea hunt.

"Runt, look at me."

Runt huffed and glared at him. The kitten squirmed out of her grasp and ran to hide in a dark gap between two cupboards.

"This is far worse than we thought. When we took down this school, I thought that was the end, but there are schools just like this one across the whole world. It isn't just one man's little thrown-together idea. This is an organized mass brain-washing. They see everything, everywhere, everyone. If you'd seen half of what I've seen, you'd realize what we're dealing with. I'm sorry you got left behind, but in another way, I'm not sorry at all."

Runt shut her eyes and shuffled away until she was no longer facing him.

"Imagine how I would have felt if you'd come back with us and got yourself captured by these people again. I don't think I'd have coped well with that."

"Well it never bothered me before. It would be better than being stuck here with all these snoring bodies."

"Listen, I need your help. Seeing as though I'm here now, let's get rid of this green stuff."

Runt shrugged, her face a carefully schooled version of *I really don't care*, but she pushed up off the floor and dusted off her hands on her skirt.

Kai led the way to the office that he'd come back into, one of those with the jimmied air freshener mounted on the wall. He hoped that the chair was still holding the doorway open. As they walked in, the freshener released a fresh burst of Affinity enhancer into the air. Kai covered his mouth and nose with his T-shirt.

Runt sniffed the air and sighed. The noxious mist had no effect on her at all.

Kai stared up at the dispenser on the wall, wondering what would be the easiest way to make it stop. Loud scraping filled the air. It sounded like someone was dragging a chair across the floor.

Kai turned to see and yelled, "Runt, no! Put the chair back!" As the doorway started closing, he ran. He grabbed the chair out of her hands and flung himself at the shrinking gap. Too far.

He fell through the opening as it slipped closed, nearly catching his T-shirt. He overshot the bridge and fell tumbling through the nothingness in between the bridges of Brio Talee. A scream built in his belly but never made it past the lump in his throat. Kai smacked down hard onto the side of a bridge. The chair hit and shattered into a hundred tiny pieces, all of them floated off in different directions. He lay there watching tiny fireworks explode on the inside of his eyelids.

Someone was slurping a milkshake, at least that's what it sounded like. A cold chill passed over him as he remembered. The soul-sucking black web made that noise. It was coming for him.

~*~

Evazee studied the cave they'd locked her in. It was made from the same holey rock as the rest of the structure, though the opening shimmered. A force field? It looked open, but she could hear the telltale whine. She found a small pebble and tossed it at the opening. It shot sparks and bounced back at her, smoking.

Right. No escaping out that door, then.

She turned her attention to the caves next to her. The walls were holey like Swiss cheese. Evazee turned to the right and peered through the lattice-like rock. Was she alone? Groans sounded from the cell next door. Evazee slipped lower and managed to catch a glimpse.

The silvery-blonde hair was pale enough to be Peta.

"Pssst! Peta. Is that you?"

"Yeah. Who wants to know?

"Evazee. I'm next to you."

"I don't like it here."

"Me neither. You never told me you had an imprint."

"What's that?"

"The mark that got you into this mess with me. How long have you had it?"

"I thought it was just a birthmark. It was always just a dark brown colour. But since we've been here, it's been changing to grey. I got grave dust on it from the graveyard, and it won't wipe off."

"Did you use it to see things the way you saw that stuff about Zulu?"

"Maybe. I dunno. Am I in trouble?"

"No. Not at all. Sometimes people are scared of other people who have special talents."

"What's yours?"

"Um, I haven't felt it for a while, but usually I know the right thing to say. Now, I seem to just blurt out whatever's in my head, and it just doesn't work."

"Is it broken? Your talent?"

Evazee snorted and bit back a laugh. "I guess you could say that. Everything we normally could do here is limited because we're under the influence of the Dark Affinity Enhancer. It's just not working like it should."

"That's not a very strong talent then, is it? If it can be broken by something else."

Evazee didn't answer as she really thought about it for the first time. Why should their talents be affected so strongly by a mere substance?

Why indeed?

~*~

Kai shot to his feet, his head spinning. It took a moment to figure out that the web was coming at him from the central platform. The only thing he could do was run toward the door at the end of the bridge and hope it would open for him.

This door was stone and it looked familiar. He ran at it and hit hard with both hands. It swung on its hinges, ponderously slow, and Kai fell out, landing on his rear and scrambling backward. He shot up, shouldered the door, and nearly popped a vein in his head with the effort of shoving it closed. This time, he'd been quick enough to close it before any of the web sneaked out, which was a good thing, as he had no handy sword-brandishing, baggy-panted soldier to sort it out.

By chance or divine will, he was back near Rei Lex, Stone City. A quick look around confirmed he was all alone. Now all he had to do was figure out how to get through the burning mist and the field of glass grass, and he'd get back to Bree.

As he hiked the path that led him to the city, he thought about Tau. He imagined the man walking with him. How nice that would be. He'd ask Tau how to get through the wall Bree so carefully built around herself. He'd ask about all the others who'd come back and who had been swept back into the system he'd just freed them from. And the network of schools. That was the most disturbing thing he'd seen yet. Cameras watching everything, everywhere, all the time. They could be watching him now.

Dropping his head, he focussed on his shoes. *Nothing happening here, nothing to see. Move along people.*

He'd also ask about that one place beyond the camera's reach. Now that would be a useful place to launch an offensive strike.

What was he thinking? He wasn't here to take down a world-wide system of corruption. He just wanted to help his friends. Yet there was nothing he could do. Only Tau could save them.

As he walked, he tested the LifeLight inside again. He wasn't sure if it would wear off or if drinking the bit of Healing Stream water was enough to flush the green gas from his system. Kai shifted his thoughts from himself and focussed on Tau. Tau who made all things better. The tingling started at the crown of his head, trickling through every vein and pore. Golden LifeLight flooded through him. He glowed.

He grinned until his face nearly cracked. He reached the mist, felt the pulsing glow of LifeLight, and kept going. Nothing stung—there was no pain, no voices. Kai's heart sang.

He came through the mist without a single burn.

But between him and Stone City stood the field of tall, swaying glass grass. His brightness dimmed as his heart sank.

Now what?

His gut told him clearly that LifeLight wouldn't stop him from bleeding if he was foolish enough to try and cross. Testing the theory, he sat down and allowed LifeLight to soak through him. He reached out a glowing hand right in between the shifting blades. Sharp pain seared through him and he pulled his hand out. It was bleeding in three places.

There had to be another way. Sitting down, cross-legged, Kai contemplated the field.

Each shift in wind made the grass sing. Gingerly, he reached toward one and felt its coolness between his fingers. Each blade was see-through with a greenish tinge, nothing like grass really, except for the shape and the suppleness.

The wind blew again and the field responded as one, shifting and whistling. Kai flicked the blade closest to him and it sounded as a harmonic would on his guitar. He flicked a few in close successions, and it made a tune.

Kai leaned in close and hummed. A shiver ran through the blades of grass and they swayed and bent in time. Kai stretched out on his tummy, opened his mouth and sang. His voice blew across the glass grass and the blades closest to him flattened out, their edges zipping together much like the tiny sections of a bird's feather does.

Kai stood to his feet and let it all wash over him. The overwhelming helplessness, the enormity of the foe they faced. His own inadequacies, his longing to see Bree fully alive again. It tumbled out of him in a song that burned through his chest. In his mind, he envisioned Tau gently take Bree's hand and leading her out of all the chains weighing her down. He brushed his fingers through her hair, restoring the bright colour, the curls, and making her smile. All of it tumbled from his lips to a tune that had lay dormant for too many years.

As the breath left his lungs, the blades of glass grass responded. They moved as one, swishing to each emotion, each word. As he sang of Tau, the glass grass blades zipped to each other, lying flat, forming one solid surface.

Kai knew what to do. His heart sang to Tau, and it poured from his mouth in music and song. He stepped onto the field of flattened glass and it held. He took another step, and another.

28

Evazee was dozing when the electric buzz of the force field shut off. The absence of noise woke her. She sat up groggily and rubbed her eyes. Peta popped into her pod.

"Are you awake? They're coming to fetch us."

Evazee leaned back on the wall of her pod, wishing that the mush in her brain would leave. "Who are they?"

"I dunno. I just heard a voice telling me to get ready because it was time."

Somehow those words didn't excite Evazee much, but she kept her thoughts to herself and followed the small girl out of her room. They met a dozen others in the central space between their pods, all of them just as confused as Evazee felt as to where they were being taken.

They didn't have long to wait. A man appeared. He was dressed in a casual cream jumpsuit. He motioned them all closer. "Have a look around. Can anyone tell me what you all have in common?"

A couple of them glanced around and shrugged. Evazee slipped a hand over the imprint at the base of her neck. She had a feeling this was what they had in common. Peta watched her closely, staring with one eyebrow lifted.

"Keep yours hidden for as long as you can. OK?"

Peta pulled at her sleeve and covered up her silvery-grey imprint. "What are you going to do about yours?"

Evazee took the ponytail out of her hair and it fell in loose waves around her shoulders. "This might help a little."

The jumpsuit man came straight for Evazee and brought her to the front. He pulled her hair back from her neck and pointed at her imprint. So much for trying to hide it.

"This is why you are all here. You all have these. We've discovered that these marks are a major hindrance to our training methods. We know that you are all here because you responded to The Call. You must understand that The Call bypasses logic but resonates with the deepest part of you, a part you may not even know exists. By responding, you acknowledged your deep, unspoken desire for more. We are here to help you find what you long for. The first step is to free yourself from this branding that limits you. You no longer need to be held captive by a simple image. You are more than that."

The group shuffled. A few looked hopeful. The rest looked worried. Evazee had no desire to lose her imprint. She was only just beginning to figure out how it all worked, and she liked it.

White showed all around Peta's eyes. It seemed she didn't want to lose hers either.

Jumpsuit man seemed entirely unfazed by their lack of enthusiasm as he herded them together. "Follow me." He led them down a narrow passage. Was that running water? They stepped into a high vaulted chamber. In the middle of the floor stood a tall, rectangular stone structure. Each side formed an arch and water cascaded off the top, flowing down in a solid sheet of liquid across each opening, hiding what was inside. Peta's cold hand slipped into hers.

"Right, folks, there's nothing to be scared of. Who will be taking the plunge first?"

No. She didn't want to do this. Losing her imprint was unimaginable. But she needed to know what to expect so she could either warn Peta, or create some miracle to get them both out.

Her nails dug into her palms as she stepped forward. "I will."

~*~

As the last note of his song sounded, Kai stepped off the flattened glass grass. The moment he drew breath, the grass swished up, tall and deadly once more. Even though he was safely across, Kai's heartbeat doubled. *Too close.*

He faced the bridges to the city now, completely unsure of which one would grant him access. There was always the risk that his name was on some wanted list and buzzing in through the front gate would bring the authorities down on him, but that was a chance he'd have to take.

It took two misses before he found a first-tier gate that would let him in. After that, it all seemed too easy. He found Tau's temple by following a group of city dwellers to the replenishing hall, and from there he used the familiar hall to re-orientate and take the right direction.

Kai walked up to Tau's temple with a plan. Get

inside and find out what's going on. On second thought, that probably didn't count as a plan. It was getting near time for another service, and the crowd of people was growing steadily.

Kai hung out on the fringes. If the authorities saw him, they would remember him as a troublemaker. There was no doubt in his mind. Being thrown out—or worse—locked up somewhere would be counterproductive. He finally settled in between two tall pillars of the building just across the street from the temple. It was a good vantage point without being seen.

The mood in the square was grim. Most of the celebrants wore troubled frowns and downcast eyes. Not a single smile amongst the lot of them. Was a glum face a pre-requisite for gaining entry? A man caught his attention, sitting outside the temple with his back to the wall, his arms hooked loosely around his knees. He watched the people as they passed, the expression on his face completely unreadable.

He looked familiar. Kai dismissed him and scanned the crowd once more, but his attention drew back to the man. In a sea of people brimming with deep concern, he carried peace as if it ran through his veins.

There was only one other man who'd ever come close.

Tau.

Could it be Tau? Kai's heart popped, and he nearly rushed over, but something held him back.

Across from him, a young girl was watching the man, too. Her midnight hair was drawn back into a single straight ponytail, much like Bree's. The man caught her eye and smiled. It was Tau.

The girl searched the crowd, maybe looking for whoever she'd come with. Whatever she was looking for, she must have found it as the tautness left her shoulders, and she ran over to Tau. He patted the ground next to where he sat, and she bottomed down next to him without a moment's hesitation. Tau leaned closer and whispered in her ear.

The girl's eyes sparkled, and she nodded. Tau took her hand in his and traced a pattern on the skin of her forearm. The LifeLight patterns underneath her milky skin danced. The Light darted beneath her skin, and she glowed. Her face lit up in sheer delight as the LifeLight settled inside her.

A brief flash and then the light dimmed and winked out, leaving a perfect silvery imprint on the inside of her wrist. The little girl threw her arms around Tau's neck and hugged him. He whispered again, and she nodded, running quickly to lose herself in the crowd.

Kai crossed the street and stopped at Tau's feet. "It is you."

"Indeed."

"Why are you sitting outside?"

"What do you mean?"

Kai waved toward the huge building. "It's your temple. Shouldn't you be inside?"

Tau leaned forward and craned his neck. "Oh this thing." He shrugged, "They don't let me in."

"Are you for real?"

Tau grinned. "Those that come here are searching but not always for me. Besides, I'm right here. Those who truly want me, recognize me."

"So what happens inside the temple then? Is it all just wasted space?"

Tau's face creased into a frown, "Not quite. I think you'd need to see for yourself."

"I don't know how to get in. The last time I made it as far as backstage, and I saw them orchestrate a whole meeting. They shammed a miracle healing. It was horrible. They also saw me, so that ruins my chances of going back."

Tau grimaced. "If they would only ask, I would do some real miracles for them. Maybe one day they will." He smiled.

Kai's emotions reset. "We can hope!"

"The area you call backstage is only one section of the temple. I think you'll find what happens there rather interesting. Here, let me show you how to get in."

Tau reached down and drew in the stone slabs of the road with his finger. His fingertip melted the hard surface, leaving grooves behind. In less than a minute, he'd drawn a complete, overhead diagram of the temple.

"Right, we are here." He marked a spot with an X. "You'll need to go down this way." his finger traced a second line around the outside of the temple, "to about here. This whole wall looks solid, but it's designed to let people in unnoticed. So if you know what you're looking for, you can let yourself in. Once inside, find the lowest level of the central court, and you should find what you seek."

"And then what?"

"And then you find a way to correct the wrong. You'll need help, but you are not alone."

"Well I'm glad to see that you are still as vague as ever."

"I try my best." Tau mock-bowed.

~*~

The soldier waved toward the tall rectangular structure. "Pick your side and enter. Be careful. What you face in there can harm you."

"What do you mean by *harm*?"

The soldier waved her forward. Evazee gave one last glance back toward Peta, who stood with her face pale and hands balled into fists.

The arches. Focus on the arches.

Inside the first arch was a familiar scene. It was the image of her dad in bed holding the letter she'd written. The same vision had plagued her with guilt for years now. Only a fool would willingly go back there.

She moved on. The next scene turned her stomach. The training ground at the OS. Peta lay in a crumpled heap at the foot of the climbing wall and darKounds prowled the perimeter. It didn't take much to hurry past that one either.

The third showed her gran tucked up and frail in her hospital bed. It had been a long time since Evazee had visited, and the twinge of guilt in her belly was enough to make her run.

The glow from the fourth arch played patterns across the floor, mesmerising Evazee before she even turned the corner. Like seeing a sunset from underwater, rippled light and colour wooed her. This was the one.

Water splashed her skin, and she flinched. It was icy, but as she passed through, she stayed dry. Beach sand crumbled beneath her feet, and sunlight warmed her skin and made it tingle. Evazee turned in a slow circle. Waves rolled in lazily, showing off their sparkling shade of turquoise on one side, but she turned her back on that scene, captured by what lay opposite.

A pathway led between the dunes, underneath overhanging banana trees with clusters of ripe fruit. She stepped into the shade and followed. Flowers grew between the feet of the trees, playfully dotting splashes of colour that glowed even in dimness. Rushing water filled the air with music. *There must be a waterfall up ahead.* She broke through the trees and sank behind a rock.

She was right. A sparkling waterfall, higher than a four-story building, threw its water into a rocky pool with the petulance of a child. Someone was swimming, unaware of her. A leaf cracked beneath her foot and she cringed.

The man in the pool turned onto his back and floated, making snow angel patterns in the water. His eyes were closed and he looked familiar, though from this distance, Evazee couldn't be sure.

"Evazee, come join me. The water is fine."

Evazee's heart thumped, and she frowned as she peered over the top of the rock. The man still floated with his eyes shut. How did he know her name?

"Don't you recognise me?"

She inched forward and squinted, tilting her head sideways. It was Elden. But not uptight Elden who was so tightly wound that one wrong word would snap him. Oh no. This Elden was totally relaxed. His skin was golden, and he smiled, stealing her breath away.

"Come on in. I've been waiting for you."

Evazee's heart pounded, and she felt more alive

than ever. She slipped out from behind the rock and padded to the edge of the pool on bold feet. Every weight she'd ever carried lifted from her heart. The water lapping her ankles made her skin tingle, and clothes and all, she slipped easily below the surface. So this is what it felt like to be alive. Truly alive. Light danced through the water, and she hung suspended, feeling weightless. Only when her lungs were bursting did she come up for air.

Elden's eyes sparkled in the sunlight as he watched her every move. "It's good, yes?"

Evazee laughed and splashed water at him. He ducked below the surface and swam to her. His arms slipped around her waist.

"Dance with me."

"But I can't feel the bottom."

"You don't need to." He pulled her close, and she surrendered to the rhythm of the water, the pounding of the waterfall and the warmth of his skin. He swam her over to a shallow rocky bowl. They settled against the side with their legs floating free. The sensations on her skin overwhelmed her, leaving her breathless.

"Do you know how beautiful you look right now?"

Evazee giggled and waved off the compliment.

But Elden wouldn't let it drop. "Wait, you have to see." He dived back into the pool and kicked down to the bottom. When he came back up, he held a shell in his hands, polished and shiny as a mirror. He settled in next to her and held it up. Their reflection in the shell looked otherworldly.

A sliver of unease shot through her belly. She reached for his arm and pulled the shell closer, angling it so that she could see the hollow between her collar bones. Her imprint had faded so much, it was almost gone.

~*~

Kai stared at the wall and scratched his head. If Tau could show up and point out this entrance to him, it would be so much simpler. He stepped in close and ran his fingers along the edges of the smooth stones. Nothing moved or shifted. This felt like such a waste of time. He pressed on the corners of the stones, wishing he had taken more careful note of what Tau had said. For all his pressing, nothing changed.

He took a step back, studying the wall. Maybe he could do the same finger thing that Tau could do. A song flitted through his mind, something about *impossible* and *nothing*. He hummed it as he reached toward the cement between the stone. It melted beneath his skin with an ease that took his breath away. He traced out a rectangular shape and pushed. The stones shifted aside, and the way in stood open. If ever Kai needed a stark reminder that the spiritual realm operated on different laws to the natural...

He climbed through and dropped to his feet inside the coolness of the room. Cold air brushed over his skin and raised goose bumps all down his arms. The silence was broken only by the sound of water flowing. It rushed and slowed with a gusting that could be mistaken for wind.

The wall in front of him was curved. Kai placed his hands on the wall, hoping for some clue as to which way to go. He shut his eyes and felt the flow going to the right. So the source may be to the left. Removing his hands from the wall, he followed the curved passage and came to a dead-end. At least that ruled out one way to go.

Smack in the middle of the dead-end wall was a button. Kai reached out and pushed it. A vibration passed through the stone below his feet, yet nothing changed.

There was nothing for it but to follow the passage the other way. His footsteps echoed. He waited for soldiers to peel out of the woodwork and drag him out of here. But nobody came, and Kai kept walking alone, following the constant curve of the walls, spiralling ever deeper into the heart of the temple.

The noise of his feet echoed, bouncing off the walls and coming back to him louder.

Hiss. The surface beneath his feet shifted. Kai looked down and yelled. The rock beneath his feet had melted and morphed into a transparent glass-like substance.

Below the surface ran a river of black ooze, flowing in the opposite direction to what Kai was walking. He kept on, following the ever-shrinking passage toward the middle of the temple. Softly at first, almost imperceptible, the noise of wind began to build. By the time Kai consciously identified the sound, it had swelled to a level that seemed like it might whip the roof of the building off.

The passage opened out into a circular room built around a central tube. At once Kai knew what was making wind sounds. The high ceiling was made from the same see-through substance as the floor, but instead of the black beneath his feet, there were four distinct colours channelled into the space from different directions. Each stream fed in at an angle and blew around the circle until they all emptied into the tall, central, glass tube. They mingled as they spun together, and halfway down the tube, all the colour blended to make sticky, black goop. He'd seen it before. In the spirit cuttings.

Kai rubbed the back of his neck and shoulders. Staring up was giving him a crick. One stream was a dull grey. Next to it was a diffused black flow. Then a glowing purple section, and lastly, wedged between the purple and grey, a sparkling gold flow that twinkled and shone. It seemed completely out of place.

Kai traced the gold stream to the section of the wall where it entered. He leaned on the wall and craned his neck to try get a better look at what the gold flecks were made from. As he touched the wall, a panel lit up, displaying a stretch of sparkly rock lighting a flat expanse, populated by small mounds. He recognised the place from the surveillance room monitor.

Kai moved across to the purple section and reached for the wall. Again, his touch activated the panel. In the image that lit up, he saw the shacks up on stilts painted in lumo purple from mushrooms.

Kai avoided the black and went straight to the grey. A night-vision image of the graveyard slowly appeared, and Kai realized where he'd seen the grey before. His friends had been covered in it until their wardrobe upgrade in Stone City.

It looked like there were different things being harvested in different places, and it all came together here to make black goo. But what was the point?

With no small measure of dread, Kai approached the panel below the black and braced himself for images of nameless horror. Holding his breath, he touched it and then stepped back a few paces. The scene that lit up the screen shocked him.

It was a worship service in the courtyard of Tau's temple.

29

Kai found a rack of overcoats hanging outside the kitchen entrance. He slipped one over his jumpsuit, buttoned it up, and walked into the kitchen looking as if he belonged. Tucking himself into the doorway to a pantry larger than his top floor bedroom at home, he searched the kitchen for Bree. She wasn't among the servers, nor those on food preparation duty. He had to go deeper into the kitchen.

Picking the ingredient closest to him—an orange, leafy thing covered in fine fuzz—Kai strode casually through the room and into the washing up area.

And that was where he found Bree.

It didn't take long to spot the type of worker he needed. One of the washers kept yawning and pressing both hands into the small of her back. A closer look showed her lower back was a mess of glowing green, the muscles all knotted into a spectacular spasm.

He dumped the orange, leafy thing on the prep table closest to him.

"Hey, you! What am I meant to do with this?" The food preparer held it out to him as if Kai had dumped an imitation leather handbag and told him to cook it.

"You're the cook, you figure it out."

Kai waited for the washer with the messed up back to step away from the row of sinks. He slipped in next to her. "I'm here to take over from you. Go see someone about that back and get some rest."

The girl blinked at him. Then her face paled and her eyes widened as she shook her head.

It didn't take a mind reader to know what was going down in her mind. "This is not a trap or a test. Tau sees you. He knows. Quickly now, before the others notice."

She left with tears in her eyes, and Kai kicked himself for not doing something about her back. He picked up a pile of dirty plates and slipped in next to Bree. She had to know that the temple she was so eager to get into was a terrible sham.

His hands sank into the soapy water, and he washed a plate before passing it on to Bree for rinsing.

Bree took it from him with her good hand. A few blinks later, it seemed she recognised him. She nearly dropped the plate. "You."

"There's something you need to see. How much longer is your shift?"

"I can't. I'm going to the temple from here. I might be able to secure an interview if my timing is good."

"OK, that's good. What I want to show you is at the temple."

"Why are you here? Don't you think you've caused enough trouble?"

"Could you stop being angry at me just for a moment? Bree, I don't think your Dad is dead. But he doesn't have much time. We need you to help us. There is something very weird happening here. I can't figure it all out. But maybe you could?"

Bree checked to see if they were being watched. The shift supervisor was over at the prep table scratching his head, while the chef-in-training waved an orange, leafy thing at him. He wouldn't be looking this way for a while it seemed.

"Let's imagine for a moment that I actually believe you. What could we do anyway? There is no room for anything here."

Kai dried his hands on his jumpsuit, patting them on his legs to get rid of the last traces of moisture. He traced a finger down Bree's soft cheek. She pulled away and smacked his hand.

He couldn't help grinning at her. This feisty Bree was the one he remembered.

"What are you smiling at? OK, fine. We'll go together after the shift ends."

"And when is that?"

Her grin was not entirely free of sarcasm. "When all of these are done."

~*~

Kai rubbed his fingers together as they walked toward the Temple of Tau. If this was the spiritual realm, why were his fingers wrinkled? As he thought about it, the wrinkles smoothed out. He sighed.

Bree pulled his hood down over his face. "I don't know what you did, but the authorities are still hunting you. Coming here was not your brightest idea, you know."

The courtyard where the meetings were held was deserted. It would only start filling up again for the next service later on. Kai ignored her comment as if he hadn't heard, but he kept the hood pulled low over his face.

"So, tell me, Bree. You want to work in Tau's

temple?"

"I've already said that."

"Have you ever been inside?"

"Of course not. Only those who are appointed can go inside."

"So, you don't know about the temple itself? Does that mean you've changed your opinion of Tau Himself? Do you believe?"

"Of course not."

"That makes no sense. How can you work in the temple without first believing?"

"The hours are shorter, the pay is better, and the rooms are bigger. Who wouldn't want to work here rather than in the food hall? It's a no-brainer really."

"So they don't even ask you if you believe or not?"

"Why would it matter?"

"Never mind. We're here."

"It's a wall. What now?"

Kai silently pleaded with Heaven for the same finger miracle he'd had earlier. He shivered slightly as a tremor passed through him. If he could show Bree, she would understand. Or maybe she wouldn't.

This is the spiritual. The wall is not really a physical wall. Kai took a deep breath and employed his finger the way he had before. Once again, like a hot knife through butter, his finger slid through the stones. Too nervous to deviate, he imitated the exact way he'd gotten through the wall before. A rectangular chunk fell through and Kai stuck his head in to check out if it was safe.

He helped Bree through and climbed in after her. This time around, he wasted no time going left but turned right and followed the curving passageway.

"Where are you taking me?"

"Let's call it an educational tour. Don't give me that look. You want to work here. I want you to know what you'll be doing. That's fair, right?"

Bree glared at him for a moment, then shrugged. The twinkle in her eye gave away her eagerness. "What are you waiting for? Let's go."

Kai walked the spiral hall as a tour guide. "Observe. Beneath your feet, a river of black sludge. Yes?"

"What is it? It is...compelling."

"That's not exactly how I'd describe it, but you're welcome to your opinion."

"Am I seeing right? It's flowing opposite to the direction we're walking."

Kai walked backward, holding up a finger, "Ah, the lady has spotted an important point. The river of black goop is indeed flowing away from the centre of the temple. Note: Exhibit A."

"Kai, cut it out. Do you have any idea how annoying that is?" She rolled her eyes and shoved him as she walked past.

They kept going, circling deeper and deeper into the temple.

Bree shook her head. "I don't understand. I thought there were many different things happening inside the temple. Not this endless spiral. And what is up with the wind? I hate wind."

"This is not your regular garden variety wind. It blows and that's about where the similarity ends." He watched Bree's face closely as they rounded the final corner into the centre room. Her gaze flicked over the streams of coloured dust flowing across the ceiling into the swirling vortex of the central tube. Her eyes narrowed as they reached the middle of the tube where all the colours smeared to black.

He took her by the hand and walked her around the perimeter, touching each monitor, which illuminated where the flow of matter came from.

"I don't understand. What is this?"

"This room is a collection point. Everything that I've come across in this section—good and wicked— they all give off substances that feed into this room, into that pipe. There they fuse together and become a living force of evil, a web that hunts." He turned back to Bree. Her face was pale. "That pipe feeds straight into Brio Talee, the spirit cuttings, polluting it. It is all part of the enemy's work. Even this temple, this city."

"You can't say that. These people saved me. They took me in and gave me a place, a family. You're wrong."

"Do you feel alive, Bree? Or are you just surviving?"

"There's not much difference between the two, now is there? Take me back. My shift will be starting soon."

"Your shift has just ended. I understand, it's overwhelming. I have one more thing to show you. Come with me."

"I don't want to see anything else. Why can't you just leave me alone? Please. I don't want to do this anymore."

"I don't think your dad is dead."

She turned on him, her eyes flashing. "Don't you dare—"

"We found his grave. Bree, it had a date of birth and a date deceased. But his death date hasn't happened yet. We have to find him."

30

Evazee floated on her back in the sunlight. Elden floated next to her close enough to bump arms. Silence settled over them, comfortable as a feather duvet. Evazee relished the sharp difference between the heat of the sunlight and the cold water. It raised goose bumps on her arms and legs. The contradiction was delicious.

Contradiction.

Why was she here? This place was paradise and her host was being most charming. She thought that the testing arches would be painful, but this was delightful.

Except for her imprint.

She shot up so fast, a mini wave dunked Elden under, and he came up spluttering.

"What was that for?"

"I have to go."

His fingers trailed a pattern down her arm, and she shivered. If she stayed any longer, it would be gone for good. Blocking her ears to Elden's protests, she swam to the side and climbed out, slipping on the rocks in her hurry to leave.

She ran through the gap in the trees and emerged in Shasta's room with its globe of earth.

Instantly, the sunlight was gone and the sand

between her toes had morphed to smooth, polished rock. Her sun-kissed skin felt the underground cold more keenly than she remembered. Hugging her arms, she checked to see if anyone was watching or if she was alone.

On cue, Shasta strode through the internal door.

"You're back."

Evazee's head swam as if it were filled with bubbles. The dizziness worsened as he came towards her. She shut her eyes tight and balled her fists, but he reached for her hand and the warmth of his fingers melted her resolve.

"Come. I need your help." He led her through a curtain and into a room full of people. They sat on the floor and lined the walls—too many to count. He slipped an arm around her shoulders and pulled her close. "You're going to persuade them to join our ranks."

"What if they don't?"

"Let's just say life will be easier for them if they do." He shrugged and the scent of sandalwood flooded her senses. "Either way, they will serve."

"I don't know what to say."

Shasta smiled, and her head spun.

"That, my dear, is the easy part." He lay one hand across her forehead and placed his other thumb over her imprint at the base of her neck. Leaning in close, he whispered words she couldn't catch with her natural ears.

He stayed behind Evazee, close enough that if she breathed in deeply, her back brushed his chest. Words swirled at her in a spiral, twisting out from a dark centre. She didn't need to read them. They echoed in her head, queuing to get out.

She opened her mouth, and the words tumbled. Though she couldn't hear them, the effect on her audience was dramatic. All across the room, individuals were standing, making their way forward. Some had tears streaming down their faces. Evazee couldn't stop the flow. She kept speaking, watching her words tear through the room like a hurricane. Not a single soul remained unaffected. All came forward and knelt at her feet, at Shasta's feet.

He moved forward, slipping a hand into the small of her back. Writhing coppery snakes flashed briefly in his palm. There was a feeling of ownership in the gesture that made Evazee's skin crawl, but she couldn't stop, couldn't walk away.

Wind picked up, fanning her hair behind her. Everything spun. Her feet lifted, and a spinning whirlwind of air sucked her backwards into a vortex of smeared reality. She shut her eyes and bit back a scream.

She came down hard on her shoulder and lay there, winded, trying to reconcile her brain with everything swirling in her mind. She peeped through her lashes. The testing arches had spat her out and the structure lit up green. Cold flashed in the hollow between her collar bones. She slipped her hand to her neck.

Her imprint was gone.

31

Kai led Bree by her good hand down the starry passage. It had taken an enormous amount of persuading to get her to come with him through the fields of Resonance Pools, all the way underground, and finally to this cave. They'd made it through without incident, and Kai marvelled at how few people they saw on their trip.

It crossed his mind—not for the first time—that a passage leading to such important places should really be under more watchful guard. Now he focussed on making sure they weren't being followed and didn't encounter anyone by accident.

"What is this place?" Bree yanked on his hand.

"Shh, someone might be here." Kai couldn't ignore the feeling of happiness that bubbled through him from Bree's small hand in his. No worries could douse the delight in his belly.

They reached the room with the hologram globe of earth floating in the centre, spinning slowly. Bree's eyes grew wide watching it.

As far as Kai could tell, they were alone. "You see how it's split up? We're in a different section than last time. I was wondering if you remembered crossing from one section to the other?"

Bree pulled her hand from his and crossed her arms, tucking both hands into her armpits. "I can't say that I remember. I wasn't exactly conscious when they carried me out of the desert."

"And I still feel like rubbish for that. But apart from that, is there nothing at all that you remember?"

Bree stared at the ceiling and frowned. "There are images, but they seemed more like dreams to me than anything else." She shrugged and went back to studying the globe. Curiosity seemed to get the better of her. "So how does this work?"

"Let me see if I can remember." Kai spun the globe and zoomed in. He focussed on the slum and zooming in took them straight to her house. A tremble passed through her arm to his.

"This is not right."

"It gets worse. Believe me." He took her down the hallway, and they crouched in the shadows outside the doorway to the surveillance room. "We might have to wait a while."

"Why is there nobody here?"

"I've wondered that myself. As far as I can tell, this is the centre of their operations. Why would they let us just walk in?" Saying it out loud made his heart cold.

"We should leave. I don't like this."

"Hold on." Kai circled the room, scanning for images of the graveyard. It was the movement of a Grave Keeper that caught his eye. "Bree, help me remember this number."

Bree hunted around on the workstation in the centre of the room and found a pen. She jotted down the co-ordinates on the back of her hand.

Kai grinned at her. "One more then we can get out

of here." He scanned the screens, homing in on the milky-grey one. He read them out to Bree and she took them down on the back of her hand as well.

"This next bit may or may not work. Come on."

Kai tried to take Bree's hand again as they left through the side door, but she was having none of it and tucked her fingers into her armpits. They reached the end of the passage and the doorway that would take them to the spirit cuttings without incident.

Kai studied Bree's face. Her cheeks were rosy and her eyes sparkled. "Are you enjoying this?"

"No. Obviously not. I'm supposed to be washing dishes and not getting into trouble. This is so much better." Her mouth pulled to a deliberate straight line, and one eyebrow popped up high. She couldn't do anything about the twinkle in her eye.

"Yeah, right. Brace yourself. This might get ugly." He hauled the navigation disc out from underneath his shirt and opened the door. The steps were deserted. The web had moved on. "Give me the first number."

"Oh dear. The last number...it smudged a little. I can't tell if it's a two or five."

"Let me see." Kai pulled her hand close and tilted his head this way and that. "I'm going with five." He pressed the centre button and the gadget lit up, humming. A holographic keypad popped up, and he typed in the number.

A second ring lit up and a beam shot out from the device.

"How do you know how to do that?" Bree seemed intrigued.

Kai shrugged. "I don't really know." For a moment, he considered telling her that his Affinity was in full swing, but this was Bree. Bree, who didn't believe in Tau and wanted nothing to do with His power. "Instinct, I guess. Come on. Let's get through this. Don't touch the rail. It'll burn you."

He reached for her hand, and this time she didn't pull away. They walked down the steps together. The beam of light blazed ahead through the darkness, not only showing them which way to go, but also lighting enough of the path for safe walking. Hand-in-hand they crossed the first bridge and made it to the central ball. Kai's ears hurt from straining to hear any sign of the web returning.

The light beam led them to the other side of the ball and across another bridge. Each step they took that didn't bring disaster built confidence, and Kai felt the tension in his shoulders ease.

They reached the doors without incident. As they stepped close to it, the light beam retracted into the navigator and shut itself off. Kai put it away and studied the doors ahead. They rose up tall ahead of them, two doors that seemed to be made of compacted sand.

"I'm not sure what will be waiting on the other side. The first time we arrived in the graveyard, it was deserted. The Grave Keepers only came later. I hope that'll be the case now as well."

Bree nodded. Her pupils were huge in the gloom. It made her look young and frightened. Kai wanted to hug all her fear away.

"Ready?"

She dipped her chin in the smallest nod. Kai shoved against the doors with all his weight, and they swung open. Heat rolled over them in shrivelling waves, but the darkness was thick and absolute. Kai stepped out of the cuttings, expecting to feel grass beneath his shoes. His foot sank into deep, soft sand. This didn't feel right.

Bree's hand trembled in his, and he gave a little tug to help her. As she stepped out, her whole body began to shake.

"I don't like being here. It feels familiar."

Kai bent down and ran his fingers along the ground. He picked up a small handful of sand and rubbed it between his fingers. This was not graveyard ash. This was desert sand. Kai allowed his light to increase as the door swung shut behind them.

A low sound from behind them stopped him. Gutteral, monstrous. He would know that snarling anywhere. DarKounds.

Bree's breathing quickened into the unmistakable pant of panic.

"Get back!" Kai flung himself toward the door and willed it to open. It began to swing but too slowly. Sleek, black darKounds eased closer on paws of smoking acid. They covered the desert sand as far as he could see. There were too many to count.

~*~

Evazee huddled on her bed in her cell. She had no recollection of how she'd gotten here. Her missing imprint swallowed her world. It was over. Moments of knowing, saying the right thing, and seeing the truth unlock people's hearts. It was all over now. There weren't even tears left in her to cry. Just a gaping emptiness that she wished could swallow her whole.

Her force field buzzed off. The bed dipped as someone sat and began to take the pins out of her hair.

It tumbled loose, fingers moved through it and then began to brush in smooth, rhythmic strokes, detangling knots and sending tingles all down her spine.

"It's normal to feel lost for a little while." Shasta's voice flooded through her, and she surrendered to the warmth in his words. She shifted so he could reach the other side. A sense of well-being seeped through her from the tip of her head, slowly working down toward her toes.

"Come here." He pulled her up toward his chest, cradling her in his arms. The now-familiar scent of him flooded her senses, and she breathed deep. With every breath, she felt the sting of her loss lighten until she held all the regret in her hand as she would a helium balloon.

"You know what to do with that balloon, don't you?"

"I should let it go." Fluffy clouds filled her brain. Thinking was hard.

"Let it fly. You don't need it any longer."

"But I'm so empty."

"I can fill you." His voice was a low baritone, full of promises of every kind, deep and soothing.

Evazee clung to him and was swept away.

32

Thoughts smacked at Kai from every side and he shut his mind to all of them. Bree had sunk into a ball at his feet with her fingers shoved in her ears, rocking and whimpering.

He threw the doors open, grabbed Bree underneath her arms, and dragged her onto the bridge. DarKounds swarmed at the doorway. One stepped inside and then leapt back, whining. It rolled on the ground as if ants crawled under its skin. The bridge in its untainted form seemed treacherous to darKound feet.

The doors slammed shut and silence settled, broken only by Bree's sniffing.

"Are you hurt?"

Bree shook her head, but a violent tremor passed through her from head to foot, rattling her teeth together.

"It must have been the smudged writing that made us wrong."

"I want to go."

"I need to show you your father's grave. It's important."

Bree shook from head to toe. She said nothing, but she didn't need to. There was no way she would cope with more. But there was one problem. Kai hadn't saved the coordinates for the doorway that would take them back. He could try and remember, but if he got it wrong, who knew where they'd end up? The best he could do was to follow the other coordinates and hope for sanctuary in the place where Shasta couldn't watch every movement. There was a chance it would work out, but it could also go horribly wrong.

Right now, they needed to move.

He read her upside-down writing and typed it into the navigator. The tiny gadget whirred and lit up, and a comforting light beam shot out across the bridge. Grabbing Bree's arm, he managed to pull her onto her feet though she clung to him. They walked.

They reached the central ball and followed the light toward the bridge that would lead them to the place beyond Shasta's sight. A sulphurous odour blew in and hung thick in the air. Kai swallowed hard.

"Bree, can you run?" He pitched his voice low, but a sliver of desperation sneaked through. She lifted her gaze, meeting his. What she saw must have frightened her, and she nodded.

"Come on. Let's go. No time to lose."

Following the light beam, they took off as fast as they could safely travel, dodging holes. There was no web on the bridge leading to the doorway, yet the moment their feet touched the bridge, a slithering sound started up behind them. Kai's blood ran ice cold.

"Run!"

Kai ran with his arm around Bree, half-carrying her when her legs gave in. Meters from the door, the web flung a loop of gooeyness and hooked Bree's ankle. She went down hard, and her chin smashed into the bridge.

"No!" Kai yelled. LifeLight quickened through

him as he ran toward the web, jumped high, and came down with two feet smack into the black goo. It severed and shot back, recoiling but leaving Bree's legs lashed together. She stared, her face a mask of horror.

Kai picked her up in his arms and ran for the door before the web could regroup and try again. He flung himself at the door at the end of the bridge. This one seemed to be made of glass, half-filled with water and tiny fish. He only hoped it wasn't submerged on the other side with water that would rush in with force and drown them.

As the door swung back, Kai heaved a sigh of relief. The water and fish were all just decorative. He bolted through. The gloom closed in around him making it difficult to see. He was on a riverbank from which fog rose like steam off murky waters. His arms burned with the ache of carrying Bree.

A light appeared in the distance, bobbing up and down in time to the lapping of the water at his feet. As the light drew closer, he could make out a boat on the river. It turned directly toward them, though how they had seen Kai and Bree was a mystery. The dark here was thick, broken only by the bobbing light. Whoever manned the boat rowed in lazy strokes, yet the boat pulled steadily closer.

Kai didn't feel the need to run. Even if he had, his legs couldn't have carried him. He stood his ground and waited.

~*~

"Where are we going?" Evazee couldn't think straight. Her mind folded every time she tried. Shasta kept her close to his side, and each time she breathed in the scent of him, she lost a little more of herself.

"There is something I want you to see."

Evazee's mind floated, detached. She glanced up at Shasta. He was staring at her face. Her knees felt weak, and she was grateful for his arm around her waist.

They passed through the holding cells containing those with implants and through to the room with the holographic map. How was it possible for some things to be a shapeless blur and yet others to be in such sharp focus, all at the same time? She was keenly aware of Shasta's fingers brushing her skin, the fine wisps of hair in the nape of his neck, the flecks of silver in his grey eyes.

"Are you ready?" He slipped his hand from her waist and took her hand.

Evazee watched every movement in his face, the twinkling of his eyes and every gesture of his hands. She nodded, not trusting her voice.

Still holding onto her, Shasta stepped over the low water fountain at the base of the hologram and into the hologram itself, drawing Evazee with him. He led her to the centre, and they sat together on the floor beneath the glowing depiction of earth. Shasta stretched out on his back with his hands behind his head. Evazee hesitated a second then joined him. The view took her breath away. The shimmery globe hung in mid-air, suspended on nothing.

"You've been wondering what this is all about. Why I'm doing what I do." It was a statement, not a question. He knew. There was no thought she could hide from him. "Let me show you."

"My, or rather our, mission is to give each and

every person a purpose, a reason for living. That is why we're gathering all those who respond to our call. Let me show you." His fingers flew, spinning the globe. It came to rest, and he double tapped to zoom in. Zulu's village appeared, glowing purple. Unlike the time she'd been there with Zulu, there were many people crossing the walkways and doing normal things—carrying water and dodging playing children. Shasta pinched and stretched his fingers and the view zeroed in on one man—the same one who Evazee had thought looked just like Zulu. He'd been one of the priests who'd performed the ritual.

"You see this one? One of our converts. He answered the call of the drums and responded so well to our training that we could plant him back in his own home village. That's always a bit of risk, but in this case, it worked. It didn't take him long to establish himself as a powerful leader."

But...

Evazee frowned, but Shasta moved right on. He zoomed in on a city of clean light, built from glowing stones. It was one of the most beautiful places Evazee had ever seen. A double tap took them close to the outside wall.

"Most of the guards who protect the city walls are converts."

Evazee had seen those uniforms on the guards here in the underground too. *Wasn't that odd?*

Shasta waggled his finger at them. "Very important job." *Slide and zoom.* "Those who work in the kitchen? Ours. Feeding people matters too, right?" *Slide.* "Temple workers. Responsible for the spiritual health of the city. I won't even comment on how important those are."

"Yours, too?"

"Oh yes. You catch on quick. "

It all seemed good, but questions swooped through her mind and bothered Evazee. Questions she couldn't find the right words to frame into thoughts, let alone ask. Not with all this sandalwood and silvery-grey filling her senses. Even so, one question wouldn't leave but stayed right there in her head, bold and strong. "But what about the others? Those who won't convert? The coerced or whatever you call them."

Evazee had never seen Shasta so unguarded, relaxed, and she watched his face, fascinated.

He shrugged. "Oh, don't worry about them. We manage to find useful things for them to do as well, in spite of the fact that they refuse to cooperate with us. It makes it all so much harder. Sometimes I don't even know why we bother when they so clearly don't want help. I honestly don't understand the way they think. But we do our best. Even amidst all the resistance. So we gather those who respond to the call, train them, and deploy them as agents all over the world. It's a beautiful thing. Almost as beautiful as you."

He turned, leaning on his elbow, and shifted his attention from the map to her. She felt beautiful and none of her *buts* seemed that important anymore.

He leaned so close his breath filled her lungs. "How about you? Are you ready to step into your role?"

33

The boat man had a hat pulled low over his face. He pulled in to stop expertly in front of Kai and Bree and tilted his chin. "You two need a lift?"

"Tau? Is that you?"

The man in the boat threw back his hat with a laugh, "Not quite. The name is Shrimp. You two need help?"

"I don't actually know what we need." There was something about this guy that made it easy to be honest. Maybe it was how much he reminded Kai of Tau.

"This is not a good place to talk." Shrimp checked the bushes behind them. "Hop in. Let's go where it's safe."

Bree hung back, but Kai gently eased her into the boat and climbed in behind her.

Shrimp saw the chunk of web coiled around her ankles. "Let's deal with that right here, shall we? Don't move." He dug around in the bottom of the boat for a knife, checked the sharpness of the blade against the wood of his craft, and stabbed the gooey blackness until it sprang loose. Careful not to touch it, he hooked it up using the knife and tossed it overboard. "That's better." He grinned at them both and turned his attention back to rowing.

Bree curled herself into the smallest ball, hugging her legs to her chest. Kai could only hope they were doing the right thing.

Shrimp called back over his shoulder, "Brace yourselves. We're coming up to the barrier."

The air in front of them lit up and the lights spun and grew, painting a picture so full of light that Kai blinked back tears. Only it wasn't a painting—it was real. A dome of blue sky melted through the darkness, and Bree gasped. The trees along the banks of the river were tall and slender, all reaching loftily toward the sky as if they had nothing better to do than play with sunrays. The river itself sparkled in glittering shades of blue.

They paddled out to the middle of the river. Its water flowed deep and peaceful, though Kai knew it was not the Healing Stream. Those waters were alive. This seemed wholesome, but ordinary.

Shrimp waved a hand, and Kai nearly fell out of the boat as out of nowhere, an enormous, glass, domed structure appeared in front of them, floating on the water, glistening in the light. Bree gasped.

"Welcome to our home." Shrimp aimed the boat sideways toward a landing gap in the base of the structure. Once the boat was secure, he climbed out and helped the others onto the stairs. They followed him inside.

"Beaver! Come on up. We have company."

They stood in what Kai assumed was the lounge, though the only pieces of furniture there were giant beanbags and a strange greeny-blue mat on the floor. Bree bent down and ran the tassels of the mat through her fingers.

The one called Beaver came up a winding staircase

through a hole in the floor. He wiped his hands on his shirt and mumbled to himself. He looked up and blinked at them all, and then his face buckled into a friendly grin. Walking straight over to Kai, he prodded him in the chest. "You can't stay here. You don't have much time."

The words were at odds with his smile, and Kai wasn't sure how to respond.

He turned to Bree, and his voice softened. "But for you, young lady, I have something special. Have you ever wanted to see an underwater garden?" He waited for her nod before motioning them to follow him back down the stairs.

The deeper they went, the more Bree's eyes sparkled. The light that filtered through the water played through the glass walls of the room. Bree held out her good hand to catch the light. Small schools of fish swam past the walls. She ran to the side and pressed her face against the glass. She looked this way and that, trying to take it all in at once. Kai glanced around, but couldn't keep his eyes off his friend, who seemed to be coming back to life before his eyes.

Shrimp called her over to the underwater garden area, and Bree went easily. It might have been imagination, but Kai almost thought he saw a curl or two reappearing in her hair.

Beaver drew him aside. "You shouldn't be here."

Kai stared past him. "Is that Healing Stream water? In those glass things?" He walked over and placed his hand on the glass. The water bubbled in response.

"It is. But I think you know that."

"I need to find the Healing Stream. Can you tell me where it is?"

"I don't actually know. I'm sorry."

"I have some friends who're in trouble." He gestured to Bree with his eyebrows, dropping his voice. "We found her dad's grave in the graveyard. The death date was in three months' time. My other friend—his death date was carved right before our eyes. And Bree herself...we watched her grave being filled up, though there was no date on the stone.

"You've been in the graveyard?"

"Yes."

"And you lived to tell me about it."

"Yes. Is that so weird?"

"Nobody has ever come out alive."

"Nobody told us that."

Beaver's gaze slid over him as if mentally recalibrating his first impression. "Well, maybe that's a good thing. I hate to be rude, but you have to leave. You can leave this one here. She'll be safe. I can see she needs some repair." He scratched his arm unconsciously. "But you must go. Now."

~*~

Shasta's fingers slid up Evazee's neck, and he leaned close to whisper, "There are some converts who are waiting to meet you. You are quite the hot topic right now."

Evazee melted under his fingertips. All the stress dissolved and left her feeling weak and weepy. "I don't believe you. Why?" She wanted to giggle at the way her tongue slurred her words the tiniest bit.

She stared at his mouth as he answered. It remained closed, but his voice echoed in her head. *It's not every girl who can claim to have won the heart of such a powerful man.*

There was a hitch in his voice that caught her off-guard. He looked away quickly and walked faster. He said nothing more until they reached a wooden double door that she'd never seen before. Her vision from the testing arch seemed to repeat as the doors opened to a crowd that filled the vast chamber. They stepped inside. Evazee's hands were slick with perspiration. There were too many to count.

Shasta moved closer to her, slipping one hand under her arm, the other caressed her neck. Reality and memory collided, and Evazee couldn't breathe. Words flew at her, sharp and piercing. They flooded through her. Just like before. She couldn't hear her own words, but they came out of her mouth like a hammer and slammed into the people in front of her. The effect was even more dramatic than it had been in her vision.

They streamed forward, pressing toward Evazee and Shasta. A shaft of cold slid down her spine. There were too many, too close. Evazee fought the urge to run. They held out their hands to her as if they'd found their savior. She felt the warmth of Shasta behind her and drew courage from his closeness. So this is how it felt to be wanted.

"Speak to them."

He slipped a hand to the base of her neck, positioning fingers over her vocal chords and sending his thoughts into her head. They flew at her like crows, black and fast. Blinding pain shot through her brain.

This was not what she wanted. She opened her mouth to tell him, but his words came tumbling out of her mouth and echoed through the chamber, amplified by the vaulted, rocky ceiling.

The more she surrendered to the flow of words, the less pain sliced through her skull. Words danced across the crowd in front of her and understanding dawned in their eyes and faces. Some embraced what they heard and threw their arms around each other, while others stood with expressions of rapture.

Surely this was good? It looked good from the outside. But why was her stomach in a knot?

~*~

Kai paddled himself away from the dome house back toward the doorway to the spirit cuttings. Beaver had decanted Healing Stream water for him, which he carried in a bag on his back. It should be enough to get him safely through the cuttings. As for navigating, he was going to trust Tau to show him the way as before.

Something splashed behind him and he spun around to see what it was. "Bree! What are you doing?"

The girl was swimming after him, even though she only had one good arm. He rotated the boat around and hauled her onboard. She was soaked through and shivering.

"You left me."

"It's safer for you here. If you thought the desert was bad, you have no idea what we'll be up against." He frowned. "I don't even know. I just can't worry about you."

Bree wiped the water from her eyes, and her hands balled into fists at her hips. "I will not be left behind again." Even as the water dripped off the tips of her hair, the waves were coming back. By the time it was dry, he'd be willing to bet his left arm that her curly mop would be back in full force.

"Your hair." He couldn't help grinning. "It's going curly again."

She rolled her eyes at him, looking so much like the old Bree that he struggled to breathe.

"What happened back there? You haven't been yourself since the desert and now..." He waved a hand over her, at a loss for words.

"I don't know. I feel like I've been asleep, trapped in an endless bad dream, but being here, woke me up." Her eyes lost focus as she tried to puzzle it out. "Anyway. It's beside the point. Apparently, you need to get a move on. So let's go."

~*~

Shasta led Evazee from the room, keeping her tucked close to his side.

"Sir, can we bring them in now?" The man who called for Shasta's attention had solid black eyes and writhing snakes on his forehead.

"Has the web filled the cuttings? You know we cannot move until it has." Shasta released his hold on Evazee and drew the man away.

Evazee stared at the man's black eyes and writhing snakes and struggled to make sense of the images. Shasta drew the man further down the passage, where they spoke in voices too quiet for Evazee to hear.

Low growls and snarls echoed from the passage beyond them, followed by the tapping of clawed feet on stone. Evazee's blood ran cold. DarKounds. She backed away instinctively and with each step away from Shasta, her mind cleared. This was all wrong.

34

Kai and Bree stood on the central ball, trying to decide which bridge to take. None of them glowed, and Kai wondered whether a drop of Healing Stream water would help. Bree was violently opposed to the idea, so they were stuck.

Bree's hair dried into a wild mop of flaming orange, and all her cheek had come back. She glared at Kai now, one eyebrow lifted. "I don't know if it will help, but I have this thing."

"What thing? We don't have time for games, Bree."

She hesitated for a moment and then pulled the back of her jumpsuit down while bending her head forward. "I have numbers. I've always had them, but I didn't know what they were. All of the slum dwellers did. We assumed they were to keep track of us. But I don't know so much now. They look like the numbers you used with that navigation thingy."

Kai stepped close and examined her neck. "You could be right." They had nothing to lose. He took out his device and punched in the number. The device whirred to life and lit up along a pathway.

Bree's mouth pulled into a tight line. Kai took her hand, and they followed. The door at the end was a solid slab of midnight-black marble. It drew back with a hiss as they got closer and stepped out into a world so familiar, it made Kai's head ache.

A tall hedge of glowing green plants stretched away into the distance, a seemingly impassable obstacle. "I know where we are."

Bree nodded. "Slums are back that way."

"And the Healing Stream is on the other side of this green mess. How do we get through?"

Bree shrugged. "We walk. There must be a gap along here somewhere."

Kai's feet hurt, but more than that, panic swelled in his chest, threatening to cut off his air and stop his heart. This was taking too long. The unbroken green hedge seemed to go on forever. "This is not right. There's got to be another way."

He turned, but Bree wasn't there.

"Hey! Get back here. Bree!"

Her head popped out from between two tree trunks. "It's an optical illusion. Try it." She turned sideways, slipped between two of the trunks and disappeared from sight.

What Kai had thought was impassable, wasn't.

She poked her head back out again. "You coming?"

Kai approached the hedge side-on. Without too much wiggling, he squirmed his way through the bank of green plants and popped out the other side, sweating. "It worked. Bree, you're a genius."

Her eyebrows wiggled expressively.

"Let's go find the stream. We're so close now."

The hike through familiar turf was quick, but when they got to the river, it was dried up. Just a dry, sandy bed remained.

"No. No. No." Kai paced with his hands in his

hair. He sat down in the dirt where the water should have been. Tears pushed at the backs of his eyes. Not manly tears either. No. These tears threatened an ugly cry. Cut off from his friends, knowing their graves were calling them and there was nothing he could do left him feeling hollowed out and sick. The one thing that gave him a constant sense of hope had dried up.

Bree sat quietly at his feet, looking up at him silently. After a while he felt silly and dried his wet face on his T-shirt.

"What would make it better?"

Kai shrugged. "Only Tau can help us now."

"Where did you last see Him? Can we go there?"

"Resonance Pools. The only way back would be the spirit cuttings, but the web has made it impassable. Without more Healing Stream water, we'll never get through. There's no hope."

Bree traced a pattern in the sand with her toe. "Not necessarily."

"What do you know that I don't? Start talking."

~*~

Evazee backed away slowly. Then she turned and ran.

Shasta called after her, swearing, but he made no effort to chase her. He didn't need to, not when he could tap into her head whenever he pleased. Evazee rushed along, taking whichever passages were open and deserted. *Jesus, help.*

She shivered when she thought of the hold Shasta had over her. Her mind ran like a hamster on a wheel, looking for solutions but finding none. She was trapped underground, lost. Her friends were all split up and out of reach. *Think, Evazee, think.*

She heard footsteps and sank into the shadows. A troop of soldiers marched down the passage, each one escorting an imprinted prisoner. Evazee shut her eyes, dropped her chin, and pretended to be invisible.

Once they'd passed, she slipped further along the passage into the next pool of shadow and slowly worked her way along behind the group, careful not to let any of them catch sight of her. Her heart caught in her throat. Peta was among those at the back of the group. Her legs were so short she ran three steps for each one of the soldier's. She hung back and peered behind.

Evazee slipped out from the hiding and joined the other implants.

Peta grinned at her, not looking surprised at all. She pulled her down to earshot. "They're splitting us up for deployment, whatever that is. Where have you been? You nearly missed it."

"It's OK, I'm here now. Be ready."

~*~

The patrol vehicle bumped along, shaking Kai and Bree as they hid in the back. Over all the years she'd lived in the slums, Bree had watched the vehicles doing routine patrols. It had been a simple matter of good timing to jump on the back and catch a lift.

Bree squinted through the darkness. "The pools are close. Get ready to jump...and...now!"

They hit the ground and rolled, knocking the wind out of Kai's lungs. He watched the stars dance.

Bree leaned over him. "Excuse me. When you're done, we should get moving."

Heat crept into his cheeks. That's right. He didn't need lungs to breathe in the Spiritual Realm. He pushed himself to his knees and got onto his feet, feeling old and broken.

Bree bounced on her toes, impatient. "This way."

The pools were as breathtaking as Kai remembered, though dotted in between the colours were a few that had lost their glow. Instead, they seemed to draw the light into themselves and swallow it. He didn't recall seeing any of those the first time he'd been there.

Tau, where are you?

~*~

Evazee and Peta followed the group out into the largest vaulted cave that she'd been into yet. The floor of the cave was carved out into a type of amphitheatre, with rows of seats graduating upwards. Sections were marked out on the floor of the cave, and the guards who'd brought them from their holding cells seated them in an area marked with blue chalk crosses on the floor. The seats filled up as more groups were led in from different sides.

Zulu's people filled a section, their dark skin glowing purple with war paint. Next to them, a large contingent from the glowing city of stone, Rei Lex, filed in and sat down. All of them wore cream jumpsuits. Slum dwellers filled a section of their own.

Surrounding the entire gathering, darKounds paced. They circled along the outer edge of the chamber.

She looked away quickly before fear got the better of her. Her eyes caught two familiar faces—Zap and Ruaan. They were both part of a group seated in the middle circle, front row to the circular stage that had been constructed. Evazee edged forward on her ledge, fingernails digging into her palms. She wished she could get their attention, slip down next to them and find out...

Find out what? If they'd been seduced the way she had? Shame flooded through her and all desire to speak to them left.

Peta slipped a hand into hers, and she cuddled up, resting against her arm with a happy sigh.

Evazee clung to the small girl's hand. This was real.

A deep drumbeat shuddered through the rock below them.

~*~

Kai couldn't see the pool where he'd encountered Tau before. No matter how hard he looked, that particular shade and shape eluded him. In desperation, he dropped to his knees at the pool closest to him. The water that lapped the sandy edges was a strange shade of maroon. Kai forced his breathing to slow and gazed deeply into the water.

Images rushed into his mind in succession. Zap's gravestone, the final number being carved. Bree's grave, a few shovels of dirt away from being filled up, her father's gravestone mere hours ahead of reality.

Kai stood up, shaking. This was not working.

Bree sat on a rock with her feet in a pool, staring at him through thoughtful eyes.

Kai rushed to the next pool. An army swirled at him out of the depths of the water, from every section. Too many to count, every single one glowing green. Damaged and ready to spread the deception.

He tore himself away. His blood flowed hot and fast. He had to do something. Panic was rising.

"Kai, you might want to see this."

"Not now, Bree. There's no time."

"Trust me. Come here."

"Fine. What?" In a few steps, he towered over Bree on her rock perch.

"Look." She drew back her sleeve with her good hand. Her damaged hand was turning black.

Kai blanched. "Let me think this through." He shut his eyes so that he no longer had to look at the terrible damage his assumption had caused.

Assumptions. Why would Tau be silent now?

Maybe he still needed to listen to the last thing Tau had said to him.

Don't be a victim.

His mind turned over what he knew about resonance. The pools were named for a reason. Of all the definitions he'd read, there was one that stuck with him.

Resonance is the place where the crystal sings back to its maker.

Up until now he'd been looking into the pools full of fear and mistrust. What if he sang back to His Maker? They may well be stuck here under the influence of dark Affinity serum, but that couldn't stop him from singing. It couldn't stop him from wrapping himself in Tau's love and protection.

He stood next to a pool, opened his mouth, and a single note rang out, clear and strong. He let his heart fill up with all the good he'd experienced from Tau, letting go of fear. Letting go of doubt. After all, it wasn't about him or his feelings. It was about the goodness of Tau.

The song built and grew, words tumbling around notes, a living revelation of being loved and loving in return. The waters in the pool at his feet churned.

Take it, Kai. Take it with you.

His insides blazed with the fiery love of Tau. Shaking from head to foot, he turned his back on the pool, flung his arms out wide and pictured Bree wrapped in Tau's overwhelming love. Words bubbled up from his belly, and he set them free on the wings of his voice.

~*~

A man slipped in and sat down next to Evazee. His face was hidden, and she pulled away. A second drumbeat shook the cave, and she felt the familiar slide. She was losing herself again. Her heart pinched and adrenalin trickled through her like needles under her skin.

"Here, put these in." The stranger handed her two chewed-up wads, and she shoved them deep in her ears. He drew back his hood just enough that she could see his face. Elden.

A low, rumbling chant built around the room. As far as Evazee could see, everybody sang and swayed. A section of the roof detached and dropped in time to the slow chanting. Upon the descending platform,

Shasta waited. The moment it touched down, he flung his arms wide, commanding the attention of the room, turning in a slow circle.

Only three of those sitting around the inner circle stood. Shasta held up his hand with the writhing snakes and the crowd went wild. He approached the first one standing next to Zap and Ruaan. Without any ceremony, he placed his hand on the boy's forehead. Suddenly, the boy jerked and screamed before collapsing in a heap.

With a satisfied smile, Shasta turned and addressed the crowd. "Those who will not be converted, must be coerced. And if they resist?" He waved toward the boy's lifeless body on the floor.

Then he turned to Ruaan.

~*~

Kai walked.

As he walked, he sang.

Bree walked behind him, sticking as close as she could without stepping on his heels. The waters of the pools followed him, drawn from their boundaries by his song, by the Life of Tau inside him. LifeLight quickened in his belly, and its brightness trailed across his skin and blazed from him as he moved, flooding through the water until it glowed like the Healing Stream.

I am in you and you are in Me.

The door to Brio Talee shattered as he drew close. Thick web blocked the opening. Kai laughed. He swept an arm toward the opening and a flood of water smashed into the web with a hiss. Screams of torment filled the air as the two elements clashed violently. A thunderclap, then silence. The water flowed into the spirit cuttings, consuming the dark web.

Urgency spiked through Kai and he ran, drawing the waters with him.

This could all be too late.

35

Evazee gripped Elden's arm. "We have to stop him."

Shasta pulled Ruaan up onto the platform. His spine stiffened, but he put up no fight. His cheek bore a deep purple bruise, swollen enough to close one eye. A taste of the cost of resistance. Shasta paced around him, sizing him up, sparks zig-zagging across his palms. He addressed the crowd.

The platform must have had some sort of built-in amplification, as he didn't need to raise his voice. But each word he spoke was clear and loud. "This one will not convert. Shall we see if he's ready to be coerced?"

The crowd erupted in a cheer. Evazee thought she might faint.

The sound of an animal in pain echoed through the chamber. Silence fell across the gathering and people peered around, looking for the source of the sound. What fresh horror was about to be unleashed?

Ruaan slipped his hands around his midsection and the animal cried out again. The crowd flinched, waiting for a dreadful beast to be revealed.

Peta pulled Evazee close enough to whisper in her ear, pointing at Ruaan. "They really should feed him."

~*~

Kai ran to the suspended ball. He took a deep breath and brought his arms up high, a conductor of an orchestra preparing for an opening note. The waters rushed toward him, absorbing his LifeLight, swirling around him. He waited.

More water.

He stood in the centre of a growing tower, the walls fashioned by water. As it reached its peak, Kai flung his arms wide, and the water dispersed down every bridge but one. The flow overpowered the black web and washed through the spirit cuttings. Each doorway it reached flew open, powerless before Tau's life carried within the water. Ordinary water, nothing special or precious, just filled with Tau. The waters flowed out of the doorways, multiplying and growing as they flowed, washing clean. Fixing what was broken. Restoring.

It was time.

Instinctively, Kai aimed toward the only bridge that remained dry, the one bridge that still felt *wrong*. He followed it and crossed through the doorway to the outskirts of the graveyard, the one that held the graves of his friends.

The perimeter fence stood tall and strong, but the gateway stood open, unguarded. Kai approached warily, but the place seemed deserted. He gritted his teeth and marched into the graveyard. The water stopped outside, refusing to follow. Should he go where the water wouldn't? Logic screamed *no*, but he walked deeper into the graveyard anyway. By the time he reached the centre, his LifeLight had dulled to a mere flicker. Grave Keepers slid out from behind the tombstones and circled him. Human and yet not, the tattered rags they wore rode the wind. They reached for Kai with metallic fingers that clicked and sizzled.

He faced them with heightened awareness. His hands and knees trembled, and his throat was dry, making it hard to swallow. For the first time, he truly saw the Grave Keepers. Within the tattered rags and gnarled fingers writhed a twisted mess of green they'd worn so long it had become part of them. Deeper still, he sensed the tangled emotional torment that had caused the green to find purchase inside them so many years ago, breaking and twisting them beyond recognition as humans. Compassion and mercy had been torn out, leaving them with nothing at their core but judgement.

Then Kai spotted Tau. Tau ambled amongst the graves, leaning down to read the stones. He moved quickly past one, but lingering at the next and whispered a few words. A slow smile crept across Kai's face as he began to move forward. He'd found Tau. Could this be real? The Grave Keepers whooshed in closer, blue sparks crackling from their palms blocking his way to Tau.

Kai stretched to peer past them. Tau was still there, crouched down next to a grave. The Grave Keepers inched forward, but Kai wasn't going to be kept from Tau. He slammed his foot into the ground. "Move." One word, spoken softly but the impact of it rippled through the ground and shook the Grave Keepers. As Kai stepped forward, they hissed and tittered but gave way before him. Another step and they fell back, rage contorted their faces. Shrieking, they closed ranks behind him as he passed.

Kai found Tau at Zap's grave. The death date was

less than a millimetre from completion. Kai turned and fixed his eyes on Tau. "What about my friend?"

~*~

Shasta turned his back on Ruaan and reached down to pull Zap up onto the platform. "Do you think your friend will allow himself to be coerced?"

"I think you should feed him."

Shasta stepped up close, palms sparking wildly. "And what about you?"

Zap shook his head. "I've seen enough. I will not serve."

Shasta shoved the lifeless body of the first boy off the platform with his foot. "You want to join him, then?"

Zap looked him straight in the eye. "It's better than serving you."

Shasta laughed, cold, mirthless. "As you wish." He rubbed his palms together and sparks shot from his hands, burning wherever they landed.

~*~

What about my friend?

Thick silence fell, and the Grave Keeper's tattered rags stuck out in mid-air as time froze. Tau waved Kai closer and slipped an arm around his shoulders.

Kai blinked at the date on the tombstone. "He's out of time." He shivered, yet warmth rippled through him from Tau's hand on his shoulder.

"Out of time." Tau rolled the words on his tongue

as if tasting them. "Time is a big deal on earth."

"It's too late to help him, isn't it?"

"Time is not relevant here in the spiritual realm."

"What does that mean for my friend? Is he stuck in limbo?"

Tau laughed, but there was no malice in it. Another flood of warmth washed through Kai at the sound.

"It means I'm the boss of time."

Kai frowned, "Can you help Zap?"

Tau drew in a deep breath. As he breathed out, the air filled with the whine from the Grave Keepers as time ticked back into operation. Tau gave Kai's shoulder one last squeeze before he began to fade.

"But what about my friend?" Kai twisted about, hoping to find something that could help.

Tau's voice drifted back to him on a breeze that seemed to sweep away the last remnants of the man, *I love your friend.*

Kai breathed out. "I thought so."

LifeLight flashed through Kai, and he gathered a growing ball of it in his palm. He pulled his arm back as far as he could and threw. It hit Zap's gravestone and shattered it into countless tiny pieces that smouldered and burned away.

The grave hole filled up and grass grew over the top until it might as well never have been there.

~*~

Shasta cracked his knuckles and held up one hand, palm aimed at the top level of the auditorium. He walked a slow circle around the edge of the platform and the darKounds stopped pacing. Their blue-black bodies trembled as they froze, eyes trained on Shasta. He patted his thigh once and half the darKounds broke away and loped through the crowd to the platform in the middle. Each tier they passed fell silent. Dread settled over Evazee at the darKounds nails clicked on the stone next to her.

Two darKounds bounded onto the platform and sought out Ruaan and Zap. The rest stood at the base. One animal sat down close to Ruaan's leg.

Evazee shot to her feet, but Elden pulled her down. "Evazee, you can't help them."

"We can't sit here and do nothing."

Elden held her hands, "I know, but do you honestly think getting caught will do any good?"

Evazee stared back toward Ruaan and Zap, hunting for a gap, a plan, anything to help them. Both were on their knees, doubled over and blocking their ears. Evazee shuddered. DarKound thoughts were too much too bear. To be bombarded by them was agony. Shasta towered over her friends, waiting.

The darKound whined, pawed the ground at Shasta's feet and lay down with its snout tucked between its legs. Shasta prodded it with his boot, but the creature pulled away from him, snarling. Shasta muttered under his breath and clapped his hand to Zap's forehead.

It bounced off.

He moved to the other side, shunting the darKound out the way with his foot and tried again. His hand jerked back as if he'd been shocked. He spluttered, swore, and tried again. This time, the rebound was so great, Shasta fell on his backside.

Zap peeped through slit eyelids and glanced

around, perplexed. Delight crept across his features and when he spoke, the platform microphone broadcast it to the entire room. "Ruaan, did you see that? Please tell me you did!"

Ruaan frowned and clasped his empty stomach. "Dude. How did you do that?"

"It's not me. I met this guy in my cell. His name is Tau."

As he spoke the name, a giant raindrop landed at his feet with a plop. All over the room, it began to rain. The water drops glowed gold and brought light wherever they landed. They didn't come from clouds, but from water that seeped through the holey rock that formed the ceiling. Above ground had been flooded.

The next drop landed on Shasta. It ran down his forehead, sizzling as it went.

Chaos erupted. Some ran from the room as if the drops were acid. Others sat in their seats with wonder on their upturned faces, palms stretched wide to catch the drops.

Evazee grabbed Peta's hand and shouted to Elden, "We have to get to the boys." They climbed over rows of seating, winding their way between a melee of bodies. Peta squealed in delight each time a drop landed on her, adding another layer of glowing light to her skin.

Evazee's heart overflowed with joy. "Someone must have flooded above ground with Healing Stream water. This must be Kai's doing."

Elden dodged the drops. "Let's get them and get out of here. If this carries on, we could all drown. Even the darKounds are leaving." Some of the falling drops landed on darKounds. They rolled on their backs as if the water were fire.

"You think this is a bad thing?"

"Drowning is a bad thing, yes."

How did she answer that? How could he not see this as good?

Shaking, Shasta shoved Zap off his platform. Zap came down hard on the stony edge of the raised seats, narrowly missing a writhing darKound. The platform rose to the ceiling with the same hydraulic whine it had descended with. DarKounds seemed to take that as a sign that their time was up. They broke ranks and bolted. Ruaan leapt from the platform before Shasta could push him and landed on his feet.

Ruaan posed with his fists ready to punch, swinging wildly in all directions.

Evazee reached him but dodged his fists. "Calm down, big guy. Look." The darKounds that had circled the gathering were all gone.

Zap's face was grim. "This is not over. We've bought some time, but he'll be back. This thing is bigger than any of us imagined, and he won't stop until the world is his, and everyone in it either serves him or is enslaved by him. His mind is full of possession."

"Converted or coerced." Evazee pulled Peta closer and hugged her, blocking the girl's ears.

Peta pushed her hands away, crossing her arms over her chest as her eyes grew flinty. "We need an army. An army of soldiers. Soldiers of Light."

~*~

Kai found Bree at her own grave.

She looked up at him with sad eyes, "I'm dying."

Kai gently pulled back her sleeve and took her damaged hand in his. She tried to pull away, but he held on. "You don't have to. Look at this." He led her a few steps further away and they were at her father's grave. "He's still alive, Bree. There's hope for him and for you. We just need to go find him."

"His time is nearly up. I wish I'd listened earlier. Maybe..."

Kai slipped an arm around her shoulders, still holding on to her damaged hand. "Hey, don't give up. Let's go find him, and then you can decide whether or not Tau is to be trusted. Yes?"

Bree nodded once.

It was enough.

36

A vast crowd stood facing the mist that surrounded Stone City. Some were dark-skinned and painted a glowing-purple from Zulu's village, Benan. Others were dressed in the cotton jumpsuits of Rex Lei, the city of stone. In between the two distinct groups were others, those with no special clothes or identity. Those who'd answered the call of the drums.

If you want to get out of this place, follow me. That's all Kai had said in the underground chamber where he'd found his friends.

Kai's heart pinched as he looked them over. He had a hunch how to get them back to the natural, but it was just that—a hunch. If wrong, he'd be responsible for more pain than he could wrap his brain around.

He held Bree's hand, and she let him. Zap and Ruaan flanked them. Zap chewed his lips and his face was pale. Ruaan glared at Kai and then at the mist and back again.

"Are you sure about this?"

Kai shrugged. "We can't get home through the spirit cuttings. They're still flooded. I've been thinking about the last time we went through the mist. I saw Runt." He held up a hand to stop Ruaan from interrupting. "I spoke to her, I was almost right there at the OS. Maybe this is just a veil of consciousness.

Maybe the dust they sprinkled was to keep our bodies asleep, but if we go in without it, we may just cross back to the natural. Think about it. Last time I was in the same room as Runt, but something kept me here. It could only be the dust."

"What about the pain?" Zap switched from chewing his lips to chewing his fingernails. "This lot," he waved an arm over the crowd who'd followed them from the underground, "they followed you here because you offered them a new start. A different life. Do you think it's fair to lead them into so much pain just because it might work?"

"Pain is temporary. They made their own choice." Kai turned to Bree. "I'm going to carry you, and you're going to let me. I'm not leaving you behind again." He swung her up against him before she could argue. Her arms clung tight around his neck, and her heart raced next to his skin.

He gritted his teeth, cast one last glance at the crowd, and stepped into the mist.

Thank you...

for purchasing this Watershed Books title. For other inspirational stories, please visit our on-line bookstore at www.pelicanbookgroup.com.

For questions or more information, contact us at customer@pelicanbookgroup.com.

Watershed Books
Make a Splash!™
an imprint of Pelican Book Group
www.PelicanBookGroup.com

Connect with Us
www.facebook.com/Pelicanbookgroup
www.twitter.com/pelicanbookgrp

To receive news and specials, subscribe to our bulletin
http://pelink.us/bulletin

May God's glory shine through
this inspirational work of fiction.

AMDG

You Can Help!

At Pelican Book Group it is our mission to entertain readers with fiction that uplifts the Gospel. It is our privilege to spend time with you awhile as you read our stories.

We believe you can help us to bring Christ into the lives of people across the globe. And you don't have to open your wallet or even leave your house!

Here are 3 simple things you can do to help us bring illuminating fiction™ to people everywhere.

1) If you enjoyed this book, write a positive review. Post it at online retailers and websites where readers gather. And share your review with us at reviews@pelicanbookgroup.com (this does give us permission to reprint your review in whole or in part.)

2) If you enjoyed this book, recommend it to a friend in person, at a book club or on social media.

3) If you have suggestions on how we can improve or expand our selection, let us know. We value your opinion. Use the contact form on our web site or e-mail us at customer@pelicanbookgroup.com

God Can Help!

Are you in need? The Almighty can do great things for you. Holy is His Name! He has mercy in every generation. He can lift up the lowly and accomplish all things. Reach out today.

Do not fear: I am with you; do not be anxious: I am your God. I will strengthen you, I will help you, I will uphold you with my victorious right hand.
                                                    ~Isaiah 41:10 (NAB)

We pray daily, and we especially pray for everyone connected to Pelican Book Group—that includes you! If you have a specific need, we welcome the opportunity to pray for you. Share your needs or praise reports at http://pelink.us/pray4us

Free Book Offer

We're looking for booklovers like you to partner with us! Join our team of influencers today and periodically receive free eBooks and exclusive offers.

For more information
Visit http://pelicanbookgroup.com/booklovers